Joy
Comes
in the
Morning

A NOVEL

by
Tamara Tilley

Joy Comes in the Morning
By Tamara Tilley

Copyright © 2021 Tamara Tilley

Library of Congress Cataloging-in-Publication Data is on file at the Library of Congress, Washington, DC.

ISBN 13: 978-0-578-91882-2

Cover design: Design 7 Studio
Cover images: Shutterstock
Photo credit: Rachel Sydlosky

ARCHER
PRESS

Books by Tamara Tilley

Full Disclosure
Abandoned Identity
Criminal Obsession
Badge of Respect
One Saturday
Just An Act
Reunion
Grace Will Lead You Home
No Secret No Lies

Dedicated to my family & friends
who continue to encourage me
in my writing journey.
My deepest thanks.

ACKNOWLEDGEMENTS

People are surprised to find out that I don't consider myself a writer. That is an esteemed moniker that I don't feel I have quite achieved. Instead, I think of myself more as a storyteller with gifted editors who help shape the words in my head until they tell the story God has placed on my heart.

So, my deepest thanks to my mom-Nancy Archer, and my dear friends Michele Nordquist and Charlene Ponzio. Thank you for the many hours you've spent pouring over my manuscripts, for seeing the story I want to tell and drawing it out of me with your helpful edits and critiques.

And what storyteller doesn't want an amazing cover to capture people's attention. A huge thank you to Scott Saunders for always sharing my vision. For taking the collage of photos and images in my head and turning them into something incredible.

As with any art form, there is a cost. I could not pursue my visions without the sacrifice my husband has so willingly made. Time spent in my office, molding and refereeing the characters in my head, is time spent away from him. To Walter—the love of my life—thank you for being my rock, my counselor, and my cheerleader when I've wanted to throw in the towel. Ten books published is a milestone I never would have achieved if not for your encouragement and sacrifice.

And to my redeemer, thank you for Your Word that reminds us —

Weeping may endure for a night, but
Joy Comes in the Morning.

1

Katie James sat in the corner of her family home, rocking the sleeping infant on her lap. Never once had she been the center of such attention, yet here she was, listening as Pa, Mama, and a complete stranger discussed her future—a future she had no say in.

She glanced at the child snuggled against her body. *I envy you, Matilda. Your pa loves you so much he's willing to sacrifice so you can have a mama, while my pa willingly offers me up as a sacrifice, so he can get a plot of land.*

Katie tried to ignore the gamut of emotions vying for her attention. Uncertainty. Fear. Sadness. But the wound that cut the deepest was betrayal, knowing it was Mama who asked Mr. Clark to meet with them.

And why is she calling me Kathryn?

It sounded strange to her ears. Even though it was her given name, she'd never been called Kathryn—not a day in her life. She'd always been Katie.

"Mr. Clark, I assure you, my Kathryn is completely trustworthy. She's nineteen, very responsible, and wonderful with children—always has been. And even though she doesn't speak, we have no trouble communicating with her."

Why, Mama? Why are you saying such things?

7

Katie thought about the years of pain she had suffered to protect her mama and her brother, Seth.

And for what? To be bartered away like the livestock in the field.

Katie dared to look at Mr. Clark as her mama continued to speak about her.

"Kathryn practically raised Seth by herself when I was taken ill. He tore me up something awful when he was born, and it was months before I was back on my feet. But Kathryn kept him fed, and clean, and took to him like he was her own. She will take good care of your Matilda."

Mr. Clark glanced her way, but Katie quickly lowered her eyes.

"Kathryn's also a good cook," her mama continued, "and she can keep a tidy house. She's sturdy too, not fragile like other girls her age. You can put her to work outside doing just about anything, and she'll give you an honest day's labor."

"But Mrs. James, I'm not looking for a field hand." Though Mr. Clark didn't raise his voice, he spoke with intention. "I'm looking for someone who can care for Matilda. Someone who is sure-minded and . . . sensible."

Mama snapped to her feet and planted her fisted hands on her slight hips. "Don't believe the gossip, Mr. Clark. I know what the town folk say about Kathryn, but I can assure you, it's nothing but lies. She's not crazy. Even though Kathryn chooses not to speak and keeps to herself more than most kids do, the cruel things people have said about her are simply not true."

Katie studied the way Mr. Clark milked the brim of his hat as he spun it between his straddled knees. Clearly, he was not convinced.

"It's not just the gossip, Mrs. James. Her own brother told me this wasn't a good idea. Wade said she was slow and not quite right."

Mama whirled around to Wade sitting at the kitchen table, his downcast eyes a sure sign of guilt.

"How dare you say such things about your sister!"

"*Step*-sister!" Wade sneered. "She's no blood of mine."

"That's enough, Wade!" Pa hollered.

But it was true.

Even though Pa forbade them from using the word step, Wade was her step-brother and Jethro James her step-father.

"Come on, Pa, you know as well as I do that Katie ain't right. She don't talk, she don't laugh. Who knows what's going on in that head of hers? She's a crazy mute." He smiled at her, but she could read the evil in his eyes. "I think she should stay right here with folks who know how to handle her."

Though Katie was chilled by Wade's menacing words, she refused to react. That's what he wanted, and she would not give him the satisfaction. Instead, she stared at Matilda, asleep on her lap. *I would never hurt you. And I would draw my final breath before I ever let anyone take a hand to you.*

Mr. Clark rubbed his jaw, looking fatigued and uncertain. "Mr. James, since this is such a big decision, maybe it would be best if Kathryn came to my place for a few days, just to see how she and Matilda get along. Then I could—"

"Absolutely not!"

Katie flinched at Pa's roar, startling the sleeping child. When Matilda squawked, Katie quickly stood and pressed the little one to her shoulder, soothing her with gentle strokes and soft words. When Pa stormed across the room, she braced herself for the punishment he so easily dished out, but he just glared at her something wicked before turning to Mr. Clark.

"How stupid do you think I am, Travis? Do you actually think I'm gonna let my daughter go stay at your house without a certificate of marriage? I guess you think if she isn't in her right mind, you can take her home and do what you want with her and not be held accountable. Well, that ain't how it's gonna work. If you want Kathryn to see to your youngin', then you'll be takin' her as your wife. I will not let my daughter's reputation—be that as it may—be sullied by the likes of you."

Katie felt nothing but compassion for Mr. Clark. It had only been two months since losing his wife, and here he was, trying to do the best thing for his baby girl.

With shoulders sagging and his head hung low, Mr. Clark let out a weary sigh. "I meant no disrespect, to you or your daughter."

"Well, of course you didn't," Mama said in the sickening sweet tone she usually reserved for Pa when he came home drunk and in a dark mood. "And Jethro didn't mean to bark at you. He just—"

"Be quiet, woman! I don't need you to speak for me." Pa sauntered from one end of the room to the other. "Didn't you hear the man? He wants to take your daughter home. Sample her. *Then* decide if he wants to marry her."

"No, sir. That is *not* what I meant." Mr. Clark stood. "And I'm offended you would suggest such a thing."

Katie cringed at Mr. Clark's defensive stance. Pa had controlled his temper so far, but if Mr. Clark challenged him, it would not end well for him . . . or Matilda. *Just leave. Take your daughter and leave before it's too late.*

"Travis, please . . . sit down. I'm sure we can discuss this calmly, like adults."

What is Mama doing?

Katie watched Pa's shoulders rise and his jaw clench. When he took a step toward Mama, she quickly pulled up a chair next to Mr. Clark and rested her hand on his forearm.

"The way I see it, Travis, you really don't have many options. You have a farm to tend to. Livestock. Chores that keep you busy from sunup to sundown. How are you going to take care of all those things and raise your daughter at the same time?"

Katie saw Mama glance at Pa. When he gave her a subtle nod, she continued.

"As you can see, Jethro is fiercely protective of Kathryn. Yet, he's sympathetic to your plight. He's willing to give you her hand in marriage, but it must be done according to God's law. On that we will not waver."

Why, Mama? Why are you trying so hard to get rid of me? Have I been such a bad daughter? Haven't I done everything you taught me—everything I've been told? Followed every rule, every command?

Even though Pa had lowered his voice and allowed Mama to do his talking, Katie watched him draw his fisted hands behind his back, his knuckles white with fury. She knew firsthand the strength of those calloused hands, the punishment they had inflicted over the years, and the many times those thick, sturdy fingers clamped down against her mouth to silence her midnight cries.

And now he was bartering her away to another man.

What if Mr. Clark is just like Pa?

Or worse!

As his wife, he would have no need for secrecy. Or to wait with patience for the house to go to sleep each night. He could take her at any time.

Katie swallowed back the bile in her throat, looked at Matilda laying in her arms, then at Mr. Clark. She studied him as he continued to talk with Pa.

He didn't seem the type to be heavy-handed or given to rage. He had yet to raise his voice—even though Pa had questioned his character—and he didn't have the reputation for such behavior. She'd never heard an unkind word spoken about him, and in their little town, people gossiped about any hint of sin, real or imagined. Not only that, but he had a daughter who looked in good health.

And his entire reason for being here is for Matilda, not himself. Surely, this isn't a man as evil as Pa.

Then again, Jethro James had the whole town fooled.

Well, almost.

Katie continued to watch Mr. Clark's mannerisms as Mama and Pa persisted with their negotiations. He didn't clench his hands or raise his voice. The few times he glanced her way, his countenance was never hard or his eyes menacing. If anything, he looked at her with an expression akin to . . . hope.

Maybe this is my chance.

2

After another hour of talk—time Katie knew Mr. Clark used to watch how she handled Matilda—the decision was made. She and Travis Clark would be married.

"Seth, I need you to ride to town," Pa said, as he clapped Mr. Clark on the back. "Find the preacher and bring him back."

Seth raced out the backdoor. Wade followed, the screen slamming behind him.

"Come on, Kathryn, let's get you packed." Mama smiled.

Katie followed obediently. What else was she to do? When she got to her room, she lay a sleeping Matilda on her bed, the fear of the unknown bringing tears to her eyes.

"Katie, please don't cry. This is an answer to my prayers."

Mama talked as she nervously flitted around the room gathering up her things. "Travis Clark is a good man. His wife had nothing but good to say about him, and she always looked happy. I know he doesn't have much in the way of possessions, but he'll treat you well. Don't you see? You'll be all right now."

Now? What does she mean by *now?*

Katie looked at Mama, her eyes sad . . . haunted . . . guilty.

She knows.

Clutching her chest, shaking her head in disbelief, Katie realized her mama had known all along.

"I'm sorry, Katie," Mama said, pulling her into a hug. "I'm so, so sorry. But there was nothing I could do. Jethro is a dangerous man, and I feared what would happen if I confronted him." Mama pulled back, imploring her with her eyes. "You understand, don't you?"

She was asking for forgiveness, but how could Katie possibly give it to her? She knew all along the suffering her husband had meted out and did nothing to stop him. She was the one person who should have protected Katie.

Her own child.

Her flesh and blood.

But she chose not to.

For so many years, Katie had kept Pa's vile secret, thinking she was protecting her mama while that same woman lay in bed each night, sacrificing her only daughter to her husband's evil desires. Did she know about Wade too? That he followed in her husband's horrific footsteps?

Letting her hands drop to her sides, Katie stepped back out of her mama's embrace and walked to the foot of the bed. Kneeling in front of her trunk, she pulled out her meager possessions and stacked them on the quilt, alongside where Matilda slept.

"I know you're upset, Katie, but you'll see. Everything is going to work out. Everything is going to be fine."

'Fine?' Katie's head spun. *How can she say that? What he took from me, I will never get back. I am a hollowed-out shell. Empty. Without worth.*

I will never be whole again.

I will never be 'fine.'

3

When Katie emerged from her bedroom, Mr. Clark turned and looked at her. His eyes immediately went to Matilda, and for the first time since he arrived, a smile brightened his face. He reached for his daughter and pulled her to his chest.

Katie returned to her bedroom and took a final look. But instead of seeing the oil lamp she read by late at night, she saw the hideous shadows that danced on the walls whenever Jethro forced himself upon her. Instead of cherishing the beautiful basin in the corner, that had been in her mama's family for generations, she heard the splash of water when Pa washed before he left. Closing her eyes against the pain, Katie inhaled the scent of depravity and evil. There was nothing here for her. *Nothing and no one.*

Gathering up the four corners of the bed quilt, she tied the ends together. Though her possessions were few, she struggled with the awkward bundle as she crossed the living room. When it caught on the leg of the rocking chair, she stumbled, nearly falling at Pa's feet.

"For heaven's sake, Kathryn, have you no pride? This man is ready to make you his wife. And what do you do? You show him you are nothing more than a bumbling half-wit. Give me that!" He yanked the makeshift bundle from her hands.

"There's no need to scold her. She merely tripped."

"Watch your mouth, Travis!" Pa nearly spit as he wagged a finger in Mr. Clark's face. "Kathryn is still my daughter, and I will speak to her any way I please. Don't be thinkin' just because you take her as your wife, she's any less kin to me. Now, come along Kathryn." He clamped his meaty hand around her upper arm and pulled her to his side. "We need to talk before you go."

Katie's heart raced as she tried to keep in step with Pa's long strides. Once he heaved her blanket of possessions into the back of Mr. Clark's wagon, he turned to her, his eyes wild with rage. "Come on, little girl, we have some talkin' to do."

Once inside the barn, Pa flung her to the ground. Katie tried to break her fall, but her head hit the solid dirt floor so hard her eyes had a difficult time focusing. Getting to her knees, she attempted to straighten her hair and remove the straw tangled in it, but Pa reached down, grabbed a fistful at the nape of her neck, and yanked her back to her feet. Pushing her against the barn's weathered planks, he pressed his body close to hers.

"You might be movin' away, but you're still my kin, understand? And so help me, if I learn you've told your new husband about our secret, I will not only slaughter your mama and brothers, but I will come after Travis and that yammering brat of his. Do you understand what I am saying?"

She nodded quickly.

"Good," his tone softened, and his expression morphed into a demented smile. "Then how about giving your pa a kiss before you go."

He wasn't asking.

With her eyes closed and tears running down her cheeks, he smashed his lips against hers, nearly swallowing them with his want. Though she could do nothing to stop his hands from roaming and groping her body, Katie was thankful he hadn't the time or the cover of night to force himself on her completely. The sound of footsteps outside the barn brought him to his senses. With a hand around her neck, he squeezed, cutting off her ability to breathe. "Remember what I said." He moved closer to her ear, his breath warm against her neck. "As God is my witness, I will kill them all if you tell anyone." He pushed away from her and stormed outside.

With her hands shaking something awful, she tried to fix her disheveled appearance, but could do nothing to hide the heat in her complexion or the puffiness under her tear-filled eyes. With her head down, Katie hurried into the house and through the kitchen. Once in her room, she collapsed onto the naked bed and silently sobbed into the worn ticking, terrified Pa would make good on his threat.

She heard Mama close the door and felt the bed shift when she sat down alongside her. "Now, now, Katie," she whispered as she tried to hush her cries. "Don't ruin this. Once you're married, he'll never be able to take a hand to you again."

Trying to regain her composure, Katie sat up and dried her eyes. Mama brushed off the dirt from her dress, then reset the pins in her hair. But when her fingers grazed the bump on Katie's forehead, she flinched.

Pulling back her hand, Mama frowned, then rushed from the room. When she returned, she held one of her bonnets, the yellow one Katie always admired.

"Here you go. A wedding gift from me to you."

She placed the bonnet on Katie's head, making sure the brim was pulled forward enough to hide the bump.

"Look at that." She smiled through tears while tying it under Katie's chin. "Right as rain." Mama grabbed her hands and held them tight. "Everything will be better now. You'll see. This is God's provision."

God's provision?

He never cared before.

Why would He start now?

4

When Seth returned with the preacher, Katie watched as the older man walked to where they stood under the largest oak tree in the yard. The look on his face was pure bewilderment.

Taking his place alongside Mr. Clark, he leaned over and whispered, "So it's true? You're going to marry Katie James?" Even though the preacher lowered his voice, she could still hear him.

"Yes, sir. Matilda needs a mama, and Kathryn has agreed to marry me."

"But Travis, marriage is a solemn vow you take before God. When you promise to love, honor, and cherish, you need to mean it."

"Then maybe I'd better come up with my own vows because this is what needs to be done. Matilda needs a mama, and I plan on giving her one."

The preacher leaned closer still. "How do you know Katie's fit? I don't usually listen to gossip, but some disquieting things have been said about her. Are you sure you want a troubled young woman seeing to your little girl?"

Mr. Clark flicked a look her way, knowing she had overheard what was said, then turned to the preacher. "I watched her all afternoon with Matilda, and I can see that

Kathryn knows her way around babies. The bond between them was almost instant. Matilda hasn't looked that peaceful since . . ."

His voice cracked, nearly breaking Katie's heart.

It took him a minute to compose himself, then in a muffled voice he added, "Besides, Pastor, no one else is offering. Kathryn and I might not share love, but that's okay as long as Matilda is cared for."

The preacher turned to her, his stare so disconcerting she immediately looked down and focused on her boots.

"Katie, is this your idea?"

He waited for her to reply, but she was silent.

"Katie," he whispered again, "are you being forced into this?"

"Pastor Holt, I take offense to that!"

It was the first time Katie heard Mr. Clark raise his voice, and it made her tremble.

"Kathryn was present the entire time I spoke with her folks. At any time, she could have refused, but she didn't."

Mr. Clark turned to her and clasped her hands in his. She stiffened, and though she tried to relax, she knew he could feel her shaking. He looked apologetic as he let go of her hands.

"Kathryn, if you don't want to do this, just say so. I'll understand. You are a young woman with your whole life ahead of you. I don't want to take from you what you're not willing to give. So, I will ask you again. Are you sure you want to go through with this?"

Katie looked up at him, not knowing if this is what she wanted to do but knowing she could no longer stay within reach of Pa and Wade.

"Don't ignore the man, girl!"

Katie jumped at Pa's booming voice.

"He asked you a question, and he deserves an ans—"

"Yes," she whispered, barely discernible.

Her family gasped in unison, as she cleared her throat.

"Yes," she repeated, her feather soft voice sounding a little stronger. Katie looked up into Travis Clark's clear blue eyes. "I'll marry you."

"Okay." He smiled softly at her before turning to the preacher. "Then let's get on with this."

5

After a short ceremony, void of any sentiment or emotion, Katie was pronounced Mrs. Travis Clark.

While the preacher spoke with Travis, she turned to Seth and saw tears in his eyes. She walked over to him and pulled him close.

"I don't want you to leave. Wade's gonna make me do all your chores."

"You got that right, runt." Wade pushed Seth aside and pulled her close. He whispered as he tightened his embrace. "I saw you givin' Pa his goodbye kiss in the barn."

Katie looked at him, shocked.

"That's right. I saw you two. Pretty brave carryin' on like that in broad daylight."

She pulled away from Wade and looked around to see if anyone had heard him.

"I ain't gonna say goodbye. I plan on stoppin' in from time to time, just to see how my baby sister is doing, you know . . . to make sure her husband is treatin' her right."

A chill coursed up her spine. *Would Wade really defile another man's wife?*

"Okay, boys, let me hug my baby before she goes."

When Mama drew her close, confusion pulled at Katie's

heart. Was this the woman she had spent the last ten years protecting, or was this a woman who thought nothing of surrendering her daughter to a vicious and vile man?

Katie did not hug her back. She waited for Mama to let go, then turned and walked toward Travis' wagon.

Pa stood a ways off and smiled an ugly smile as she walked by. "Well, *Mrs. Clark*, you finally paid off," he said, chewing a piece of straw and spitting it into the dirt. "Here I thought I would get stuck with you for life, being stupid as you are. But instead, I fetched me a mighty fine piece of land. I guess you weren't good for nothin' after all."

Katie didn't know why his words hurt her so. She hated him and held no regard for him. But still . . .

No! You will not let that man hurt you more than he already has. He is not your pa, not your blood. He used you in the most despicable ways. And when he was done, he traded you for a plot of land. Don't do this to yourself. You are finally free from his abuses, no matter the circumstances.

She tried to believe her own thoughts, but tears wet her face. She pulled the brim of her bonnet forward to hide her emotion.

If only a bonnet could hide all the hideous things Jethro and Wade did to me.

She walked over to where Travis stood, thankful he hadn't heard Jethro's ugly words.

"Are you ready?" he asked.

Not trusting her voice, she nodded.

Travis lifted her up onto the splintered seat of the wagon and walked around to the other side. Katie reached in the back where Matilda lay in a blanket-cushioned box and pulled the wide-eyed baby to her chest.

When Travis settled on the seat next to her, he gathered the reins and started them on their way. He glanced at her, then back on the road in front of them. "Matilda will fall asleep in the box. You don't have to hold her."

But Katie held her anyway. She looked down at the precious infant and realized this child, just shy of three months old, was her savior. If it weren't for Matilda's needs, Travis would not have married her. And though the haunting of Jethro and Wade would always be with her, never again would they be able to sneak into her room at night or corner her in the barn. Even Wade threatening to visit held no weight. He would not be able to *visit* her repeatedly without explanation.

But what if all men are the same? What if Travis is heavy-handed or brutal with his touch? What if something happens to Matilda, and he blames me?

Despair swallowed her brief ray of hope, making her wonder if she had just traded one prison for another?

Please God—

She stopped herself.

She would not beg God for help. She had pled for His mercies over and over again, but never once had He seen fit to rescue her. She had decided God did not exist. And if He did, He had little use for her.

———— • ————

Travis sat on the rickety bench next to his wife.

His wife!

Oh God . . . what have I done?

He could barely believe it. He'd taken Kathryn James as his wife.

24

No . . . not his wife.

Someone to care for Matilda. That's the arrangement.

As the silence stretched out between them, Travis wanted to say something to ease the awkwardness, but what could he possibly say? And if he tried talking to Kathryn, would she even answer?

He was shocked when she had spoken earlier. Though her whispers were barely audible, it was proof she could still speak. *Then why did she choose not to?*

His thoughts wandered.

And then there was the way she looked when she came in from the barn, disheveled and emotional, with her hair askew and her cheeks wet with tears. It was unsettling.

Had she fought with her father?

Had he forced her into this marriage?

But I asked her. The preacher asked her. She agreed. Was she lying?

He didn't know.

In fact, he didn't know anything about Kathryn, except for what he'd heard in town. Just the thought of his precious Matilda being in the hands of a girl not in her right mind, someone who didn't have control over her emotions, sent him straight to God.

Please, God, keep Matilda safe.

Keep us all safe.

Shifting his attention before he panicked and turned the wagon around, he looked at Kathryn.

"So, your mother tells me you like to read?" he blurted, startling her slightly.

Kathryn nodded.

"Mary loved to read. She has a collection of books her

mother gave her when we married. She planned to add a new book every year, then give them to Matilda when she married."

Kathryn didn't say anything, she just smiled before turning toward the countryside.

Travis stared at the road ahead of him.

Mary, why did you have to go?

What am I going to do?

How will I ever make this work?

6

Katie looked at the small cabin as Travis pulled the wagon to a stop.

She was here.

Her *new* home with her *new* husband and her *new* daughter. It was almost more than she could take in.

She stared at the weathered door and the small panes of glass that made up the front window.

"I know it isn't much," Travis said, apologetically. "But I'm planning to add a bedroom off the back for me. I mean us . . . uh . . . not that I expect us to sleep in the same . . . room . . . bed . . . at least not . . ."

Katie listened as Travis stuttered and stumbled over his words. Though the only reason he had married her was so she could care for Matilda, she was still considered his wife. And a wife had specific *duties* expected of her.

What if he demands that I . . .

Surely he wouldn't.

We've barely exchanged a handful of sentences. I'm a stranger to him. Would he really bed me just because I share his last name?

Travis jumped down from the wagon and circled around to take Matilda from her arms. He cradled his baby girl next to his body, looked at her, and smiled adoringly.

With an extended hand, Travis helped her down from the wagon. His grasp was warm and sturdy, and he didn't let go of her until her feet were firmly planted on the ground. Following him up the plank steps, Katie crossed the threshold, then scanned the one-room cabin.

She was surprised but thankful to see a cook stove alongside the massive fireplace. It was the one luxury she'd had growing up, learning to cook on a real stove. It gave her a small sense of relief knowing she wouldn't be expected to cook over an open fire.

A diminutive cupboard sat next to the stove, with a stack of pots on its top shelf and a bouquet of utensils sticking out of a tin can. A table was pressed against the opposite wall, two chairs pushed up next to it. And at the back of the cabin, a large bed was nestled in one corner with a washbasin and dresser sitting in the other. A tiny cradle rested at the foot of the bed, and it was there that Travis laid Matilda.

He turned to her, his hands clasped together, looking awkward and uncomfortable. "I'll get your things out of the wagon. Then I need to see to my chores."

As if on cue, Matilda let out a whimper.

"I'll be milking first thing," Travis said as he walked past her to the door. "And then I'll show you how to prepare Matilda's bottle."

Katie stepped toward the stove, still taking in her surroundings.

"Uhh . . . can I ask you something?"

She turned to Travis standing in the doorway.

"Do you prefer Katie or Kathryn?"

She thought a moment. She'd always been called Katie.

Except today when I was being bartered away like a secondhand workhorse.

Kathryn. She repeated in her mind a few times. *Kathryn.* It sounded mature. Strong. Refine. So unlike the little girl who shied away from people. Sat silent in the schoolroom. And went to bed terrified at night.

But that person is gone. Katie James no longer exists.

"Kathryn," she whispered.

"Kathryn it is." He nodded, then pulled the door closed.

7

The instant the door closed behind Travis, Katie pushed back her bonnet and picked up a displeased Matilda. She gently bounced her on her shoulder as she paced at the foot of the bed. It was then she saw a small set of shelves to the left of the dresser. It held the books Travis had mentioned, a tiny wooden box, and a framed photograph of Travis and Mary.

Katie picked up the frame and studied the pair, realizing it was their wedding photo. Mary wore a simple white dress, and Travis looked sophisticated in his morning coat and string tie.

She remembered Mary from church and even saw her a time or two in the mercantile. She was a tiny little thing—even though she was pregnant—and was what some people might describe as plain, but she always looked happy.

Katie studied the photo and the smile Travis showered on Mary; the same smile he shared with Matilda. She looked at the cherub in her arms. "You have your daddy's blue eyes."

"What are you doing?"

Startled, Katie spun around, the frame slipping through her fingers, the glass shattering on the floor.

When Travis rushed forward, she instinctively flinched,

squeezed her eyes shut, and pulled Matilda close to her chest to protect her. She waited for the retribution, but it never came. Daring to open her eyes, she saw Travis squatted down, the splintered wood frame in his hand. When he stood and looked at her, his eyes were red, his face drawn, his jaw clenched tight. She wanted to apologize but was too afraid to speak.

"I need to get something to clean this up," he said, before storming out the door.

Katie didn't know what to do. She wanted to hurry and clean up the mess; it was her fault after all. Even so, with Matilda fussing, she was afraid to put her down and give the infant a reason to squawk.

When Travis returned, he had an old wooden box in his hand. Crouching, he carefully picked up the crystal shards and splintered wood, then gently laid the picture on top. Staring at the photo, he brushed his fingers across a scratch that had damaged the pictured. He stood, glanced at her, then left.

When Travis returned a few minutes later, he picked up the milk bucket he had dropped by the front door and carried it to the counter by the stove.

"Mrs. Shaw showed me how to mix up some milk. Cow's milk is a bit strong for Matilda and not as healthy as Mary's was, so we need to doctor it up a little."

Katie watched as he poured a portion of milk into the narrow glass bottle, and half again as much water. Then, he sprinkled in a helping of extra fine powder.

"This is wheat. I mash it up extra fine, so it doesn't turn to mush, then mix it all together." He pulled the rubber nipple over the top of the bottle, fastened it with a thin leather cord, and shook it vigorously. "Here you go."

He handed her the bottle just as Matilda was ready to wail.

Katie quickly pressed the nipple to Matilda's heart-shaped lips and watched as she immediately latched on.

"Yep. You're a smart one, aren't you, Mattie," Travis cooed over Katie's shoulder. "You know when you've got something good." He reached around Katie and let Matilda squeeze his finger tight. "You're gonna be as beautiful as your mama, you know that? And when you're older, you're going to get an education. A good education. Your mama wanted that for you."

Katie's heart swelled when she heard the catch in Travis' throat. He coughed and stepped away from her, but not before she saw a tear on his cheek.

"I need to get to my chores before I lose any more light. I'll be back in a while." He hurried outside, closing the door behind him.

Katie looked at the infant in her arms, crystal blue eyes staring back at her. "I'm sorry about your mama. She didn't leave you on purpose. But don't worry, I can tell your pa loves you something fierce. And I promise to love you with everything that I am. And you can be sure I won't let anyone raise a hand to you. Ever."

8

After Matilda had her fill and was fast asleep, Katie looked around the cabin. When she caught her reflection in the dresser mirror, she moved closer and studied her profile. Pushing her hair back from her forehead, she fingered the purplish-blue lump and winced.

It was tender to the touch, but that wasn't what worried her. She didn't want Travis to see it or have to explain how she got it. She just wanted her former life to go away. This was a chance for a brand-new start.

A start she never even imagined possible.

Playing with her hair, she let it fall closer to her cheek instead of pushing it behind her ear as she was in the habit of doing.

As long as I don't fiddle with it, it should be fine.

She walked to the small cupboard on the right-hand side of the stove and poked through Travis' supplies. They were meager, but she'd seen less. Long winters were always rough on her family because Jethro didn't like hunting in wet weather, and especially not in the snow. However, that didn't change the fact that they had five mouths to feed. So, Mama taught her how to be creative with items they could store all winter. Biscuits were a must. They were fast, easy, and always filling.

Biscuits it is.

Using flour from the cupboard and water from the pail by the stove, she made dough in no time. Next, she stoked the fire until the fading embers reignited and set the pan of biscuits in the oven. She glanced at Matilda to make sure she was still asleep, then walked across the way to the vegetable patch she had noticed when they first pulled into the yard.

Looking over the little picket fence, she sighed. The tattered garden was nearly dead. Obviously, Travis didn't have time to tend to it, along with his other chores and caring for Matilda.

Katie pushed the little gate open and knelt next to the parched soil. She tugged on the withered greenery and pulled out a pencil-sized carrot.

It won't win any prizes, that's for sure, but it's edible.

She pulled up a few more carrots and dug out a couple of potatoes. The onions in the patch looked the worse for wear but would still add some flavor to a stew. Taking the meager ingredients into the house, Katie prepared her first meal in her new home.

It had been dark for hours when Katie heard the front door creak open. When Travis walked in, she jumped to her feet. He stopped abruptly as if he'd forgotten she would be there.

Their eyes met for only a second before he crossed the room to Matilda's cradle. He knelt next to his baby girl and smiled. Seeing that she was wide-eyed and content, he stood and turned back around, glancing at the stove then at her.

"I'm sorry I took so long. I had a lot of catching up to do.

Just give me a minute to wash up," he said as he headed for the backdoor.

"There's water in the pitcher."

He walked over to the basin in the corner, looking perplexed or irritated, she wasn't sure which.

"I used the water in the pail by the stove. I figured you would want to wash up before supper, and that you could bring in more water later."

He offered a half smile then poured the water into the basin.

Turning her attention back to the stovetop, Katie ladled broth into two bowls. She made sure Travis got the lion's share of vegetables then set them on the table. Placing the biscuits in a handkerchief-sized cloth she'd found in the cupboard, she set the bundle on the table and waited for Travis to take a seat. As soon as he did, she poured them coffee and sat in the chair opposite him. He bowed his head, said a quick blessing over the food, then picked up his spoon.

Katie watched as he brought the seasoned broth to his lips. She had hoped to make stew, but with no meat, she had to settle for vegetable soup; a pitiful vegetable soup to boot. But it was better than nothing.

He split a biscuit, then eyed the table.

"I'm sorry there's no butter," she said, bracing herself for his disapproval.

"No matter." He shrugged, dipping the biscuit into the broth and popping it into his mouth.

She sighed with relief. The absence of meat and butter didn't seem to hinder his enjoyment of the meal in the least. Convinced he was satisfied with supper, Katie raised a spoonful of broth to her lips.

"Can I ask you something?" he said around the biscuit in his mouth.

Choking on the broth that had just passed her lips, she accidentally dropped her spoon back into the bowl, the hot liquid splattering on the table and splashing her face. She coughed and sputtered, trying to swallow fast enough to answer him. *You are nothing more than a bumbling half-wit.* Jethro's hurtful words pierced her thoughts.

"I'm so sorry," she said as she quickly mopped up the spill. Then, with her head down, eyes squeezed tight, hands in her lap, she waited.

"No need to apologize. Spills happen."

She looked up and watched as Travis continued to spoon the broth and eat the biscuits.

No screaming.

No shouting.

No calling her names.

After a few minutes passed, he leaned back in his chair. "Can I ask that question now?"

She nodded.

"I was under the impression you didn't speak, but here you are talking to me like any nor—"

Even though he stopped himself, she knew what he was going to say.

"I'm sorry. I didn't mean to suggest you were abnor—I mean that you were diff—"

Embarrassed, she watched his fist tighten around his spoon and his jaw clamp shut. She'd made him mad. She didn't mean to, but she knew the signs. With her hands folded together on the edge of the table, she waited for the yelling to start.

"Kathryn . . ." He reached across the table and covered

her hands.

She flinched, turning her cheek out of instinct.

"What is it? Your hands are ice cold and you're trembling. Are you ill?"

"No, sir." She spoke with her head down.

"Kathryn, look at me." His words were soft but firm.

She swallowed deep then looked up to see his eyes trained on her.

"I didn't mean to hurt your feelings. It's just that I was surprised to hear you speak. I'm sorry. Please forgive me."

She looked down in confusion. *Why is he apologizing to me? I angered him and made a mess. It's my fault.*

Thinking this was some sort of trick or a game, she didn't know what to do, so she remained silent and waited for Travis to finish his supper.

"This broth is mighty good. You found all this in the cupboard?" Travis asked as he dunked another biscuit into his bowl.

"No, sir," she continued to talk to her lap. "I went to the garden and pulled some vegetables."

"You left Matilda alone?" His tone went up an octave.

"She was asleep, and I only stepped outside for a min—"

"But she is why you're here! The *only* reason you're here!" He turned to look at his sleeping child, then back at her. "I didn't ask you to cook for me *or* tend the gard—"

He stopped abruptly. And even though Travis tried to mask his anger, she could tell he was still mad.

"I brought you here to care for Matilda, and that's what I expect you to do. Do you understand?" he asked calmly.

"Yes, sir."

"You are not to leave her alone, not even for a minute."

"Yes, sir."

Katie fought the tears that stung her eyes. She'd only been in Travis' home half a day, but she'd already made him mad.

Twice.

But she knew better now. He expected nothing from her but a nursemaid for his daughter. She could do that. She would care for Matilda like she was a fragile little bird. He would have no reason to be mad at her again.

Travis pushed away from the table and stood. "I have more chores to do—chores I haven't gotten to for a while." He crossed the room and grabbed his heavy coat. "I'll be coming in late. There is enough milk in the pail for Mattie until morning. She'll be up at least two more times tonight and again at first light. You stay with her, understand?"

"Yes, sir."

When Travis closed the door, Katie expelled the breath she'd been holding and started to clear the table.

But what am I to do with the dishes?

There wasn't enough water to wash them, and she was forbidden to leave the cabin. Resigned to the fact that she would have to wait until morning, she finished clearing the table.

After pouring the remaining broth from her bowl back into the pot, she pulled the piece of cloth snug around the leftover biscuits and set them on the shelf.

When Matilda fussed, Katie picked her up right away and pressed the child to her chest, afraid the smallest chirp would bring Travis back in, angrier than ever.

Swaying from side to side, she was thankful the child didn't let out another peep. Instead, Matilda looked at Katie like all was right in the world.

"I guess I would get bored too, just lying in that cradle," Katie cooed as she walked Matilda around the cabin. "See this," she pointed to the stove, "that's where we will cook our meals. And the fireplace will keep us warm in winter."

She moved about the cabin as she spoke, pretending Matilda understood everything she said. "I will teach you how to roll biscuits and knead bread and make a crust that will have your pa's mouth absolutely watering with delight. Of course, we will have venison stew, and duck, and whatever else your pa hunts. He will provide for your sustenance, and I will provide for your needs."

The infant looked at her with dazzling blue eyes, her face the picture of contentment. Tears pooled in Katie's as she clenched them shut and held Matilda a little tighter to her breast.

Protect her, Lord. Don't ever let her know the anger of a man.

Katie was surprised at her mumbled prayer, having given up asking God for help a long time ago.

But seeing the innocence in Matilda's eyes, she had to hope there was someone out there who would protect her, even if it was from the people who were supposed to love her.

I ask nothing for myself, Lord, but help Matilda to have a good life.

9

With the midnight moon casting shadows around the cabin, Katie fed Matilda, wishing she shared even an ounce of the child's peace and calm. Travis never returned after storming out during supper, and Katie didn't know what to make of that. Though she was grateful he didn't take out his anger on her, or demand she share the marriage bed her first night there, she was worried.

What if he doesn't return?

What if he leaves us for days on end?

Alone.

To fend for ourselves.

"No," she whispered to Matilda. "Your daddy loves you too much. He wouldn't leave you, even if he is angry with me."

Katie continued to question Travis' action as she stared at Matilda pressed against her nightgown.

With her bottle finished and her tummy cleared of air, Matilda fell back to sleep without so much as a whimper. Katie carefully laid her in the cradle, then stood over her in complete awe. The light from the lantern played with Matilda's hair, transforming the little wisps into spun gold, and her soft eyelashes rested against her porcelain skin, like feathers on a drift of snow. She looked so beautiful, so perfect, Katie felt her heart constrict.

Tucking the small blanket around Matilda, Katie stepped toward the kitchen table to extinguish the light. But a soft glow from outside the cabin drew her attention.

Peering through the small windowpanes, Katie saw light filtering from beneath the barn door. She glanced at the timepiece on the mantle.

One o'clock.

Is Travis still working?

Confusion swirled inside her as she turned down the lantern and crawled beneath the musty quilt. Katie's eyes and nose stung as she fought back the emotion welling inside her. She didn't know why she was struggling so much with her feelings. She was thankful Travis hadn't required her to consummate their marriage. And even though she knew *that* wasn't why he married her, it was well within his right to claim her as his wife.

Did he believe what people said about her? Did he think she was crazy?

No. It can't be that. He wouldn't leave Matilda with me if he thought I was unfit.

But if it wasn't her disposition, it had to be what he saw when he looked at her.

She gathered her hair together and pulled it across her shoulder, the tips nearly reaching her waist. She always thought her hair was her best quality. Her mother used to call her 'her little Rapunzel.' She said the fairy tale beauty had long, golden hair. Katie's hair was nearly the color of Matilda's, and Travis beamed when he looked at his daughter.

So it can't be my hair.

She moved her hands and allowed them to rest upon her

slight chest. She wasn't ample like some girls her age, but her figure was fuller than Travis' deceased wife. Her hands drifted to her hips. She was by no means portly. Though on occasion she had tried to add to her figure, thinking she could make herself look less appealing to Jethro, but it never worked. His lecherous behavior could not be diminished by a few pounds.

That left her face.

He must think I'm unattractive.

Jethro was right. She was a nothing. A waste.

She would never amount to anything or be loved by anyone.

Katie hadn't even realized she was crying until a tear trickled down her face and wet the pillow.

It's not true, she encouraged herself.

Matilda loves me. I can see it in the way she stares at me.

Their bond was instant as they sat in the rocker in her living room, their parents deciding their futures.

Katie closed her eyes, wishing away the turmoil inside her.

I am here for Matilda.

Nothing more.

And for that I will be thankful.

10

Katie woke abruptly, not knowing why.

She quickly tossed back the quilt and looked over the edge of the bed into the cradle. As she did, she heard the front door creak shut.

When she saw Matilda was still fast asleep, she took a deep breath in relief. With the cabin just beginning to awaken with the light of day, she glanced at the kitchen table and noticed a basket and a pail.

Travis must have slipped in and back out again.

And since he'd never come to bed last night, she could only assume he had bedded down in the barn.

Curious what was in the basket, she tiptoed to the table and saw several eggs nestled together next to a pail of fresh milk.

She glanced at the timepiece on the mantle and counted on her fingers how many hours Matilda had been asleep. Knowing the baby would be up soon, Katie realized she needed to get dressed and fix breakfast if she hoped to eat before Matilda woke up.

Lifting her bundle from the corner, and laying it on the bed, she pulled out her brown skirt and shirtwaist. Once she was dressed, Katie stared at the basket of eggs and thought about what Travis had said.

'I didn't ask you to cook for me.'

But how can I not fix him breakfast? There are plenty of eggs, and he needs to eat too. But if I disobey . . .

Katie struggled, not knowing what to do.

Even though Travis' only interest in her, was for Matilda's sake, she wanted to help him too. Matilda hadn't just lost a mama; Travis had lost a wife. And even though she could never replace Mary, that didn't mean she couldn't do the things a wife would do.

Looking around the dusty cabin, at the empty pantry shelves, and the stack of soiled clothes near the backdoor, she sighed.

He didn't just need a nursemaid; he needed a wife.

Someone to care for *him.*

Katie prepared breakfast and hurried to eat her portion. She'd made enough scrambled eggs for Travis, hoping he would come in and eat, but he didn't. Matilda, on the other hand, woke with an infant-sized roar and a tiger-sized appetite.

After changing Matilda's diaper, Katie settled them in the rocking chair and watched with amazement as the little girl guzzled her bottle like a hungry calf. The wonderment she saw in Matilda's eyes was magical. She didn't know yet that there were people in the world who could hurt her. She didn't understand about pain and sorrow. Katie longed for the time when she was that innocent, before her life had turned into a never-ending nightmare.

When Katie laid Matilda in her cradle, she watched the child's eyes as she took in her tiny, little world. Every day would be exciting for her, filled with new curiosities, leading to wonderful discoveries.

And I will be there to protect you every step of the way.

Katie waited until five-thirty before putting Travis' breakfast in a pail and gathering Matilda in her arms. She crossed the yard to the barn and slipped through the slightly parted doors. When she heard scraping and shoveling, she followed the sound to the far side of the barn.

"Travis?" she called out, her voice low and scratchy.

She thought it strange that she no longer sounded like herself. Years of silence had changed her voice, or maybe it was puberty. Or both. She cleared her throat and tried again. "Travis?"

He walked out from one of the stalls and looked at her, sweat glistening on his forehead, irritation in his eyes.

Forcing a smile, she held out the pail in front of her. "I brought you breakfast."

He looked at Matilda in her arms, then at her. "That wasn't necessary. I had some jerky."

"But it was no trouble. You gathered plenty of eggs, and the biscuits are left over from supper." She handed him the pail and watched as he accepted it reluctantly.

"But I told you, I don't want you worrying about me. You're here for Matilda."

"But she is so easy to care for, and a good little sleeper. I could easily handle garden work when she's nap—"

"No!" his voice boomed. "I don't want her left alone, not even for a minute."

"But—"

"I said no!"

She flinched at his shout, causing Matilda to stir. She saw Travis clench his fist and take a deep breath. She took a step back and held Matilda a little tighter.

"Please, Kathryn." His words were softer, more controlled. "Just take care of Mattie. I have a lot of work to catch up on, and I won't be able to do that if I'm worried about her."

Katie stared at the dirt floor. "I understand. I'm sorry I upset you." She turned around and was almost out the barn door.

"Kathryn . . ."

She looked over her shoulder.

He lifted the pail slightly. "Thank you for breakfast."

She smiled, even though she was fighting back tears.

Hurrying to the cabin, her heart thrashing about in her chest, she laid Matilda on the bed, afraid her shaking hands would drop her.

"What is wrong with me? How is it I bring out such anger in men?" she whispered while she paced, kneading her fingers, brushing tears from her cheeks.

Finally, she sat down at the kitchen table, her head in her hands, taking deep breaths until her racing heart settled.

When Matilda cooed, Katie moved to the cradle and looked down into her little cherubic face. She couldn't help but smile.

"Don't worry, Mattie, I might not be your mama, but I'm going to care for you like you're my very own."

Sitting at the kitchen table, Katie glanced at the clock on the mantle then to the amber sky. She swallowed the last of her supper, but it held no taste.

She had spent the whole day in the cabin keeping watch over Matilda, waiting for Travis to come in for dinner and then supper.

But he never showed.

With sagging shoulders, she walked to the stove and scraped the cold congealed gravy from her plate into a makeshift trash bucket. Wrapping the remaining biscuits in the piece of cloth she'd been using, Katie set them aside for breakfast.

Again.

Groaning from boredom, she walked to the small bookshelf tucked in the corner and tilted her head so she could read the spines. Even though each title intrigued her, she didn't reach for a one. Instead, she watched Matilda as she slept.

"What a wonderful world you live in," she whispered. "You're content with a full belly, a dry backside, and a hummed lullaby. If only life could always be so easy."

Katie watched Matilda's steady breathing, her chest rising and falling. It became hypnotic and soon she felt her own eyes flutter shut. With resignation, she undressed, slipped into her nightgown, and crawled under the cold bedcovers.

11

As Katie dressed Mattie for church, she thought back over the last few weeks. Though she really didn't know what to expect when she rode off with Travis three Sundays ago, she certainly wouldn't have guessed the weeks would go by as they had.

Travis had all but ignored her. Though every morning fresh eggs and milk were on the counter, and every other day, he left some kind of meat or a plucked chicken, Travis spent very little time in the cabin.

The few instances he did come in during the day, he immediately went to the cradle. Katie knew Travis was checking up on her, making sure Mattie was getting the care she needed. Even so, it warmed Katie's heart to see such a strapping man melt at the sight of his little girl. He would pick her up, smile at her, and talk in gentle whispers.

However, when he turned to her, a blank expression would cover his face.

A few times Travis asked if she needed anything, but for the most part, they had shared very few words.

Katie had spent her time cleaning and re-cleaning the small cabin she now called home. Every corner, every window, and every surface had been washed, scrubbed, or dusted. She made breakfast and dinner for Travis every day and left it in a pail outside the barn door. For supper, she would leave a plate of food sitting on the stovetop, and in the morning it would be empty.

She didn't understand what it was about her that Travis didn't like, or why he insisted on staying away. And even though she felt lonely, she was at peace, knowing she was doing what she was brought there to do.

Care for Matilda.

Though fear of Jethro and Wade still lingered in her thoughts, she did her best to ignore them. Despite their taunting words, she was convinced they weren't foolish enough to ride onto Travis' property and follow through with their threats.

Even they are smarter than that.

When Mattie's cooing interrupted Katie's woolgathering, she walked over to the cradle and smiled at her rescuer. "Well, little miss, are you ready to meet the world?" she asked, then scooped up Matilda and brought her to her shoulder.

Today would be Mattie's first trip to town. In fact, other than being at Katie's house when she and Travis were married, Mattie hadn't gone anywhere. This would be her coming out trip, and in many ways, it would be Katie's as well.

But the thought of facing the townspeople made her shudder.

What would they say? What would they think?

Would they treat Travis like they treated her, as an outcast, a person to be kept at a distance? Would they think he was foolish for allowing a crazy woman to care for his daughter?

Immediately, Katie felt protective of Travis. Though he hardly talked to her or showed her any attention, he didn't deserve to be shunned.

He was a good man.

With a beautiful daughter.

In a desperate situation.

People should look for ways to help a man in his circumstances, not turn their backs on him.

And if the townsmen chose the latter, it would be because of her.

Overwhelmed with sadness, she held Mattie a little tighter.

"Maybe I can convince Travis it's too soon for you to go to town, that it would be best if you were a little older before being surrounded by so many people."

After all, Travis still insisted they stay indoors, as if he feared a wild animal would carry Matilda away if they were outside. The only fresh air they got each day was when they left Travis' breakfast and dinner at the barn door. And as the days stretched into weeks, Katie walked slower and slower, sometimes even circling around the back of the cabin. Anything to allow them a few more minutes outside.

Maybe I could—

When the door swung open, Katie turned to Travis.

"Are you ready?" he asked.

"Uh, yes, but I was thinking . . ." Her words were so soft, she could barely hear herself. Clearing her throat, she tried to sound stronger. "I don't know if Mattie should go to town."

"Why?" Travis rushed across the room, panic in his eyes. "Is something wrong with Matilda?" He circled behind Katie and bent to look at his daughter where she was perched on her shoulder.

"No. She's fine. I promise. I was just thinking maybe we could wait another week or so. You know, until we're . . .

better adjusted."

Travis stepped in front of Katie and looked her in the eyes. "Why don't you want to go to town?"

She looked away.

"Kathryn, if this is about the town gossip, you need to move past it. You're my wife now. Eventually, people will accept you as such. Besides, I have to talk to Mr. Dudley from the mercantile while we're in town."

Defeated, Katie walked over to the kitchen table, where she had placed Matilda's things.

"Here, let me take her." Travis reached for Mattie, and with the most adoring smile, he took her into his arms and whispered, "Everyone is going to see how beautiful you are. You're going to make your daddy so proud."

After filling the blanket-lined box with every imaginable thing Matilda might need, Katie carried it outside and put it in the back of the wagon. Once she was seated on the buckboard, Travis handed Matilda up to her. She watched as he closed the front door, then settled on the seat beside her. And with a flick of his wrists, the horses headed for town.

Though Travis was quiet, Katie did her best to enjoy the scenery. It was all new to her, never having gone this route before. So, she studied the different trees and the unique rock formations that popped up here and there, anything to keep her mind off what lay ahead.

"How is Mattie doing at night?"

Caught a little off guard, she glanced back at Matilda, then turned to Travis. "Very well. She only wakes up once now."

"Really. Is that okay?" Concern creased his brow as he looked at her. "I mean . . . is she getting enough to eat?"

"She's doing fine. I read in the evenings . . . to help pass the time. So, I feed her before I turn in for the night. She doesn't wake again until about two. Once she has her fill, we rock for a few minutes, and then she sleeps until dawn. She's a good little sleeper."

"Not before you got here, she wasn't." Travis shook his head. "I would walk the floors with her half the night, just knowing something was wrong. She would fuss and wriggle and look at me like she was trying to tell me something."

"Well, babies are very smart. Mattie probably sensed your worry, so she worried too. She was just copying her pa."

"Maybe so." His shoulders drooped.

Instinctively, Katie placed her hand on his forearm, trying to comfort him. "It's not your fault, Travis. You didn't know. This is all new to you."

He looked at her hand, then at her. "I don't want your pity, Kathryn."

His words scorched her, and she quickly snatched back her hand. "That's not what I was doing. I just didn't want you to feel—"

"Don't worry about how I feel. Just take care of Matilda. That's all I'm asking from you."

Katie fought back tears that threatened to fall. She'd been enjoying their conversation. She didn't mean to upset him or hurt his feelings.

Why is it I keep saying the wrong thing?

Something triggered inside her, the same protection mechanism that helped her shut the world out for over five years.

She was silent.

12

When they arrived in the church yard, all eyes were on them. Katie looked at Mattie, straightening the little white gown she wore, not wanting to make eye contact with anyone. Travis set the brake on the wagon and walked over to help her down. Katie could see the nervous look on his face, his eyebrows dipping, his lips pressed tight.

After passing Mattie to Travis, he held out his hand to help her down. She brushed the wrinkles from her dress, made sure her hair was still in place, then reached for Mattie, but Travis took a step back. "I'll hold her. She is my daughter after all."

Though she was sure Travis didn't mean for his words to hurt, they cut like a knife. *Of course he wants to hold Matilda and show her off.* But Katie had counted on having the child to care for—a distraction—so she wouldn't have to interact with the other churchgoers.

When Travis stepped away from the wagon with Matilda in his arms, Katie quickly grabbed a few items from Matilda's box and caught up with them. Immediately, a cluster of women gathered around them, cooing and smiling.

"Why she's just a little angel, Travis," Mrs. Hathaway gushed.

"Look at that golden hair. A real beauty she is," Mrs. Dudley added then smiled in Katie's direction. "She's beautiful . . . just like her mother." Katie stood a little straighter. A nicer complement no one could've ever given her. "*Mary* always was a beauty . . . in her own way."

Crushed. That's how Katie felt.

Utterly crushed.

It wasn't the first time Mrs. Dudley had humiliated her. The way she used words as weapons, Katie was convinced the woman had vinegar flowing through her veins.

"Everyone," the pastor spoke from the church steps. "If we can all find our seats, it's time to begin services."

It took all the willpower Katie could muster not to burst into tears. Travis seemed oblivious to Mrs. Dudley's cruel statement. Then again, it wasn't cruel to him. He loved Mary and could see her reflected in his daughter's eyes.

Katie clenched her hands at her sides, doing her best to smile. *Don't let them win. Don't let them know they've hurt you.* She walked a few paces behind Travis, sensing all eyes on her. She felt like a circus sideshow, a freak people gawked at with curious stares.

When fingers dug into her upper arm and spun her around, she gasped.

"Aren't you going to say hi to your pa?"

Jethro James smiled, but it was the gleam in his eyes that frightened her.

"Where are your manners, ignoring your kin like that." Wade glared at her over Jethro's shoulder. "We have some catching up to do. But you go on. We wouldn't want to miss services. We can talk about a reunion later."

13

Katie didn't hear a thing the preacher said. The only words echoing in her ears were Jethro's and Wade's.

Reunion? Surely, they aren't that foolish or that bold. I'm married now. Another man's wife. A husband would know if his wife was . . .

But Travis wasn't her husband, not really. Yes, he married her, and yes, they lived together, but their marriage wasn't . . . complete.

But Jethro and Wade don't know that. They couldn't. They're only trying to scare me. Scare me into silence.

After the closing hymn, and the handshake of fellowship from the preacher, Katie followed Travis down the church steps. She wanted to leave before Jethro made some sort of scene, but Travis seemed to linger.

"We should probably get Matilda home. This has been a long day for her." Katie took a few steps toward the wagon, but Travis didn't follow.

"I still have some business to discuss with Mr. Dudley. Go ahead and take Matilda; I'll meet you at the wagon."

Just as Travis placed Matilda in her arms, she began to fuss. And even though it wasn't quite feeding time, Katie hurried to the wagon, not wanting others to think she couldn't handle caring for a baby.

Pulling herself up onto the wagon, she watched as Matilda continued to fret and whimper. Knowing she was getting ready to speak her peace, Katie grabbed a bottle from the box in the back and pressed the tip against Matilda's lips. Immediately, she opened wide and started drinking with gusto. Katie rocked her slowly, humming a lullaby while Mattie stared at her with big soulful eyes.

"You're a natural."

Katie looked over her shoulder and saw her mama standing alongside the wagon. Feeling the sting of tears, she turned back to Mattie, not knowing what to say. She had so many questions she wanted to ask but wasn't sure if she could handle the answers.

"How are you doing?" Mama asked.

"Fine."

"Is Travis treating you all right?"

"Yes, ma'am."

"And Matilda, how are you two getting on?"

"We're getting along just fine, Mama."

Katie's words were sharp . . . cold, but she couldn't help it. She no longer knew if she considered Mama kin or enemy.

"Katie, I'm so—"

"It's Kathryn, remember?" She watched as her mama withered.

"All right . . . Kathryn," her mama repeated, "I am so sorry. What I did . . . or should I say what I didn't do, there is no excuse other than I was in fear of our lives. Jethro is a very dangerous man. I didn't know that when I married him, and then it was too late. I didn't know what else to do."

"How long?" Katie whispered.

Her mama frowned. "I don't understand?"

"How long did you know what he was doing?"

Mama stared off into the distance. "It doesn't matter, not now. You have Travis and Matilda. Your own little family. Things will be better now. You'll see."

"How can you say that?" Katie snapped, but hushed her tone for Matilda's sake. "He hurt me, Mama. He hurt me something awful. And you let him. How could you?"

"He told me he would kill you if I said anything."

"But don't you understand? What he did to me . . . he *did* kill me. On the inside." She looked away, trying to hold back her tears, but it was no use. "Do you know how many times I sat under the oak tree by the barn, a rope in my hand, wondering if I could climb it . . . if I could tie a knot tight enough? I just wanted the pain to stop. But I didn't do it. Because I was terrified what he would do to you and Seth."

Crying, Mama laid her hand on Katie's skirt. "I'm sorry, Kathryn. I was just so afraid."

"And what about Wade? Were you afraid of him too?"

Mama frowned. "What are you talking about? Did Wade know?"

"Yes, Mama, he knew. Wade is just like his pa. He—"

"Kathryn, what's wrong?"

She quickly brushed the tears from her cheeks before turning around. "Travis, I didn't hear you walk up. Are you ready to go?"

"What has you so upset?" he persisted.

She froze, knowing she couldn't explain.

"Oh, you know us women folk, Travis," her mama said as she dabbed her eyes. "We cry over the craziest little things. Just seeing my baby sitting with a baby in her arms, well it's enough to make a mother weep."

Mama turned to her, smiling through her tears. "Well, I'll be seeing you, Kathryn. I know you're busy with this little one and all, so I won't be bothering you none at your place. I'll just see you next week at church." She laid a hand on her knee and squeezed. "You've made your mama awfully proud."

———— • ————

Wade watched as Travis pulled out of town. Looking at his pa, he could tell what he was thinking, because he was thinking the same thing. Sooner or later Travis would leave Katie alone. Once he trusted her enough with that brat of his, he would leave her. And when he did, Wade would do the brotherly thing and check in on her, make sure she was treating her new husband right. And let her know how very much he missed having her around.

14

Riding in silence, Katie kept her attention on Matilda, though out of the corner of her eye, she could see Travis kept looking her way.

No sooner had Matilda finished her bottle and fallen asleep, Travis cleared his throat and asked, "Are you sure you're okay?"

"Yes, sir." She looked out over the prairie, anywhere but at Travis.

"Are you homesick?"

"No," she answered softly.

"You seemed pretty upset talking with your mother. I didn't hear what you were saying, but you sounded like you were . . . angry."

"I'm fine, Travis."

They rode only a short distance more when he spoke again.

"Kathryn, can you look at me for a minute."

She took a deep breath, then turned his way.

"I need to apologize. I was short with you today and said some unkind things."

She teared up at the sincerity she saw in his eyes.

"This is all just so different for me. So new. I don't know what to say or how to act, but it's not fair to take my confusion out on you."

She didn't trust herself to speak; her feelings were such a jumbled mess.

"I'm sorry I've been ignoring you and Mattie," he said, staring at the road in front of them. "That first week, I had so much to do, so many chores. I had allowed everything to fall into ruin and had to work hard to bring it back. One day ran into the next, one week into another. With each day that went by, it got easier to be by myself, to do what I knew how to do. So, I stayed in the barn."

He glanced at her, but quickly looked away.

"I was selfish and didn't consider the changes going on in *your* life. Separated from your family. Living in a strange place. I was only thinking about Matilda. But . . . seeing you crying with your mother made me realize how selfish I've been. I'm sorry, Kathryn. I hope you'll find it in your heart to forgive me."

She quietly cried into the sleeve of her dress.

"I forgive you, Travis," she said after gaining her composure. "And I'm sorry you lost Mary and felt pressured into giving Matilda a mama. I don't want to be a burden to you, and I know you're grieving. I just want to help anyway I can."

"You are helping me. The way you've taken to Mattie is a real answer to prayer."

"But I could do so much more if you'd just let me. When Mattie's napping, I could help with the garden, collect the eggs, see to the milking. Then you wouldn't have to work so hard or such long hours."

He didn't say anything for a long while, long enough Katie figured he wouldn't. But then he sighed, his shoulders drooping like the weight of the world had settled on them.

"One day I was out milking," he whispered. "When I walked back into the house, Mattie's lips were blue. She wasn't breathing. I picked her up and shook her, pinched her, anything to get her to squawk. Finally, she gasped and let out a terrifying cry."

Travis turned to Katie, tears wetting his face. "What if I hadn't checked on her? What if I had gone on to my next chore? She would've died." He turned back to the road. "I don't know what I would've done if I lost Mattie too."

Katie couldn't imagine how horrible that must've been for Travis. Wanting to comfort him, she reached for him, but quickly withdrew her hand, not wanting to make him angry again.

"Travis, I can understand how terrifying that must have been for you, but Mattie has been doing fine these last few weeks. She's eating good, sleeping well, and just the sweetest little thing when she's awake. Mattie is strong and in good health. I don't think you have anything to worry about. Even so, if you don't want me to leave her alone, she could go with me when I'm doing chores."

Travis shook his head vigorously. "No. She doesn't need to be outdoors. Going to church is one thing, but I don't want her outside more than she needs to be."

"But Travis, babies need the sun and the strength it provides. They also need to breathe fresh air. It's good for them."

"But what if she gets sick or catches a chill or something?"

"That could happen even if I keep her indoors. In fact, I think being cooped up in a stuffy house can be just as bad on little ones."

"But you don't know that for sure." His tone grew rigid.

"Okay, Travis, how about I only take Mattie outside after the noon hour? The day will be at its best, the morning chill chased away by the sun. You would still have to bring in the milk for morning, but I could work in the garden and maybe even get some of the laundry tended to. Nothing has gotten a thorough scrubbing since I got here."

She watched Travis, his jaw rotating as he mulled it over. She wanted to say more, convince him she knew what she was talking about, but didn't dare.

"Okay. You and Mattie can be outside in the afternoon but watch her closely. The least little sign she's doing poorly, you tell me. Don't go hiding it because you don't want to admit you were wrong."

Determined not to be wounded by his words, Katie sat up a little taller. "Travis, I can assure you, I would never let ego get in the way of Matilda's well-being, that I can promise you."

Choosing to focus on the positive, Katie celebrated on the inside. She had just dispensed her first bit of parenting advice, and Travis had listened to her like she was a real person. It was a small victory, but a step none the less toward a better relationship with Travis.

15

It had been six weeks since marrying Travis, and for the first time in Katie's life, she felt hopeful about her future.

Even though Travis still spent most of his time away from the house, and bedded down in the barn each night, when he came in for meals, conversation was easier between them. And though Jethro and Wade taunted her every Sunday with their wicked stares and evil comments, they had not made good on their threats.

Matilda continued to be an absolute delight. They had fallen into a simple routine, spending most afternoons outside tending the garden and seeing to the wash, even taking naps under the large shade tree outside the backdoor. Katie would strip Mattie down to nothing but her diaper, lay her on a blanket, then watch as she looked around with her big blue eyes, clearly stimulated by her whole new world.

However, Katie hoped to accomplish a little bit more today.

Tired of the bucket wash she had settled for on Saturday nights, she was desperate for a good bath—a complete soaking.

Having already scouted out the ideal location where she could lie Mattie down but still keep an eye on her while she bathed, she'd just been waiting for a day warmer than most.

So, today when she stepped outside and felt the intense rays from the sun, she considered it.

Then, when Travis told her, he would be on the far side of the pasture fixing some rotted posts, she decided it was the perfect chance to take a bath without being seen.

After dinner, she gathered everything she needed, picked up Mattie, and headed for the creek. Situating the blanket just right, Katie stripped Mattie down to her diaper and watched her coo and smile as the breath of the wind brushed across her face, and the warmth of the sun kissed her skin.

"Enjoy it while you can, little miss, your fair skin can't take too much of this sun. But you'll be fine while I take a quick dip and scrub some soap through my hair."

Katie pulled off her skirt and shirtwaist, pressed a towel to her chest, and walked to the water's edge. After taking a swift look around, she removed her underthings and slipped into the slightly chilled water. Wading to where it was deepest, she sat down and let the water flow over her shoulders.

Not wasting any time, she tipped her head back to get her scalp completely wet, then scrubbed her hair with her special bar of perfumed soap. She worked it into a lather, massaging her head more than necessary, but it felt so luxurious she didn't want to stop. She couldn't remember the last time she'd taken a bath without worrying that Jethro or Wade was lurking among the shadows, so she allowed herself to indulge a few minutes longer.

After rinsing the suds from her hair, she soaped her body, all the while keeping a watchful eye on Mattie, laughing at the way the infant cooed and punched the air, mesmerized by the branches dancing above her.

When it came time to get out of the water, Katie carefully

navigated the rocky creek bed. But as she reached for the towel on the bank, she heard a twig snap.

Startled, she dropped back into the water, arms crossed against her bare chest. Looking at Matilda, she sighed with relief to see the baby still babbling and squirming, carefree and happy.

Darting a look at the far side of the creek, Katie scanned the shore, terrified she would find Wade lurking behind a tree, ready to make good on his threats.

But no one was there.

With her heart racing, Katie dashed out of the water, collected her underthings, and tossed them on the blanket next to Matilda. Pulling her skirt and shirtwaist over her still wet body was difficult, but she didn't dare waste time drying herself off.

Looking around for any signs of a predator, she scooped up Matilda, gathered her things in the blanket, and hurried to the backdoor. Once she was safely inside the cabin, she crossed the room and laid Matilda on the bed, not trusting her shaky hands to hold her.

Taking several deep breaths to slow the pounding of her heart, Katie watched Mattie as she smiled and wriggled, completely unaware of the danger she'd been in.

Thank goodness.

After dressing Mattie, Katie twisted her wet hair over the basin, squeezing out as much water as she could, then pulled Matilda to her chest. "I'm sorry, sweetheart. I'm so, so sorry. Anyone could've been out there."

Wade could have been there, wanting to cause trouble.

Or a wild animal could have come and carried Matilda away.

How could I have been so careless?

"I am so, so sorry," she repeated, tears wetting her cheeks as she paced the cabin, rocking Matilda, scenario after horrifying scenario taunting her.

Katie wasn't sure how much time had passed, but when she realized Matilda was asleep on her shoulder, she stopped pacing and gently laid her in the cradle.

Looking down at her sopping clothes, she pulled off her skirt and shirtwaist, slipped on her underthings, then dropped her head into her hands, her wet hair falling loose around her face.

Travis was right to be overprotective.

I was careless and irresponsible.

I never even considered Matilda would be in danger.

What kind of mother would do such a thing?

16

Travis was stunned.

So stunned, he wasn't sure what to do next.

When he heard splashing coming from the creek, he thought it might be game.

He had no idea Kathryn was bathing.

And even though he knew he should have turned away immediately, he was so captivated by her ivory skin glistening in the sunlight, he stood there gawking like an adolescent schoolboy.

When he finally came to his senses, he turned to leave but stumbled over a brittle tree limb, sending Kathryn running for the house, a look of terror on her face.

Now he wasn't sure what to do.

He wanted to make sure she was okay. However, if he explained what happened, he'd be admitting to watching her.

Not that he did it intentionally.

She just looked so . . .

Maybe I'll go to the house to see how she's doing. If Kathryn seems fine, there will be no reason to bring it up.

Travis' rapidly beating heart confused and frustrated him. He had no right to look at Kathryn *that* way. Even if they were married, it was only for convenience. The sole purpose was to provide Matilda with a mother. He wasn't looking for a wife. He loved Mary with all his heart, and to gaze on another woman betrayed that love.

Stopping at the cabin door, he took a deep breath before walking in. He tried to act normal, like coming home in the middle of the day was part of his routine, but as soon as he saw Kathryn grab for something to cover herself, he realized he had only made matters worse.

———— ● ————

Katie stood with her wet skirt pressed against her chest, not knowing what she should do.

Travis was her husband after all, but he had never seen her in her underclothes, and with her wet hair hanging in her face, and eyes that were sure to be red from crying, she had to be quite a sight.

But to explain why she was undressed in the middle of the day would require her to tell him what she'd been doing and how careless she'd been.

Just when I've started to gain Travis' trust, I've gone and ruined everything.

"Kathryn, are you okay?"

She didn't know if it was the caring timbre of his voice or the fact that she would have to explain her carelessness, but Travis' simple question opened up the floodgates of emotion she had tried so hard to press down.

———— ● ————

Instinctively, Travis crossed to where Kathryn was

standing beside the bed and reached to pull her close, but when she flinched, he took a step back, not knowing what to do.

"Are you hurt?"

A second of panic had him looking for Matilda, but when he saw her sound asleep in the cradle, he sighed with relief.

Turning his attention back to Kathryn, he noticed how her body shook. From fear or cold, he wasn't sure which.

"Kathryn, you need to sit down."

When she lowered herself to the edge of the bed, he took a seat next to her, then reached for the corner of the bed quilt and draped it around her shaking shoulders.

"I'm so sorry, Travis. I . . . I didn't mean to be so care . . . careless. I just wanted to take a bath and wash my ha . . . hair. I never let Matilda out of my sight. But then there was a no . . . noise. Someone or something was watching us. I don't know who or what, but Matilda would've been help . . . helpless against anyone or anything if they had wanted to hurt her."

Kathryn was hysterical, her words barely discernible through her sobbing.

"It's my fault. All my fa . . . fault. I thought it would be okay. I was no more than a couple of yards from the house. I thought it would be sa . . . safe."

"It's okay, Kathryn. It's okay."

Travis wanted to comfort her but felt any attempt would probably do more harm than good. He looked at her hands, shivering as she clutched her wet skirt to her chest.

"You need to put on some dry clothes. You're chilled."

She didn't move. She just kept repeating how sorry she was, and that it was all her fault.

"Kathryn," he said firmly, "I need you to get dressed. Then we can talk about what happened."

She didn't move. She just rocked, her shaking hands pressed to her chest. "I'm so sorry, Travis. I should have listened to you. I should have been more careful. How could I have been so foolish? I'm so sorry."

With a sigh of guilt and resignation, Travis finally blurted out the truth. "Kathryn, it was me. What you heard was me."

There. I said it.

Slowly, as if it took a moment for his words to sink in, she turned to him in disbelief.

"I didn't know you were bathing," he continued. "I heard noises and went to see what the commotion was. It was me who snapped the twig. You did nothing wrong. Matilda was never in danger."

Tears once again flooded her eyes, making him feel even worse than he already did.

"I'm sorry I startled you, really I am."

He waited for her to gather her composure, feeling clueless on what he should do or say.

Finally, her tears stopped, but her body continued to shutter and rock.

"Kathryn . . . look at me."

Travis sighed, irritated she was ignoring him. Or was he really just irritated with himself?

Crouching in front of her, he pushed her wet and matted hair back from her face, hooking it behind her ears. Then, as gently as he could, he cupped her face in his hands and tipped her head up until he could look her in the eyes. "Kathryn, you did nothing wrong, understand?"

Slowly, she nodded, but the guilt never left her eyes.

"Now . . . I need you to let go of those wet clothes and

put on something dry before you catch your death."

Travis stood and stepped back, giving her some room. Slowly, she pushed the quilt off her shoulders and stood, her wet skirt still pressed to her chest. As she walked to the dresser on the wall opposite the bed, Travis couldn't help but notice how ill-fitting and worn her camisole was. It was clear, by the way she held the strap on one shoulder, that it was far too big for her and from the tattered stitching and mismatched thread, he could see it had been mended several times.

Dropping her skirt on the floor, she pulled a dry set of under things from the dresser. Finally letting go of the tattered strap, she allowed it to slip from her shoulder, exposing her back.

A back marred with scars.

17

"Sakes alive, Kathryn, what happened to you?"

She knew the second Travis gasped, that he had seen the ugly stripes that crisscrossed her back. She quickly pulled the camisole strap onto her shoulder and took a deep breath.

You just have to sound convincing. He'll have no reason to doubt you.

Having prepared for this moment—knowing it was only a matter of time before she'd have to explain the hideous scars—she just wished it didn't have to be now. Her heart was already racing, and the fact that she was standing before Travis in nothing but her underthings didn't help matters.

"It was an accident," she said, matter-of-factly. "I got twisted up in a barbed wire fence. The more I tried to get loose, the worse I cut myself. It happened a while ago. It's no big deal. It's nothing. Really."

When she felt Travis' fingers slide the camisole strap from her shoulder, she shuddered. Clutching the thin cotton garment to her chest, she sensed his eyes on her, studying her scars, not believing her.

"That had to be some pretty thick barbed wire to leave marks like that."

"Like I said, I made it worse by trying to get free. Pa said

I got what I deserved, that I was being punished for my disobedience."

"Disobedience? How is getting caught in a fence disobedience?"

Shut up, Katie, you're only making it worse.

This is why she chose to be silent for so many years. Talking only got her in trouble.

"Kathryn, tell me what—"

"Travis . . ." She cut him off, not wanting to explain further in her frazzled state. "I could really use some water. The bucket is outside. I took it with me so I could fill the basin. Would you mind bringing it in?"

"But Kathryn . . ."

"Please, Travis," she pled, waiting for him to leave.

When Katie heard the soft click of the cabin door, she exhaled and nearly crumbled to the floor. With what little strength she had, she quickly dressed and tried to run a brush through her tangled hair.

When she glanced at Matilda, Katie smiled, relieved all the commotion had not affected the sleeping child in the least.

Closing her eyes, she said a quick prayer.

Thank you, God, for protecting her. She is an innocent. And though I no longer deserve Your protection for the things I've allowed, Matilda deserves only the very best. Help me provide that for her.

———————— • ————————

Travis knelt alongside the creek, splashing water on his face, his head spinning.

Kathryn was lying to him.

No barbed wire fence could make the ugly marks that scared her back. He knew a whipping when he saw one, but never had seen the results of one so severe. It was clear Kathryn had been punished something awful.

But why?

What could she have done that would call for such a beating?

In Travis' mind, there was nothing so bad, so wrong, that a father should take a strap to his daughter.

His first instinct was to go to Jethro James and question him about it, make him admit he'd been too harsh. But Travis didn't like the man much.

What would come of it if I did confront him? It wouldn't change anything. I would just be stirring up dissension with her family, and that's not fair to Kathryn.

No, I'll give her some time, then I'll ask again.

When Travis returned to the cabin, Kathryn sat on the far side of the bed, dressed and brushing her wet hair.

Crossing the room, he poured some water into the basin, and set the bucket down on the floor beside it. "I brought enough for evening."

"Thank you." She raised her eyes to meet his but quickly looked away.

"If you're okay, I need to get back to my chores."

"I'm fine. Thank you."

"Kathryn . . . I—"

"I'm fine, Travis, really."

Even though she spoke with confidence, he could see her hands were still shaking as she gripped the brush and ran it through her hair.

He didn't want to leave. He wanted to wrap her in his

arms and assure her everything would be okay. But knowing that could make matters even worse, Travis clenched his hands at his sides and willed his body to move toward the front door.

"Okay then. I'll be in at supper."

Once outside, he crossed the yard, the realization of his current situation sinking in. Kathryn wasn't just Matilda's mother; she was also his wife. And as her husband, it was his responsibility to protect her, provide for her, and keep her safe.

Though he loved Mary with all his heart—something that would never change—Kathryn was his wife now. And even if he married her for practical reasons, she had sacrificed a future she could've had with another man in order to provide Matilda with a mother.

Because of that, she deserved better.

Kathryn deserved a husband.

And starting tonight, that's what she is going to get.

18

When Travis came in for supper, Katie watched as he hooked his hat on the peg by the front door, then turn to her, questions clouding his eyes.

She quickly grabbed the basket of biscuits and set it on the table. "It's all ready," she said with a smile, pretending the earlier debacle never happened.

"Okay. I'll just wash up."

She stopped for a moment, surprised. Travis always washed up *before* coming in for meals.

Katie watched as he crossed the room to the washbasin, poured some water, soaped his hands, and splashed his face. After using a towel to dry off, he lifted Matilda from her cradle.

"How is my little lady tonight? Did you enjoy the sunshine this afternoon?" Matilda giggled and cooed. "All that sun is making you grow like a weed."

Katie watched Travis as he carried on with Matilda.

Lord, I pray Travis always loves his daughter the way a father should and protects her from anyone who would want to do her harm.

"Kathryn, that ham you're frying is spitting something fierce."

Katie gasped and turned to the stove. She was so caught up watching Travis, she completely forgot about dinner. Wrapping her apron around the handle of the skillet, she moved it from the licking flame.

"Ouch!" She quickly pulled her hand back.

"Kathryn, are you all right?"

She turned away and looked at her palm. Pressing the red blotch on her hand, she silently winced. "It's nothing."

"It's not *nothing*," Travis said from where he peered over her shoulder. "Let me see it."

"Really, Travis, I'm fine."

She picked up the bowl of mashed potatoes and set it on the table, while out of the corner of her eye, she watched Travis lay Matilda in the cradle.

Moving back to the stove, she stacked slices of ham onto a plate, feeling Travis hovering behind her.

"Let me see your hand," he insisted.

Not wanting to anger him by refusing, she held her palm out for Travis to see.

"Kathryn, that's going to blister. You need to put something on it."

Before she could protest, he retrieved a jar of salve from the small utility cupboard, twisted off the lid, and scooped a dollop out with his calloused finger. Gently, he touched the ointment to the angry red blotch on her hand.

She sucked in a breath at the pain.

"I'm sorry. It's going to hurt at first, but you'll feel some relief soon."

In slow, circular motions, Travis spread the ointment over her burn. Somehow, watching his large fingers stroking her skin with such tenderness made her completely forget the pain. She didn't dare look at him; she just watched his fingers continue their ministrations.

"There, does that feel better?"

Not trusting herself to answer intelligently, she just nodded.

"Good."

She was ready to pull her hand away when Travis lifted it closer to his lips and blew softly across her palm. The chill against the burn was nothing compared to the chill that filled her entire body.

Without thought, she looked up at him, only to be caught in his stare. He blew again on her hand, but his eyes never wavered from hers.

The moment was so intimate, so unsettling, she didn't know what to do, and the look in Travis' eyes was like nothing she had seen before.

She was terrified, but not afraid.

His stare was dangerous, but surprisingly, she'd never felt safer in her life.

The rest of the evening was a strange mix of normal and daydream.

Travis ate supper, talked about what he hoped to accomplish tomorrow, and spent time playing with Matilda like normal.

However, for Katie, the evening was anything *but* normal.

Though she ate dinner and listened as Travis talked about his plans, all she could think about was the intimacy they had shared. The way Travis held her hand, how his fingers soothed the burn on her palm, the feel of his breath against her skin. She even found herself imagining what it would be like if Travis thought of her as more than just a mama for Matilda. But then she would catch herself, knowing it wasn't to be.

Travis still loved Mary, and Katie knew he always would.

With the dishes done, and everything ready for tomorrow's breakfast, she prepared Matilda's evening bottle and waited for Travis to tell her good night and leave for the barn like normal.

But he continued to linger.

Katie watched as he played with Matilda long after supper. It was adorable to see a man of Travis' stature on his hands and knees playing peek-a-boo or hear his baritone voice rise to falsetto as he recited nursery rhymes and silly poems.

But soon enough, Matilda started to fuss. Travis tried his best to cajole her, but she would have none of it. She was hungry, and no amount of playtime would quench her appetite.

"She's just hungry, Travis," Katie yawned, feeling the late hour. "Here, I'll take her." She walked over to where he stood and put her arms out to take Matilda.

"Actually, I would like to feed her this evening," Travis said, even though he looked hesitant. "I admit, feeding time was always a struggle. Matilda would squirm and fuss, and I would end up with milk all down her front. But now that she's sturdier, I would like to give it another try."

"Of . . . of course," Katie stuttered slightly. "I'll just get her bottle." She turned and walked toward the stove, her mind racing.

Travis no longer trusts me. That must be it. That's why he hasn't left for the night. Because of what happened this afternoon, he's afraid to leave Matilda alone with me.

Feeling light-headed and fearful, Katie thought she might be sick. *If Travis no longer trusts me, there's no reason to keep me around.*

Reaching for the bottle on the stovetop, she winced, then picked it up with her good hand.

Please God, I can't go back home.

No . . . I won't go back home.

If Travis no longer needs me, I have nothing.

And if I have nothing, I don't want to live.

When Matilda squawked, Katie realized she still had the bottle in her hand and took it to Travis. "Here you go." She gave it to him then stood at the stove, trying to look busy. But as she listened, Matilda would be quiet for only a few seconds then cry, be quiet again then fuss.

Turning around she saw that Travis held Matilda in an awkward position and was fumbling with the bottle.

"Here . . ." Katie moved to the rocking chair and rearranged Travis' arms. With Matilda cradled in a better position, Katie shifted the bottle so it was angled properly. ". . . you need to hold her like this."

"But won't she choke?" Travis asked, even as Matilda nestled more comfortably in his arms and suckled the bottle with gusto.

"No. She'll be fine. She's just a little impatient. If you keep the bottle tipped just so, the milk flows easier, and she doesn't have to try as hard. I just remove the bottle every once and again, so I know she is swallowing everything in her mouth, then I give it back."

"How will I know when she's swallowed everything?" he asked, sounding like a scared little boy.

"Oh, she'll let you know," Katie chuckled softly as she looked at the content child, her eyes closed in satisfaction.

"She's an angelic little thing when she's sleeping, and playing, and just enjoying the day. But, if you mess with her food and make her wait, she turns into quite the little scamp."

Katie watched as Travis pulled the bottle from Matilda's mouth. Matilda took a couple of deep swallows, pursed her lips, opened her eyes, and let out a yelp.

Travis chuckled as he slipped the bottle back between her lips, then smiled at Katie. "She doesn't have you fooled, does she?"

Katie returned the smile even though her heart was breaking. "We've learned to communicate quite well these last several weeks." Feeling her eyes well up at the thought of having to leave, she reached for her wrap by the door.

"Uh . . . I think I'll step outside for some fresh air."

"Wait!" Travis gasped. "I don't know what to do next."

"You're doing fine. I scratched a mark on the bottle when to stop and burp her. Then she can finish the rest. Burp her again and change her diaper before you lay her down. Matilda usually puts herself to sleep."

After rattling off the instructions, Katie knew she had to leave before her emotions overwhelmed her. Once she was outside, she ran to the far side of the barn. When she reached the smokehouse, she leaned back against the sturdy wood structure, slid to the ground, and sobbed uncontrollably.

19

Travis followed Kathryn's instructions to the T. And sure enough, when he laid Matilda in the cradle and toed it with his boot a few times, she went right to sleep.

But where was Kathryn?

He could tell she was upset about something. The red in her eyes spoke of tears yet to come, but why?

Was she still shaken up from this afternoon?

Or was she upset with him for interfering with her routine?

If that were the case, she'd have to get used to it. They were a family now and needed to start acting like one. He knew it would take some getting used to, but it had to be done.

As he waited for Kathryn to return, he glanced every few minutes at the mantle, watching as time ticked away on the clock.

He needed to go look for her, make sure she didn't wander off somewhere, but the thought of leaving Matilda alone all but stole his breath. The last time he did that, she nearly died.

Standing over her cradle, he looked at Matilda nestled under her little pink blanket, her chest rising and falling with every breath. Glancing at the timepiece again, he sighed.

Okay, Lord, I need Your help. It's clear Kathryn was upset, and I want to go look for her, but I need You to protect my little girl. She . . . she's all I have.

Travis waited another five minutes, but when Kathryn didn't return, he went looking for her. Walking toward the barn, he called out. "Kathryn."

When he didn't get a reply, he tried again. "Kathryn."

Rounding the corner of the smokehouse, he was ready to yell for a third time when he nearly tripped over a heap on the ground.

A soft heap.

Squatting in front of her, he asked, "What's wrong?"

She didn't answer.

With his hands to her shoulders, he helped her stand, but she refused to look at him. With her back pressed against the smokehouse wall, Travis tipped her chin up, but she still avoided his eyes.

"Kathryn, talk to me."

She tucked her head and wiped her tears with the sleeve of her dress, looking so much like a child.

"What has you so upset?"

"You . . . staying tonight . . . feeding Matilda."

Travis bristled slightly. "She's my daughter. I have every right to feed her, play with her, take care of her."

Finally, Kathryn looked at him, fear in her eyes.

"Please, don't send me away," she pleaded, as if her very life depended on it.

Caught completely off guard, Travis was momentarily speechless. Finally, he asked, "What are you talking about? Why would I send you away?"

"You don't trust me anymore. That's why you stayed inside tonight. That's why you fed Matilda. You said it wasn't my fault what happened today, but clearly, you don't trust me. Please, Travis, don't send me away."

He had refused to comfort her earlier when an entire room stood between them. However, feeling the tremors shaking her body, he pulled her close and wrapped his arms around her.

"Kathryn, I have no intentions of sending you away. I meant what I said. What happened today was *not* your fault."

Her shoulders quaked against him, her tears wetting his shirt. Stroking the back of her head, he tried to hush her cries.

"Kathryn, please stop crying. Everything is going to be okay."

She mumbled something into his chest.

With his hands on either side of her face, he tipped her head back slightly so he could look at her. Though her face was still shadowed, he could at least hear her words.

"What did you say?"

"If you no longer trust me, you no longer need me."

Kathryn tried to turn away, but he wouldn't let her. Bending so he could look her in the eye, he asked, "Why do you keep insisting that I don't trust you?"

She swallowed deep. "Because you stayed inside tonight longer than you ever have. And you wanted to feed Matilda. Obviously, you're afraid to leave her alone with me after what happened this afternoon."

With a heavy sigh, Travis stood straighter. Moving his hands to her shoulders, he stroked her arms up and down, wanting to comfort her as he tried to put his feelings into words.

There's no easy way to say this. I just have to be honest. Blunt but honest.

After another deep breath, he looked at Kathryn, but her face was still veiled by shadows. Taking a step back, he pulled her closer to him. When he looked at her porcelain skin, honey-colored hair, and doe eyes filled with fear, his heart skipped a beat requiring him to take another deep breath.

"Kathryn, the reason I stayed tonight is because I no longer want to bed down in the barn."

A different kind of fear colored her eyes. It was subtle, but he saw it.

He continued to stroke her arms reassuringly. "Not because I want . . . relations, but because it's the right thing to do."

Nervously, she fiddled with the buttons on her bodice. "But I don't understand."

"Kathryn, I married you so Matilda would have a mother. But I didn't realize what you were sacrificing."

She looked up at him clearly confused.

"You gave up your chance to choose your own husband, to have your own child."

"No, I didn't. No one would ever marry me. Not when they think I'm crazy."

"But you're not crazy. I know it, and you know it. You're smart, resourceful, caring, and when you love, you love with your whole heart. My insides turn to mush when I see you with Matilda. And today . . ."

She quickly turned away, but he gently touched his fingers to her chin, forcing her to look at him.

"When I saw how upset you were about what happened today, I knew it came from deep within your soul. You're protective and maternal, as if Matilda's your own."

"I love her, Travis. I would do anything to protect her. I would give my life for her."

He smiled. "I know you would. You proved that today. And it got me thinking. Matilda deserves a mother *and* a father. She deserves a family."

"But she has that."

"No, she doesn't. She has a father who sleeps in the barn and spends most of his day away. That's not a real family."

He looked deep into her eyes hoping he was getting his point across.

"I want us to be a real family, Kathryn. I know it will take time, and we have a lot of adjusting to do, but we have to start sometime. So, it starts tonight."

20

Katie paced the cabin not sure what she should do. Travis had gone to the barn to gather his things, leaving her only a few minutes to absorb what had just happened.

Though she was incredibly thankful Travis still trusted her and had no intentions of sending her away, the simple routine she'd fallen into over the last several weeks was in for a change.

A very big change.

When Travis returned from the barn, he quickly tossed his pillow and blanket on the floor, then hurried to Matilda's cradle.

Katie watched as the tension in his shoulders softened with relief. Picking up the pillow and blanket, she set them on the bed.

"See, I told you she would be okay. She's strong, Travis. You don't need to worry."

"She might be, but I don't think I'll ever stop worrying."

"I guess that's what being a parent is all about."

Travis chuckled as he took off his hat. "I remember when I was a kid, my father used to say, 'You're going to make me gray with worry.' Now I understand what he was talking about."

"Do you get much chance to see your parents?"

He shook his head. "They died five years ago. Cholera."

"Oh, Travis, I'm sorry."

"Me too. My father was my best friend. He taught me everything. The importance of family and faith. What to look for in a plot of land. Being a businessman with integrity. And he made sure I knew the measure of a man's success has nothing to do with his bank account or the amount of land he owns. It comes from somewhere inside."

"Your pa sounds like a wonderful man."

"He was. He loved God and never allowed others to influence the way he lived his life. So, when the Lord took him and my mother from me, I didn't understand. I was pretty bitter. Sometimes I still am. But I believe what he taught me."

Travis stopped—gazed out the window as if lost in a memory—then continued.

"My father lived by faith every day. So, I figured the best way to honor him is to honor the God he served, but some days are harder than others." He coughed, masking the heaviness in his throat. "Like losing Mary."

Katie's heart ached for the man who was now her husband. How would she ever be able to replace the woman he lost, the woman he felt so much love for, the mother of his child?

Travis would never feel for her what he felt for Mary. Especially if he learned she was soiled and used.

Ugly memories filled her mind. Violent scenes from her childhood. The pain she'd been forced to endure because of the evil that dwelt inside Jethro and Wade.

"Kathryn—"

She jumped when Travis placed his hand on her shoulder. She hadn't meant to, but with the horrid thoughts racing through her mind, he caught her by surprise.

"Are you okay?"

She quickly stepped away from Travis and fiddled with the kettle on the stove. "Yes, of course." She moved to the bucket, scooped some water into the kettle and put it on to heat.

"But you didn't answer me?"

"Answer you?" She turned and looked at him.

"I asked about your parents."

"You did? I'm sorry; I guess I didn't hear you. What about them?"

"I was just wondering how you get along with them. Your mother seems a bit frail, timid even, while your father seems to be . . . well . . . he seems pretty . . . firm."

She quickly turned back to the stove and brushed at some stray crumbs. "Mama's health has always been poor. Having Seth nearly killed her, and Pa . . ." her heart hammered so hard she was sure if she turned around Travis would see it beating against her shirtwaist. ". . . he only wanted sons. He thinks women are a nuisance. The only reason he married Mama was so she could care for Wade. He didn't like it much that I was part of the bargain."

"But I'm sure he didn't feel that way as you grew older. Your mother talked about how you took care of your younger brother from the day he was born. And you're obviously a good cook. Your first day here you made a meal out of next to nothing. I'm sure, even if he never said it, he came to appreciate your talents."

Katie's stomach rolled, knowing the only thing he appreciated about her was what he took by force.

"Kathryn?"

She had to change the subject before she fell apart. "I think the water is hot enough, so I'm going to make myself some tea. Would you like some? Or I could make you some coffee?"

He chuckled. "At this late hour? I don't think so. The morning comes early and with it a list of chores. I'm thinking it's time to go to bed."

She stood frozen in front of the stove, chastising herself for being so naive. *You knew the time would come for this. You agreed to be his wife, and with it comes certain . . . duties.*

But somehow, with the routine they had fallen into, she had put the thought of them sharing a bed out of her mind. She had come to believe—true to his word—Travis' only intention toward her was giving Matilda a mama.

Even so, with the words he'd spoken tonight about being a real family, she felt nervous and self-conscious.

He said he wasn't expecting . . . relations, at least not right away.

But what if he turns out to be like Jethro?

What if his own manly urges make him demanding and self-indulgent?

No.

Travis was not like that. He'd been angry on occasion and raised his voice to her, but she could never see him being cruel or forceful.

Hearing a clunk, she turned to see Travis sitting on the edge of the bed, one boot on the floor, his hands anchored on the other one. With a second clunk, he sat up and caught her staring.

"I like to sleep on the side closes to the door. For protection."

90

She nodded, not trusting herself to speak.

Realizing she wasn't going to get her tea, Katie moved the kettle so it could cool, then rounded the foot of the bed. Pulling her nightgown from the dresser, she glanced at Matilda asleep in her cradle, then stood on her side of the bed, her body numb, unable to move.

She watched as Travis unbuttoned his shirt, pulled it off, and hung it over the knob on the headboard. He wore no undershirt, and she couldn't help but look at him, mesmerized by his sculpted arms and the muscles that crisscrossed his back.

Feeling her cheeks heat up and her blood swooshing through her veins, she was completely taken by surprise.

Never in a million years would she have thought the physique of a man would stir such a reaction inside her.

She assumed because of what Jethro and Wade had done to her, she would never be able to look at a man *that* way.

Apparently, she was wrong.

Travis released his belt, then lowered his trousers and sank to the bed in one fluid motion. In just a matter of seconds, he was under the bed covers, all while she stood frozen, her nightgown in her hand.

When he glanced at her from where he lay, she looked away, embarrassed. Though she wanted to know what he was thinking, she couldn't bring herself to look him in the eyes.

"Why don't you turn down the lamp before getting undressed. It will give you some privacy."

Without a word, she scurried to where the lantern sat in the middle of the kitchen table. After extinguishing the light, she waited a second for her eyes to adjust.

With the moon glow filtering through the window, she could still make out Travis' silhouette—laying on his side, facing the door, eyes closed.

Tiptoeing around the foot of the bed, she sat on the edge, unlaced her boots, and tried not to disturb Travis as she tugged them off.

As quickly as she could, she removed her skirt, shirtwaist, and chemise, then slipped her nightgown over her head, wishing it wasn't so tattered and worn.

She was careful as she crawled into bed, not to pull the covers from Travis' shoulder, but that was the least of her problems.

The mattress sagged.

Horribly.

And even though she hugged her body to the outer most edge of the bed frame, the worn mattress pulled her toward the middle.

I'll be fixing that first thing tomorrow.

Slowly, she worked the ticking with her shoulder and hip, creating a good-sized niche for herself so she wouldn't drift toward the middle.

However, just when she thought she was through, Travis rolled to his back, causing the mattress to sag.

As hard as she tried, she couldn't keep her back from resting alongside him or ignore the way the heat of his skin warmed her.

"It's bound to happen, you know?"

She gasped, having thought he was already asleep. "What is?"

"It's a small bed," he whispered. "We're going to brush up against each other. Try not to think about it and just get some sleep."

Get some sleep!

Easy for him to say. He's shared his bed with a loving wife. Touched her with desire and love.

I laid awake night after night for years, terrified by the insatiable sins of a horrible man.

Lying with the covers clutched under her chin, and her eyes open wide, Katie stared at the wall.

It's going to be a very long night.

21

Katie sat up like a shot.

When did I fall asleep?

She had lain awake for hours, unable to adjust to the feel of Travis' body next to hers.

It didn't help that he moved a lot in his sleep, and each time he did, the mattress sagged a little bit more, pulling her closer to the middle.

And even though she tried holding on to the bed frame, the burn on her hand made it difficult to hold tight.

When Matilda squealed for a second time, Katie remembered why she was awake and carefully slipped from the bed, trying not to disturb Travis' last few hours of sleep.

He let out a sigh, tossed from one side to the next, then came to rest on his back, his head pillowed in his left hand.

Katie picked up Matilda before she let out another cry and walked to the stovetop where her bottle sat already prepared. After giving it a few gentle shakes, she crept to the rocker, trying to avoid the floorboards that creaked.

Once she and Matilda were settled in the chair, Katie chanced a look at Travis. He was still asleep, and though she knew she was spying on him, she couldn't look away.

The fading moon offered just enough light to see the

outline of his body, and with all the tossing and turning he'd done in his sleep, the bed quilt had slipped to his hips, leaving his upper body exposed.

Katie was unprepared for how captivated she was by his form. Like his back, Travis' chest was all muscle, sculpted and defined, with deep ridges lining his torso.

For a second time, she felt heat rush through her veins, and it angered her. She felt betrayed by both her body *and* her mind. *How?*

After all she'd endured at the hands of Jethro and Wade, how could she even look at a man with anything but fear and disdain? But that was just it, Jethro and Wade weren't men; they were monsters.

But Travis . . . Travis was a true man.

Even though he was brokenhearted over Mary's death, and had every right to be angry and bitter, he chose instead to focus all his energy and love on his daughter. He pushed his private pain aside and sacrificed his future with another woman, all for the sake of Matilda. A lesser man might have taken her to an orphanage, dropped her off at a church or abandoned her on someone's doorstep, then spent his days drowning his sorrows in liquor or crude behavior.

But not Travis.

And even though they had a bumpy start, and he made it very clear he'd married her only so Matilda could have a mama, he had shown himself to be kind and compassionate.

Katie didn't know if it was his declaration about wanting to be a family, or the way he held her close and tried to reassure her everything was going to be all right, or how he gently stroked the burn on her hand, but something had changed.

She realized she was attracted to Travis.

Better still, the thought of the three of them becoming a real family warmed her both inside and out.

It wasn't long before Matilda's sleepy eyes closed, but Katie didn't rush to put her down. She gazed at her like she always did during the silence of night. With her elfin lips pursed and feather-soft lashes resting on her rosy cheeks, Matilda was the essence of innocence, and it never ceased to take Katie's breath away.

Knowing she needed to get some more rest before sunup, Katie quietly tiptoeing to the cradle, laid Matilda down, then crept alongside the bed.

The bed she now shared with Travis.

The bed that seemed so much smaller with him in it.

Slipping under the covers, careful to avoid Travis' outstretched elbow, Katie huddled against the edge, trying to take up as little room as possible.

She had just closed her eyes when she felt Travis shift behind her.

"Kathryn . . ."

She shuddered when she felt his breath flutter her hair.

"You don't need to be afraid."

"Afraid?" Her voice was hardly more than a squeak. "I'm not afraid." *Liar.*

"But you jump every time I speak to you."

"You just startled me is all. I thought you were asleep."

"Is that why you were staring at me, because you thought I was asleep?"

She cringed with humiliation, knowing he caught her ogling him.

"Kathryn," he laid his hand on her exposed shoulder causing gooseflesh to chill her body. "I know this is going to take some getting used to—you and me. I'm guessing you've probably never even been kissed by a boy, and now you're sharing your bed with a man. And even though I want to provide a proper home for Matilda, I won't lie to you. I loved Mary deeply, and I don't know if that will ever change."

The emotion in Travis' voice was so raw, Katie's heart broke for him.

"But I need to move forward—for Matilda's sake—and I know Mary would want that too." He paused, removing his hand from her shoulder. "I can't promise you love, Kathryn, but I do promise to provide for you and Matilda. You will never be in want."

She didn't know how to respond. Was she supposed to assure Travis she wasn't looking for love, that she was willing to live her life as a stand-in for Mary? Was this his way of telling her she would never have a child of her own, that he could never open his heart to her completely? Even though he had said last night that he wanted to be a family for Matilda's sake, could they be a real family without love?

I don't know, but I can't go back home.

"I understand, Travis."

"Thank you." He rolled away from her.

The tears wetting her pillow came as a surprise. She should feel grateful that Travis was such a gentleman. He was her husband after all, and could expect, even demand so much more of her, regardless of if he loved her or not.

But he didn't.

She should feel relieved but instead felt empty inside.

Unable to get back to sleep, Katie watched the light of dawn dance across the wall. It wasn't long before Travis stirred, then swung his legs out of bed. She listened to the jangle of his belt buckle as he dragged on his pants, and the soft grunting sounds he made when he pulled on his boots. The dresser drawer creaked open and closed, and when Katie heard the click of the front door shut behind him, she rolled to her back and stared at the ceiling, feeling utter exhaustion.

The jumble of emotions she experienced yesterday and last night had her waking up more tired than when she'd gone to bed. The calamity in the creek. Fear that Travis didn't trust her and would send her away. His declaration that he wanted to be more like a family, even if he could never love her. Her feelings of attraction.

It was all so confusing.

However, what puzzled her even more was the safety she felt lying next to him last night. Safety, not fear.

Could I be falling in love? Is this what it feels like?

She daydreamed about the future. The three of them a family. Rides to town. Picnics next to the creek. Sharing quiet evenings when the weather turned cold. But what Travis said kept poking at her. That even though he wanted Matilda to have a family, he wasn't sure he would ever feel for her what he had felt for Mary.

Closing her eyes, she wondered, *can I love someone who doesn't love me back?*

22

Katie went about her day, doing her best to ignore her wandering thoughts. Even so, there were several times she found herself remembering how Travis looked in bed, moonlight shining on his chest, and when she closed her eyes, she could almost hear his whisper-soft voice telling her not to be afraid.

He was a good man—a kind man.

And today would mark a new beginning.

She felt giddy more than nervous when she thought about this evening, the three of them together.

Like a family.

And even if Travis can't bring himself to love me like he loved Mary, my life will still be so much richer than I ever could have imagined.

Lifting Matilda from the cradle, she perched the infant on her hip. "Okay, little miss, we're going to try this again." Carrying Matilda outside, Katie laid her on a blanket under a low-hanging branch and watched as she kicked and squirmed at the quaking leaves dancing above her. Though Katie wouldn't soon forget the panic she felt, thinking Matilda was in danger, she was glad Mattie was completely unfazed by yesterday's fiasco.

Turning her attention to the laundry she'd hung out earlier, Katie watched as sheets and shirts floated on the breeze, the same breeze that caught strands of her hair and blew them across her face. A telltale sign that fall was in the air.

As she worked her way down the clothesline, she found herself glancing at Matilda every time she unpinned a garment and put it in the basket. She couldn't help it. Even though she knew Matilda wasn't in any danger, she was having a hard time dispelling yesterday's fear.

Finally, with the laundry finished, Katie lay down on the blanket next to Matilda and studied the precious little girl.

"You look so much like your pa, you know that?" She stroked the little wisps on top of Matilda's head. "His hair is a shade darker, but you've got his crystal blue eyes." Mattie wriggled; her eyes open wide as if she were agreeing. "And you know what else you have? You have your pa wrapped around your little finger." Matilda wriggled some more, making Katie laugh. "You, little miss, are going to be a heart breaker."

"Ahem."

Katie whirled around to see Travis and another man standing behind her.

"Sorry. I didn't mean to startle you." Travis smiled, looking genuinely happy. "Kathryn, this is Caleb Marshall." He turned to the man next to him and laid his arm across his shoulders. "He's an old friend from home; we grew up together."

Katie jumped to her feet but got tangled in the edge of the blanket. Catching her balance, she quickly smoothed out her rumpled skirt and pushed her tousled hair behind her ears. Embarrassed, she chanced a glance at Travis and caught him hiding a snicker behind his hand. He was laughing at her, and that smarted.

Caleb tipped his hat. "Howdy, ma'am. It's a pleasure to meet you."

"Caleb will be staying with us for a spell. He's going to help out with a few projects, and if we have time, work on that room addition I talked about."

"Oh." Katie didn't know what to say.

"He'll bed down in the barn, but he'll take meals with us. I just thought you should know before supper."

"Of course. Of course." She milked her hands and smiled, feeling . . . to be honest, she didn't know how she felt. "I'll make sure there's plenty."

"And this here must be Matilda." Caleb squatted down next to the blanket. "She has your coloring, Travis." Katie was ready to agree when Caleb continued. "But she gets her beauty from her mother. I can see Mary in her for sure."

Caleb's words cut like a knife.

And for the first time, Katie realized Mary would never be far from Travis' thoughts. Matilda would serve as a constant reminder of the love he once had and lost.

The love he had no intention replacing.

"Well, I better get supper underway." Katie scooped up Matilda and draped the blanket over her arm. "I'll see you in a little bit." She glanced at Travis, then quickly looked away, but not before she saw a worried expression on his face.

"Uh, Caleb, why don't you put your things in the barn while I help Kathryn with the laundry. I'll be along in a minute to show you the lay of the land."

"Sure thing." Caleb tipped his hat at her, picked up his

satchel and walked toward the barn.

Katie headed for the house, Travis with the laundry basket a few paces behind her.

"Kathryn . . ."

She kept walking, but Travis caught up to her. With a gentle tug on her elbow, she turned around, but didn't want to look at him because she was sure he would see the disappointment she felt.

"Are you okay?" Travis asked.

"Sure. Why wouldn't I be?" Katie fiddled with Matilda's gown giving her reason not to look up.

"He didn't mean anything by it."

Katie forced a smile and mustered the courage to look at him. "I don't know what you're talking about, Travis."

He sighed. "Caleb loved Mary . . . a lot. In fact, he proposed to her before I did."

"What?" Katie was sure she hadn't heard him right.

Travis took off his hat, ran his fingers through his hair, then put it back on, the brim low on his forehead. Whatever he had to say was giving him a hard time.

So, she waited.

Letting out a deep breath, Travis cleared his throat. "Caleb, Mary, and I grew up together. We were best friends. Inseparable. Both Caleb and I fell in love with Mary. However, Caleb beat me to the punch and proposed first. But Mary turned him down. She said she had loved me since the day I tripped her in the school yard and was just waiting for my feelings to catch up to hers. When I proposed a few months later, she accepted. Our engagement was hard on Caleb. It broke our friendship, and he left town shortly after that."

Travis took another deep breath as he toed the dirt.

"When Caleb heard about Mary's death, he wrote me a letter, saying how sorry he was. He also explained that he regretted leaving town and never should have let his feelings for Mary come between us. He'd come to accept our marriage and wanted to apologize to both of us, but his realization came too late. He asked for my forgiveness and wanted to know if he was still welcome in my home. He also said he had other things he needed to discuss with me. That's why he's here."

Katie didn't know what to say. She was glad Travis had his friend back, but selfishly she couldn't help but wonder if having Caleb around was going to interfere with her, Travis, and Matilda becoming a real family.

23

When Travis walked in with Caleb, he saw that Kathryn already had supper on the table and was working at the stove. Carrying a stool in from the barn, he set it next to the table.

"It smells mighty good in here, ma'am," Caleb said as he pulled off his hat and held it to his chest.

"It's nothing special, but it's hearty. And please, call me Kathryn."

"Here." Travis took Caleb's hat and put it on the peg next to his, then offered Caleb one of the chairs while he took the stool. He watched as Kathryn glanced at Matilda one more time before sitting down. Once she did, he folded his hands together to say grace. Caleb quickly followed suit and bowed his head. Travis waited until Kathryn closed her eyes before he began.

"Thank you, Lord, for this meal and for Kathryn who worked hard to prepare it. Thank You for bringing Caleb here safely and for the help he's offering. Watch over Matilda and keep her healthy as she grows. In Your matchless name we pray. Amen."

Travis thoroughly enjoyed the evening and the easy banter he shared with Caleb. Seeing him after all these years was good for his soul.

They reminisced about their growing-up years, the angst they caused their parents, and of course, Mary. Travis hardly had a childhood memory that didn't include her. But as they talked, Travis watched the expression on Kathryn's face teeter-totter. Once he realized why that was, he purposefully steered the conversation to the present, and the projects he hoped to accomplish with Caleb's help.

When Kathryn sat down in the rocker, Matilda in her lap, he stood, Caleb following suit. "I'll be right back. I'm just going to walk Caleb out."

Kathryn smiled up at them. "It was nice meeting you, Caleb. I'm glad you're here."

"I feel the same, ma'am. Thank you for having me."

Closing the door behind them, Travis walked Caleb to the barn.

"It's good seeing you, Travis. I was worried how you would fare out here on your own. I know your father taught you about land, and what to look for, but it's not like you were raised on a farm. Then, when I heard about Mary, I thought for sure you would come home. But you've done well for yourself. And Kathryn seems like a fine young lady."

"Meaning?" Travis asked, feeling defensive.

Caleb stopped in his tracks. "*Meaning* Kathryn seems like she's good for you and Matilda."

"But you think she's too young, is that it? I mean, I know there are some years between us but Kathryn's of age and consented to this arrangement."

"Travis, calm down," Caleb laughed. "I didn't mean

anything by it, other than, Kathryn seems like a lovely young woman. You're lucky to have her."

"And she's great with Matilda."

"I can see that."

They walked a little further before Caleb asked, "But it was her mother who approached you about getting married?"

"Yeah, that's right. I was terrified I was going to lose Matilda too. The day she turned blue I knew I needed to find someone to help. Doc Hammond must have said something to Mrs. James, because she came over and spoke to me about Kathryn."

"But there's no way she would've known about your family, right?"

"No. Mary and I never talked about it with anyone in town. We wanted to do this on our own."

"But you know it's just sitting there, waiting for you to claim it?"

"I know."

24

It had been three weeks since Caleb had come to live with them. Though the days went by slowly—since Travis and Caleb were always outside working on one project or another—the evenings were quite enjoyable.

Katie loved listening as the men reminisced over dinner and late into the night about their childhood; the antics they pulled, the close calls, their rebelliousness. It was so fun to watch Travis' amusing expressions and hear his deep peals of laughter.

Unfortunately, even though Katie relished this glimpse into Travis' past, it was difficult to hear Mary's name on his lips or see the look in his eyes when he spoke about her, a look Katie knew was reserved only for Mary.

As for their *family* time . . . it had yet to happen.

Though Travis came to bed at night, it was long after she'd fallen asleep, and in the morning, he was gone by dawn. Katie enjoyed the warmth of him lying next to her as she slept, and she studied him by moonlight when she fed Matilda, but she longed for more intimate conversations, like the one they had shared the night before Caleb arrived.

Travis had talked about them being a *real* family, but with Caleb around, nothing more had been said. And with the memory of Mary always getting stirred up, maybe nothing would be again.

"More coffee, Caleb?" Katie asked.

"No more for me but thank you." Caleb got to his feet. "I need to be turning in. If I'm not rested tomorrow, I'm liable to fall asleep while the preacher's preaching."

"I'll walk with you." Travis put on his hat and followed Caleb out the door; just like he had each night since Caleb had arrived.

Katie watched him go with regret, knowing Travis wouldn't return until late into the night.

———————— • ————————

"You know, I don't need a personal guide to get to the barn each night," Caleb said, sounding annoyed. "I'm capable all on my own."

"What's that supposed to mean?" Travis asked.

Caleb tossed his hat onto the makeshift night table next to his bed of straw and dropped his suspenders around his waist. "It means it's time for you to move on."

"Move on?" Travis took a step back. "What are you talking about?"

Caleb just shook his head.

"Come on. It's obvious you have something you want to say, so just spit it out."

"Fine." Caleb pointed to the scratched wedding photo hanging on the beam. "I'm talking about that."

Travis looked at the picture he had rescued from broken glass the day Kathryn arrived. He couldn't bear to part with it, so he pinned it to a beam where he could see it every day.

"You need to take it down, Travis."

He balled up his fists and anchored them on his waist, trying to control his anger. "That's none of your business, Caleb."

"She's gone, Travis. Mary's been gone for almost five months now, and as much as you loved her, as much as you miss her, you need to move on."

"You don't know what you're talking about, Caleb, so I suggest you leave it be."

"Oh really? You don't think I know what a broken heart feels like?" Caleb took a step closer and jabbed a finger in Travis' chest. "Are you forgetting who you're talking to?"

Travis took a step back, not wanting to come to blows, but Caleb was asking for it.

With another poke to his chest, Caleb unloaded on him. "Mary broke my heart when she turned down my proposal, and if that wasn't enough, you smashed it to smithereens the day you made her your wife. So, don't tell me it's none of my business. You're my best friend, Travis, and I refuse to stand by and watch you throw your life away, a life you could have with that young bride of yours.

"Leave Kathryn out of this!" Travis clenched his fist harder.

"She's your wife, Travis. You can't leave her out of *this*!"

Caleb grabbed at the picture and ripped it from the nail.

"Why you—" Travis charged Caleb, plowing him into the ground. He landed a right hook to his jaw and followed with a left. Caleb took the blows but didn't back down on his verbal assault.

"Is this helping, Travis? Is this what makes you feel better, so you don't have to deal with the truth? Is beating me black and blue going to make the pain of losing Mary go away?"

In one lightening swift move, Caleb rolled over and pinned

Travis to the ground. He picked up the picture that had fallen to the dirt and shook it in Travis' face.

"Staring at this picture every day is not helping anything. You have to start a new life. You need to move on. Loving someone new is not betraying Mary. She would've wanted you to live and love again. She would've wanted that for you *and* for Matilda."

Travis shoved Caleb away, got to his feet, and snatched the picture from his hand. He brushed the dirt from it and looked into Mary's smiling eyes.

"Don't you see what you have?" Caleb got to his feet and continued his lecture in a more civil tone. "You have a chance to start over. You have a beautiful young wife who sacrificed everything for you and Matilda. Doesn't she deserve to have a husband who cares for her? The way you're treating her, ignoring her like you do, it's not fair. Not to Kathryn, not to Matilda . . . and not to you."

"It's not that easy," Travis mumbled, trying to put words to his emotions. "And don't you dare tell me you know how I feel, because you don't know the half of it. When I look at Kathryn at night, lying next to me, I want nothing more than to circle my arms around her and pull her close, to feel her skin against my chest. But it's only because I miss Mary. It has to be. Because if it's anything other than that, I would be the lowest of the low. To bury my wife, then bed another woman just like that, it's not right. I care for Kathryn. I do. But I still love Mary."

Caleb sighed. "You *loved* Mary, but for different reasons than you love Kathryn."

"No!" Travis vehemently shook his head. "I didn't say I love Kathryn. I don't know what it is I feel for her, but it can't be love."

"Take it from me, Travis. It's love."

Hands on his hips, Travis snapped back. "How can you say that? You've been here all of three weeks."

"Because you look at her the same way you looked at Mary when we were fifteen years old. You didn't know it was love then either. It was too new. It was a love of discovery. Every new thing you discovered about Mary you loved. It just took you four more years to realize it."

Travis looked away, not wanting to hear anymore.

"That's what's happening between you and Kathryn, if you want to admit it or not. You see the way she cares for Matilda. The way she talks to her and coos with her, encouraging her to smile. The way Kathryn tucks her hair behind her ear when she blushes. The way she glances at you and tries to hide her smile. You're falling in love with her, Travis. But this time you don't have four years to come to your senses."

They locked eyes.

"If you wait too long to reveal your feelings to Kathryn, you're going to extinguish the love for you I see in her eyes. Sure, she'll stay with you. But her love for you will grow cold."

Travis couldn't breathe.

He laced his fingers together and rested them on his head, pacing the barn, trying to gather a deep breath. He wanted to punch Caleb, tell him he was wrong, tell him he didn't know the least little thing about love. But he couldn't. Because everything he said was true.

In fact, he felt jealous that Caleb had noticed Kathryn's little quirks. After all, she was *his* wife. But Caleb had obviously been watching her closely.

Maybe a little too close.

After several minutes of struggling with his newfound feelings, Travis turned to Caleb. "I should punch you; you know that?"

Caleb spit blood from his cut lip and rubbed at his swelling jaw. "What? For making you face the truth?" He stood his ground, obviously waiting for Travis to take another shot at him.

"No. But the way you're talking, it sounds like you're smitten with Kathryn. And if that's the case, I'm going to have to knock some sense into you."

Caleb smiled, stepped forward, and wrapped Travis in a man-sized hug. "You won't have to do that. Believe me, I learned my lesson the first time. Kathryn only has eyes for you."

Travis took his time returning to the cabin, pondering what Caleb had said. He wasn't convinced it was love, but he couldn't ignore the fact he did have feelings for Kathryn. Closing the door behind him, he quietly crossed to the bed, undressed, slid between the bed covers, and lay on his back.

Her love for you will grow cold.

Kathryn only has eyes for you.

The way she glances at you and tries to hide her smile.

With Caleb's words taunting him, Travis rolled toward Kathryn, rested on his elbow, and stared, wondering if she was still awake.

As his eyes adjusted to the darkness, he studied the outline of her delicate form. Reaching for her shoulder, he saw the jagged scars peeking from the neckline of her nightgown and pulled his hand back.

She lied to me about her scars, but why?

And if she lied once, what else might she be lying about?

Like stream water on a frigid winter's night, Travis got a chilling dose of reality.

Though Caleb might be right that his feelings for Kathryn were more than just gratitude, the scars on her back reminded him how very little he knew about her.

But that would change very soon.

He was committed to learning all he could about Kathryn.

His wife.

The woman he was indeed falling in love with.

25

Something was different.

Katie wasn't sure what it was, but Travis was acting strange. Each time she looked at him, he smiled. But it wasn't his normal smile. It was like he was hiding a secret or knew something she didn't know.

Trying to ignore him, she continued to work on breakfast while he got dressed in his Sunday best. However, when he stepped outside to tend to his personal needs, she hurried to the mirror above the dresser.

She looked at her face, her hair, her dress. Surely something had to be wrong with her appearance for him to be acting so strange. But after several glances, she couldn't see a smudge on her face or a hair out of place. She turned from side to side, not seeing a tear or a stain on her dress.

Then why is he acting so strange?

Katie went on with her morning chores but couldn't put Travis' peculiar behavior out of her mind. Then she gasped out loud but quickly covered her mouth.

"Has he been drinking?" she whispered to herself. "Did he and Caleb go to town last night?"

That's ridiculous!

She scolded herself for even thinking such a thing.

Travis is not that type of man. He would never . . .

After nearly burning the biscuits and ruining the gravy, she told herself enough was enough. She would just ask him. She would simply look Travis in the eye and ask him what had him so bothered.

The truth certainly couldn't be any worse than the scenarios she'd conjured up all on her own.

When the front door swung open, Katie turned. "Travis what has you—" She stopped the minute Caleb walked in. "For heaven's sake . . . what happened to you?"

Standing in the doorway with his eye almost swollen shut and his lip a sickening shade of purple, Caleb looked sheepish, as he twirled his hat between his hands, while Travis walked in behind him, looking guiltier than a fox in a hen house.

"Well ma'am, Travis and I got into a little scrape last night."

"A *little* scrape?" She walked over to him, and with her finger to his chin, tipped his head back to get a better look. "That looks like more than a little scrape." She turned to Travis surprised he was capable of such violence. She didn't know if she should be angry or fearful. However, when both men broke out in laughter, she decided she was mad at the pair of them.

"Men!" she huffed and went back to the stove. "Why is it you have to settle disagreements with your fists? Why can't you be more civilized and talk things through?"

She carried the basket of biscuits to the table and then the pan of gravy.

"What was it this time?" she asked as she poured their coffee and took her place at the table. "Who could shoe a horse faster, or maybe it was something really important like who could eat the most flapjacks?"

Both men sat down, looked at each other and grinned.

"Caleb was just being his know-it-all self," Travis said as he slid several biscuits onto his plate. "I didn't mean to hit him so hard. He used to be better at ducking."

Travis and Caleb filled their plates, not looking the least bit mad at each other. Katie just shook her head and peered over to where Matilda was making silly noises and boxing the air.

"Oh no you don't, little miss. I'm going to teach you manners and grace. You will not be using your fists for anything other than kneading bread; you hear me?"

Again, both men laughed; Caleb winced, but laughed just the same.

After breakfast, Travis and Caleb left to harness the horses and bring the wagon around. Katie tidied up the cabin, then walked outside just as Travis jumped down and started across the yard toward her.

He is so handsome. She thought to herself. Though Travis was attractive no matter what he wore, his Sunday shirt with the dark-blue yoke made his gorgeous blue eyes stand out even more.

"Here, let me help you with that."

He took the bag she was carrying, the one with all the essentials Matilda might need, and with a hand pressed to the small of her back, he led her to the side of the wagon.

Her heart fluttered at the simple, but unexpected gesture.

Once they reached the wagon, Travis took Matilda and laid her in her crate, then placed his hands to Katie's waist and helped her up into the wagon.

After she scooped up her dress and situated herself on the seat, Travis laid a hand on her thigh and asked, "Are you comfortable?"

So flustered by the warmth of his hand through her skirt, she just nodded and smiled.

Feeling awestruck by Travis' show of affection, they had driven clear out of the yard before she even realized Caleb wasn't with them. "Wait, Travis, what about Caleb? Isn't he coming to church?"

Travis chuckled. "He decided it would be better to stay home than have to explain his bruises."

"Oh. Well, yes, I could see where that might be difficult." She thought for a moment. "You know . . . you never did tell me what happened."

Travis looked at her so intently she was sorry she'd brought it up, but then he turned his attention back toward the road and smiled. "Just guy stuff. You wouldn't understand."

When Travis started to whistle a tune, she decided to let the subject drop. Whatever had happened between him and Caleb couldn't have been all that bad, not with Travis being in such an exceptionally good mood.

Instead, they shared polite conversation and quiet moments, but the closer they got to town, the more Katie tensed in her seat, just like she did every Sunday.

Although each week the townspeople treated her with a little more kindness and no longer stared at her like she was a freak from a traveling circus, it was knowing she would see her family that bothered her most. Mama always teared up and talked in hushed tones, drawing questions from Travis on the ride home. But it was seeing Jethro and Wade leering at her from across the yard that nearly caused her to empty her stomach right there for all to see.

"Give me a second," Travis said as he set the brake then walked around to her side of the wagon. Helping her down, he allowed his hands to linger on her waist longer than usual. When she looked up at him, he smiled.

"You look lovely today, Kathryn."

"Oh?"

"Not to say you don't look lovely every day, but today in particular, you seem different. You're glowing."

"Thank you, Travis, that's nice of you to say. It's probably the extra sun Matilda and I have enjoyed of late."

His eyes lingered on her a moment longer before Matilda's timid mew stole his attention. "Here you go, little lady." Travis scooped her up and held her to his chest, then reached for her bag.

"That's all right, Travis. I shouldn't be needing any of her things until after services. Just grab her rattle in case she gets fussy."

Travis pulled out the small wooden rattle he'd made for her and slipped it into his back pocket. Then, extending his elbow to Katie, he asked, "Shall we?"

Katie slipped her hand through his arm and rested her fingers on his shirt sleeve, wondering what had gotten into him. He was being so attentive, so warm. She didn't know what to make of it but was loving it all the same.

"Katie!"

She heard her name and turned just in time for Seth to wrap her in a hug, nearly knocking her off balance.

"Why, Seth," she squeezed him, then steadied herself and smiled. "I didn't even recognize your voice. You are sounding more like a man every day. Why, let me look at you."

He took a step back, standing taller with the compliment. She circled him, squinting as if he was under some sort of inspection.

"Yes, I do believe you've grown at least two . . . no, three inches since I've been gone."

"And I'm stronger, too."

Before she knew it, he picked her up and twirled her around. She couldn't help but laugh. When her feet were firmly planted back on the ground, she held him at shoulder's length. That's when she saw a tear escape his eyelid.

"I've missed you, Katie. I've missed you something awful."

"Oh, and I've missed you too."

"What about me, Kathryn, have you missed your pa?"

Turning, she saw Jethro leering at her with a demented smile, Mama cowering at his side.

Before she could say anything, he wrapped his lecherous arms around her and grazed her neck with his sour breath. He pressed himself against her and whispered for only her to hear. "I've missed your sweetness."

He took a step back, and for that she was thankful, but it did little to settle her stomach. She felt ill. Dizzy. Pinpoints of light danced before her eyes and the ground swayed beneath her feet.

"Kathryn, are you okay?" She felt Travis loop his arm about her waist, steadying her. "You're white as a sheet."

"And plain as one too," Jethro cackled.

Travis turned his head and snapped, "Don't speak to my wife that way."

"She's my daughter. I'll speak to her anyway I please."

"*Step*-daughter," Katie clarified, knowing Jethro hated the term.

"Don't you dare disrespect me, girl." Jethro sneered. "I'm the only pa you've ever known. But it's plain to see you got your weakness from your mama and your no-nothing father."

"That's enough, Mr. James," Travis warned.

But Jethro continued with a taunting laugh. "Why look at you, a few minutes in the sun and you're swooning like a hothouse orchid. I raised you to be tougher than that. But just a few months under someone else's roof and you've become as pathetic as your mama. You were supposed to be a help to Travis, not a burden. I think it's time you come home and put a stop to this ridiculous arrangement. Travis doesn't need to be takin' care of two babies."

"Why you—" Travis took a step toward Jethro, but Katie held him tighter, not wanting to cause a scene.

"It's all right, Travis. Let it be," she whispered.

"It's not all right! I will not stand here and let him talk to you like that." He turned to Jethro. "I don't care if you raised Kathryn or not. She's my wife now, and you will treat her with respect. And for your information, Kathryn is doing a fine job with Matilda."

Jethro rolled his tongue around his mouth before turning his head and spitting a lump of tobacco. He then leered at Travis with a snarly grin. "And what about you, Travis? Is she doing a fine job by you?"

Katie was horrified Jethro would be so bold, so wicked with his words. Travis took another step toward him, a flush of anger reddening his complexion, but this time she was unable to stop him. "Not only is your question rude and unsuitable, but it's well out of line, Mr. James."

Jethro laughed with satisfaction. "I'll take that as a *no*."

"How dare you speak to—"

"Katie!"

She heard Seth shout and felt her body sway right before everything went black.

Travis turned just in time to catch Kathryn as she collapsed against him.

"Kathryn!"

He quickly passed Matilda to Mrs. James, then scooped up Kathryn and carried her to a nearby bench. Setting her down gently, he patted her cheeks.

"Kathryn? Kathryn, can you hear me?"

Her eyelids fluttered but did not open.

"Travis, what's wrong?"

He turned to see Doc Hammond approaching.

"Kathryn fainted."

The doctor squatted down next to him, opened the little black bag he always carried, and pulled out a vial of smelling salts. Passing the small bottle underneath Kathryn's nose, she flinched and tossed her head from side to side before opening her eyes.

She looked up at him, to the doctor, then back to him.

"You fainted," Travis answered the question he saw in her eyes.

"Katie . . . I mean, Kathryn," Doc Hammond corrected himself. "Can you look at me?"

She turned his way.

"I want you to close your eyes and take a long, slow, breath."

She did what the doctor said, then opened her eyes.

"That's good. Let's do that a few more times."

She complied.

Travis wasn't sure, but it looked as if a little color returned to her cheeks.

"Okay, Kathryn, now let's see if you can . . ." The doctor paused as he rummaged through his bag and pulled out a stick. ". . . follow this stick with just your eyes. Can you do that for me?"

Kathryn followed the stick as the doctor slowly moved it from side to side.

"Good." He tossed it in his bag, then reached for her wrist. Pushing back the cuff of her sleeve, he pulled a chained timepiece from the pocket of his vest.

Travis, along with Mrs. James and Seth, watched in silence as the doctor held her wrist and stared at his gold watch.

After what felt like an eternity, the doctor let go of her wrist and put his timepiece back in his pocket.

He looked at Travis with a reassuring smile. "It's a little fast, but nothing too alarming."

The doctor turned back to Kathryn. "How are you feeling, now?"

She looked around at the small semicircle of people. "Embarrassed."

The doctor smiled good-naturally. "Besides that, do you have any other symptoms?"

———— • ————

Katie didn't know what to say.

She felt sick to her stomach, her skin tingled like the prick of a thousand needles, and her mouth was so dry she was sure it was lined with cotton. But she didn't need a doctor to diagnose what she was feeling.

When she thought Jethro and Travis were going to come

to blows, she'd fainted.

Clear and simple.

She'd collapsed out of fear.

"No. No other symptoms," she whispered.

"Kathryn spent a lot of time outdoors this week," Travis offered, worry evident in his tone. "Could it be she got too much sun?"

The doctor shrugged. "Possibly, even though the temperatures have been pretty mild." He turned his attention back to her. "You're sure you have no other symptoms? Nausea, exhaustion, loss of appetite?"

Katie forced a smile. "I'm fine. Really. I don't know what came over me."

The doctor stood. Travis followed suit and helped her stand. She could feel all eyes on her, everyone waiting to see if she would faint again. But she didn't. Subconsciously, her body had done what she needed it to do. Distract Travis long enough to keep him from throwing the first punch.

"Well, if she has no other symptoms," Doc Hammond continued, "a day of rest should do the trick. If she's still feeling poorly in a day or two, have someone come and get me. I'll give her a thorough exam and see what I come up with."

With a snug arm around her waist and Matilda in his other arm, Travis walked her to the wagon, his steps slow and cautious. He settled Matilda first, then helped her up into the wagon. When he sat down next to her, he asked again if she was okay.

"I'm fine, Travis, really. I'm more embarrassed than anything."

"Okay, but you tell me if you start feeling poorly. I don't want you falling out of the wagon."

As Travis unwrapped the reins from around the brake, Mr. Dudley waved to him as he trudged across the yard.

"Travis, I'm glad I caught you." The older man panted. "With all the commotion, I forgot to tell you that the lumber you ordered came in on Friday. If you'd like to wait until after services, I'd be willing to make an exception and meet you at the mercantile so you could load it up."

Travis shook his head. "I appreciate that, Mr. Dudley, really I do, but I need to get Kathryn home. I'll come by later this week to pick it up if that's all right with you."

"That would be fine. But I would be obliged if you could pick it up no later than Friday. I have a large order coming in, and I don't want the two of them getting mixed up."

"Sure thing. I'll see you Friday morning."

Mr. Dudley tipped his hat first to Travis, then to her. "I hope you're feeling better soon, Mrs. Clark."

———— • ————

Wade waited until Travis pulled away before stepping from the shadows of a nearby tree. "Friday it is," he whispered. "It's time I pay my little sister a visit."

26

They traveled in silence, but Katie could feel Travis' watchful eyes on her, his attention switching back and forth from the dusty road ahead of them to her.

Glancing at Matilda as she slept, Katie wished she would wake up. She could better ignore Travis' stares if she had Matilda to keep her occupied.

After several minutes of fidgeting, she sighed, "I'm fine, Travis. Really I am."

"You're not fine," he said, not with accusation but concern. "A healthy woman doesn't just collapse in the middle of the day for nothing."

"Well, I'm fine now." She offered him a smile, wishing he would forget it even happened.

After several more minutes of quiet, Travis turned to her and asked, "Why does he treat you that way?"

She shrugged. "Because I'm not his own."

"What happened to your real father? If you don't mind me asking."

"He was thrown from a horse. Snapped his neck."

"How old were you?"

"Almost three. I don't remember much, just Mama crying a lot."

"How did she come to marry Jethro?"

"It was a marriage of convenience, much like—" Katie stopped herself, refusing to compare her marriage to that of her mama's. She cleared her throat and started again.

"Jethro's wife died of the fever two weeks before my pa died, leaving Jethro with both Wade and his farm to look after. When he realized he couldn't care for both, he decided to ship Wade off to his sister. But his sister told him about my mama needing a husband. Even though Mama was much younger than Jethro, his sister convinced him it would be better if he took a wife, someone who could not only care for Wade, but tend to his house as well. We came by stage the next week. They were married the day we arrived."

Travis was silent, staring straight ahead. When he spoke again, his words were hushed but matter-of-fact. "Those scars on your back, they're from him, aren't they?" It was more a statement than a question.

She turned away, tears instantly springing to her eyes. "It was my fault. I left the gate open and—"

"No," he shook his head, his tone controlled, but she could sense his anger. "There is nothing you could've done to deserve a beating like that."

She fiddled with the gathers of her dress, wishing Travis would change the subject.

"Is that why you stopped talking?"

Katie kept her eyes fixed on her dress. *Not the change I was hoping for.* Choosing her words carefully, she offered an explanation.

"Jethro threatened things would get worse if I told anyone. So, it was just easier to be quiet than accidentally say something I shouldn't."

"Did he take a hand to Wade and Seth too?"

She shook her head. "No. They're his blood."

"So, he beat you because you didn't have his blood flowing through your veins? What possesses a man to do that?" Travis snapped.

Again, she shrugged. "He gave me lots of reasons."

"Like what?"

"He said I was an addle-brained girl and completely useless. A bumbling half-wit. Jethro thought females were weak and needed a firm hand."

"So, he beat your mother as well?"

"I'm not sure."

"How are you *not* sure? Either he did or he didn't!"

Travis' anger woke Matilda, and she was none too happy. Katie reached around to lull her back to sleep, and once she was quiet, Katie turned in her seat.

"I'm sorry, Kathryn. I didn't mean to raise my voice."

"Then maybe we could talk about something else. Because there is nothing to be done about it now."

"But Kathryn—"

"Please, Travis," she cut him off, resting her hand on his knee. "What can be accomplished by talking about the past? What's done is done."

"But Jethro should pay for what he did. He shouldn't be allowed to get away with hurting you like that, you or your mother."

Katie realized at that moment, she could never tell Travis the other atrocities she had endured at the hands of Jethro and Wade. She knew that was wrong; she should be able to share everything with her husband.

But not that.

As angry as Travis had been today with just words, what would he do if he found out the whole story?

"Promise me, Travis. Promise me that you will leave the past in the past."

"I don't know if I can do that, Kathryn. You deserve better."

"And that's what I have now." She looked at him. "With you and Matilda, my future *will* be better. Much better. Please don't ruin it with anger about things you cannot erase."

He was quiet for some time. Then he laid his hand on top of hers and twined his fingers with hers. "Okay, Kathryn, I promise."

"Thank you." She squeezed his fingers and turned her attention back to the road ahead of them, hoping they would never have reason to talk about her past again.

When they pulled into the yard, Caleb came out of the barn, a puzzled look on his face.

Travis stopped the wagon in front of the door to the cabin and hurried around to help her down.

"Wow, the preacher must have been short-winded today," Caleb joked.

"Kathryn doesn't feel well," Travis said as he set her down beside him.

The smile left Caleb's face as he studied her from head to toe. "What's wrong?"

"She fainted dead away."

Katie rolled her eyes at Travis' over exaggeration. She looked at Caleb with a shake of her head. "It was nothing. Travis is making way too much of it."

Travis ignored her as he circled his arm around her

shoulders and tucked her close to his side. "Can you grab Matilda for me?" Travis asked Caleb as he ushered her inside the cabin.

Caleb followed right behind with a smiling Matilda.

"I want you to lie down." Travis led her to the side of the bed and lowered her to the edge.

She sprang back to her feet. "Travis, I'm not about to lie down in the middle of the day. I have dinner to prepare and Matilda to tend to."

With his hands on her shoulders, Travis sat her back down. "You will do as I say and not argue with me. Caleb and I can throw something together for dinner, and I will see to Matilda. You need to rest. Doctor's orders."

27

Katie spent the next few hours tiptoeing around Travis and his doctoring. He and Caleb had done a fair job on dinner and had entertained Matilda until she had fallen asleep. But anytime Katie swung her legs over the side of the bed, Travis would look down his nose at her and tell her to stay put.

When Matilda woke, Travis laid her on a blanket in the middle of the floor, and he and Caleb got down on their hands and knees and played with her. Katie had to turn her head and cover her mouth to keep from laughing out loud at the two grown men talking baby babble.

After a while, even though she tried to fight it, sleep crept up on her. What else was a body to do when lying in bed all day?

When Katie awoke, the cabin was silent, and she was all alone.

Quietly, she got to her feet and was surprised to feel the same dizziness that had struck her earlier in the day. She was sure her early collapse had been from fear and worry, but now she wasn't so sure.

Maybe I am coming down with something.

She sank to the edge of the bed and pulled on her boots. When she stood for a second time, she made sure she was steady on her feet before heading out the backdoor.

Well, Travis and Caleb couldn't have gone far with Matilda in tow.

After looking behind the house—their favorite place to throw down a blanket and enjoy the outdoors—Katie headed toward the barn.

As she got closer, she was relieved to hear voices filtering through the weathered boards. However, she took only a few more steps, then stopped.

Giggling to herself, Katie decided to have a little fun.

She would get as close to the door as she could without being heard. Then, when they least expected it, she would jump out and put a scare into them.

That should prove to Travis that I'm feeling just fine.

Taking small, quiet strides, she was almost to the door.

Just a few more feet and I can—

"I think you might be right about Kathryn."

As soon as she heard Travis speak her name, she froze.

"So, you admit it; you're falling in love with her?"

Katie stumbled back against the wall, feeling dizzy all over again.

"I didn't say it was love. But I know I care for her deeply. I was ready to come to blows with her father on account of how he was talking to her. Then, when I found out he's the one responsible for the scars on her back, I'll tell ya, Caleb, I was seeing red. If it weren't for wanting to get Kathryn home so she could rest, I would've high tailed it back to that church yard and exposed Jethro James for the vile piece of trash that he is. The man needs to pay for what he's done to her."

"Calm down, Travis, before you upset Matilda."

"I can't help it. You should see them. The scars on Kathryn's back are worse than any whipping I've ever seen."

"But you're not thinking about doing anything foolish, are you?"

Katie took a step closer, needing to hear Travis' reply.

"If it was up to me, I would strip Jethro bare in the middle of town and rip his back up just like he did Kathryn's."

"But you're not going to, are you?"

Just then, Matilda let out a squawk and a whine.

"What's the matter little girl, are you missing Kathryn?"

Katie listened as Travis soothed Matilda with soft words and humming. When she was quiet once again, Caleb spoke up.

"Travis, you didn't answer my question. You're not going to do anything foolish, are you?"

The long silence terrified Katie. *Please, Travis, just say no. Please.*

"I can't."

"What do you mean, you can't?"

Travis' pause felt like an eternity to Katie. She took another step closer, willing Travis to explain himself.

"I promised Kathryn I'd leave the past in the past."

Katie exhaled with relief.

"But I'll tell you this much, she's my wife now. And if Jethro James thinks he can raise as much as an eyebrow to her, he has another thing coming. Let him pick on someone his own size and see what happens."

Matilda began to fuss and whine, bringing the men's

conversation to a stop.

"Okay, little lady. Let's get you back to Kathryn. I'm sure she's wondering where we've gotten to."

28

Katie raced to the cabin, knowing she had to get there before they did, or she would have a whole lot of explaining to do.

She hurried through the backdoor, then rushed to the bed. Flipping off her boots, she lay on top of the covers and propped herself up against the headboard. Breathing hard, she had to concentrate on slowing it down.

Slow, deep breaths. Slow, deep breaths.

The door pushed open, followed by soft footsteps.

"It's all right, Travis, you don't need to be quiet. I'm awake."

Walking across the room he asked, "How are you feeling?"

She reached out for Matilda and smiled. "A hundred percent."

"You don't look a hundred percent." His brows furrowed with concern as he laid Matilda in her arms then pressed his hand to her forehead. "You're flush, and you feel a little warm."

Of course. My dash across the yard.

Katie fiddled with the hem of Matilda's dress, thinking of an excuse. "That's what I get for resting in this heavy skirt. When I woke up, I was all tangled up in it. But I feel fine, really I do." She thought she sounded persuasive, but Travis didn't look convinced.

When Matilda's whimper turned into a wail, Katie used it to her benefit. "Now, enough about me, Travis. This little miss isn't so fine." She turned to Matilda. "You're hungry, aren't you?"

"I'll take her." Travis reached for her.

"Please, Travis, let me. Just bring me her bottle."

"But you should be resting."

"I've rested all afternoon. If I rest much more, I'll go crazy. Now, please, give me Matilda's bottle before we have an all-out war on our hands."

Matilda suckled the bottle as she stared up into Katie's eyes. This was usually Katie's favorite part of the day, holding Matilda, wondering what was going on in her little brain. However, it was her own brain that was going a mile a minute.

Travis has feelings for me?

Could it really be?

That explains his behavior today. Smiling at me the way he did, resting his hand on my back, making sure I was comfortable in the wagon.

Her heart pulsed faster, and her vision blurred.

Don't cry! She scolded herself. *That will ruin everything. Travis will worry all the more.*

She thought again about what he'd said. *'I didn't say it was love. But I know I care for her deeply.'*

It was almost too good to be true.

Travis' words replayed over and over in her head as she fed Matilda. Once she finished her bottle, she drifted off, her little shoulders lifting with every breath.

"Is she asleep?" Travis asked as he walked over and angled his head to see his precious little girl.

"Out like a light," Katie whispered.

"Would you like me to take her?"

"No. Not just yet." Katie smiled down at the angelic little girl. "I love holding her after she's fallen asleep and imagine what's going on in that little brain of hers."

Travis walked around to the other side of the bed and lay down next to Katie. Resting on his elbow, he brushed his large, work-worn finger through Matilda's feather-soft hair. "She's growing fast."

"Yes, she is." Katie didn't trust herself to say much more with her heart pounding like it was. Surely Travis could feel it beating as he brushed up against her.

"I need to apologize to you, Kathryn."

"Apologize?"

"Yes. I keep messing up."

"Messing up?"

He chuckled. "Are you going to keep repeating what I say?"

"Repeat?"

He laughed again.

"I'm sorry." She turned away, embarrassed.

But, with his calloused hand, Travis gently cupped her chin, and turned her to face him. "Don't be sorry." He smiled. "I'm the one who's sorry, remember?"

"For what?" She swallowed deep, not sure she was ready to hear what he had to say.

He looked down at Matilda, like he was having a hard time gathering his thoughts. He stroked his daughter's chubby little arm and cleared his throat. "Before Caleb showed up, I said I wanted us to be more like a family. And I meant it. But reminiscing with Caleb about our growing-up years—memories that included Mary——made it difficult for me to deal with my emotions. It was easier for me to slip in at night when you were already asleep than have to explain my muddled feelings."

Katie's heart sunk. "You don't have to explain yourself, Travis. She was your wife. Of course you'll always have feelings—"

He reached up and pressed his fingers to her lips, gently silencing her. "Kathryn, the feelings I'm talking about are the ones I have for you."

She dared to look into his crystal blue eyes, as his hand sunk to his side.

"Feelings you have for . . . me?"

He smiled. "You're repeating me again."

They were too close. She couldn't think with Travis lying right beside her, talking about his feelings for her. She needed to get up and put some distance between them. "Ah . . . I should probably put Matilda down if I expect her to sleep."

"I'll take her."

"That's okay." Katie scooted to the edge of the bed. "I've got her." But before she could get to her feet, Travis had circled around to her side, scooped Matilda out of her arms, and gently laid her in the cradle.

Taking a seat next to her on the bed, Travis reached for her hands, gave them a squeeze, then looked her square in the eye.

"Kathryn . . . I don't know how to say this. I mean, I'm not sure what I want to say." He shook his head. "No, I know what I *want* to say, I just don't know *what* to say. Oh, for cryin' out loud." Travis stopped trying to explain himself. Instead, he leaned toward her and pressed his lips against hers.

His kiss was soft, gentle, timid even. Before she had time to react, he pulled back and looked at her with guarded eyes.

His skin was flush, and Katie realized he was blushing. He looked like a shy schoolboy instead of the rugged man she'd come to know. She felt her own skin heat up as a smile pulled at the corners of her lips.

"Now, Kathryn . . . laughing at a man who just kissed you doesn't do much for his ego."

"I'm not laughing, Travis, I promise." She quickly assured him, amazed she could even speak. "You just surprised me is all. You didn't ask for a kiss . . . not that you had to. Of course you wouldn't ask. I'm your wife. A husband doesn't ask his wife; he just kisses her. Not to say that a husband is demanding. Because I don't think of you like that. I mean, I think of you like a husband, just not a demanding one."

What am I saying?

She threw her hands over her face, simply mortified. "I'm sorry, Travis. I've completely ruined this special moment with my blathering."

He rested his hand on her knee, "Can I assume that means it's okay that I kissed you?"

If her face was red before, now it had to be downright crimson. Was he asking if she was *glad* he kissed her? Or if she'd enjoyed the kiss? It didn't matter. How was she supposed to answer either question?

"Kathryn," he gently pulled her hands away from her face and held onto them, his thumbs brushing against her knuckles, stroking them, doing crazy things to her insides. "Caleb helped me see that having feelings for you isn't a betrayal to Mary. I loved her. I think I will always love her. But that doesn't mean I can't have room in my heart for you."

She studied Travis, wanting to memorize the look on his face the first time he put his emotions into words.

"I guess I didn't realize how strong my feelings for you already were. That is, not until I stood toe-to-toe with Jethro. The thought of him laying a hand on you had me seeing red. I wanted him to pay for what he'd done to you. I still do."

She shook her head, her heart racing. "But you promised to leave the past in the past."

"I know I did. And I plan on keeping my promise. I just want you to know my feelings for you run deep. And Kathryn . . . I was hoping in time . . . you might feel the same way about me." He looked at her, staring clean through to her soul.

At that moment, there was only one way Katie knew to show Travis her feelings for him were just as strong. Slowly, with heart fluttering, hands shaking, and her eyes closed, she leaned toward him.

Before she knew it, they were sharing their second kiss. But it was so much better than the first, because this time Katie returned Travis' affection with that of her own.

29

Katie spent the rest of the afternoon in what felt like a daydream.

After their kiss, Travis insisted she spend the remainder of the day resting. She wanted to tell him that would be impossible with her heart doing a loop-da-loop each time she thought about them kissing. But out of respect, she didn't argue. And surprisingly enough, she felt herself drifting off.

She sensed the moment Matilda was awake, but just as quick, the cabin grew silent and still. Travis had taken Matilda outside and left her alone with her thoughts, thoughts that see-sawed between hope and betrayal.

In her heart, she wanted to believe God was allowing her a fresh start with Travis and Matilda, and that her days of fear and nights of treachery were a thing of the past.

But how could that be?

How could she say she loved Travis, yet not tell him the truth?

Her heart tried to convince her head that he didn't need to know the sordid details. That she deserved to be happy, and she was better off putting the past behind her and never looking back. But her mind taunted her with ugly words. Unclean. Unwanted. Unfit.

But Travis believes in the power of forgiveness.

He told Katie he forgave God for taking his parents, even his precious Mary. But would he forgive her? Forgive her for not telling him sooner? Could he comprehend the filth that was thrusted upon her by no choice of her own? Could he forgive her completely?

Was she willing to take that chance?

And what of Jethro's threats? He swore Travis and Matilda would pay with their lives if she divulged his repulsive . . . no, *their* repulsive secret. Could he really be that wicked? She knew the abuse he was capable of—knew he'd murdered before. But was Jethro demented enough to kill again? Or worse, take the life of an innocent child?

Katie tossed and turned all afternoon and finally came to the only conclusion that made sense.

She could not take that chance.

She couldn't let Travis and Matilda fall victim to Jethro's unpredictable behavior.

And even though she told herself that her decision was based solely on Matilda's and Travis' safety, Katie knew in her heart of hearts, she was protecting herself as well. She could not bear to see the look of horror on Travis' face when he found out the woman he'd taken as his wife had been violated by another man.

By supper time, Katie could not lie still a moment longer. Though she felt fatigued by the psychological battle she'd struggled with all day, she was convinced she'd made the right decision.

Getting up, she splashed some water on her face, then went

about preparing the evening meal. Since Travis and Caleb had picked at scraps for dinner, Katie decided to prepare a hearty feast—stew with all the fixings.

After gathering the needed ingredients, she worked quickly cutting vegetables, mixing biscuits, and searing the meat. However, as she prepared the meal, she caught herself leaning, rather than standing, her body weak, her soul weary. Even her subconscious worked against her, filling her mind with horrible thoughts and painful memories.

No! God has given me a new start.

I need to concentrate on the good not the bad.

So, when she caught herself dwelling on the past, or felt the sickening feeling knot her stomach when she thought about Travis finding out her secret, she quickly pushed those feelings aside and thought instead on all the good that had happened. The kisses she'd shared with Travis. The warmth in his eyes when he tried to explain his feelings. The trust Matilda put in her every time she held her.

She smiled and sighed, feeling a little better.

When the front door creaked, Katie hastily stroked her hair and straightened her shirt waist, wanting to look her best.

As soon as Travis walked in and their eyes met, she felt the blush that started at her heart immediately race up her neck and heat her complexion.

Travis cocked his head with a questioning glance and walked toward her. With his hands resting on her hips, he bent close and whispered, "What are you doing out of bed?"

"I couldn't lie still another minute. Besides, you and Caleb deserve a good meal after such a meager dinner."

He leaned down and pressed a gentle kiss to her

forehead—sending shivers down her spine—then pulled back to look into her eyes. "You feel warm." He lifted his hand to her cheek to confirm what he felt with his lips.

Flustered, she turned to the stove. "I'm only going to tell you this because I don't want you to worry and send me back to bed. The heat in my cheeks is not from fever." She picked up the basket of biscuits and set it on the table then nervously wiped her hands on her apron. "Before you walked in, I was thinking about . . . well, what happened before." She quickly crossed back to the stove and stirred the stew. "It made me blush," she mumbled under her breath.

"What was that?" he asked, as he leaned over her shoulder and plucked a chunk of meat out of the pot.

Katie swatted his hand. "Never mind," she huffed. "Just get washed up."

He stood his ground behind her. "I washed up in the creek."

"Where's Matilda?"

"She's with Caleb, and don't go changing the subject."

"I'm not changing the subject."

"Then what did you say?"

"Nothing. I'm just flush from working over the stove."

"That's funny, I thought you said you were blushing."

She stood up straighter. "And I thought you didn't hear me."

"Oh, I heard you," he chuckled. "I just wanted to hear you say it again."

She tried to step away from him, but Travis reached out and tugged on her dress, pulling her dangerously close. "Now, don't get in a dander," he teased, his words laden with amusement.

"I'll show you a dander," she said, slapping his hands away. "Caleb will end up with a bunkmate if you keep pestering me."

"I don't think so!"

Both Katie and Travis whirled around to see Caleb standing in the doorway, a bright-eyed Matilda in his arms.

"Travis makes a lousy bunkmate. He snores too much. Besides, why should I get punished if he's the one in trouble?"

Travis stepped back from Katie and rubbed his jaw with a chuckle. "Sorry about that, Caleb, Kathryn and I were . . ."

"I saw what you were doing, Travis. I'm not blind." He walked over to the table and took a seat. "I'm just saying you two need to settle your *differences* among yourselves. Isn't that right, Miss Matilda?" Caleb sat Mattie on the edge of the table and spoke to her. "I think your mother and father need to make sure the door is shut tight if they're going to be settling their *differences* in the middle of the day, don't you?"

Katie chanced a glance at Travis and saw that his complexion was as red as hers felt. They shared a knowing smile as he lifted the pot from the stove and set it on the table. Though she was embarrassed Caleb caught them in a cozy moment, the way he just naturally referred to her as Matilda's mother made her heart melt.

Picking up the coffee pot, Katie carried it to the table, sat down, and reached for Matilda. Once she was settled on her lap, Katie turned to Travis and asked him to say the blessing.

He looked at her with starry eyes and a wink. "I most certainly will."

"God, I want to thank you . . ." Travis paused, and in his silence, Katie glanced his way. His eyes were squeezed shut, and he was pinching the bridge of his nose. He cleared his throat, but she could still hear emotion in his words. "Thank you for . . . unexpected blessings. Amen."

30

Though Katie had very little appetite, the evening meal had been perfect.

Travis and Caleb talked about the addition they were ready to add to the house as soon as Travis picked up the lumber, and they reveled in the rumor that the price of wheat was predicted to go as high as .65¢ per hundred weight.

She gathered from their enthusiasm that was a good price.

The men continued to chatter while she cleaned up after their meal and gave Matilda her evening bottle. She was just laying her down when Caleb stood and stretched. "Well, I think I'm gonna call it a night," he said as he sauntered toward the door.

"So soon?" she questioned.

"Yeah. Travis has been keeping me up way too late these last few weeks. I'm looking forward to a full night of shut-eye."

"Hey, it takes two to have a conversation, and you held up your end just fine," Travis defended.

Caleb chuckled. "I guess I did at that." He removed his hat from the peg on the wall and tipped it toward her before placing it on his head. "Supper was delightful, as always. Thank you, Mrs. Clark."

She felt her cheeks heat up. "You're welcome, Caleb."

With Matilda settled in and the dishes done, there wasn't

much else left to do. Katie normally read until Matilda's next feeding, but with Travis in the cabin, she wasn't sure what to do with herself.

She fiddled around the stove, cleaning up imaginary crumbs while Travis sat in the rocker.

"I think Caleb and I are going to get started on that addition I was talking about."

"Oh?"

"Yeah. When Mary got pregnant, a second room was only common sense. Originally, I'd planned on getting it done before winter. Then, well . . . Mary got sick, and I . . ."

Katie felt the sadness in Travis' silence and wished she could think of something to say to lessen his grief. But she knew only time would be able to accomplish that.

After clearing his throat, Travis started again. "I planned on waiting until spring, but with Caleb here, I'm thinking we might be able to get it done before the first snowfall. He's real handy with a hammer, and even better at coming up with a good plan."

She turned to him. "But I thought you already had a plan?"

"I did, but I hadn't put much thought into it. Caleb convinced me that we should add two rooms instead of one."

"Two rooms? Well, I guess that would be nice when someone comes to visit. They wouldn't have to bed down in the barn."

"And it would give us some privacy when Matilda gets older."

The thought of needing privacy made Katie's already sensitive stomach flip-flop.

"I was even thinking about ordering a bit more lumber,

so I could add on a small room for a tub."

"A bathtub?" She clasped her hands together, barely containing her excitement. "I saw a real honest-to-goodness bathtub in Danby Falls. It was amazing!"

"Well, I don't know what you saw, but we could sure use something bigger than the washtub we have now."

"Oh, Travis, that would be wonderful." She beamed, but her smile quickly turned to a frown. "But that would be so extravagant. I'm sure there are more important things you could buy, practical things."

He stood and walked toward her, a gleam in his eye. "But seeing you smile like that makes it important."

She glanced away, feeling her skin blossom. She didn't know what to make of Travis' change in behavior. She'd gone from being Matilda's mother to becoming Travis' wife overnight. It was as if his confrontation with Jethro had forced Travis to stake his claim. And now that he had, it lit a fire under him that fueled his need to protect her, even romance her.

"Why are you blushing?" he asked as he reached for her hands, a devilish smirk on his face. "Is it the thought of us needing privacy?"

She turned away.

"Kathryn, I promise I won't rush you. I know you need time to . . . adjust to our situation. I just want you to know you don't have to be afraid. And you don't need to keep your feelings all bottled up inside. We're married now. And the best way for us to grow our relationship is with trust. We're not two but one. You can tell me anything, and I promise to . . ."

Travis was still talking, but Katie didn't hear him. Her stomach shifted, and her mouth soured. Before he could finish, she raced for the backdoor and stumbled in the dark until she fell on her knees and allowed her stomach to give up what little she'd eaten.

"Kathryn!" Travis shouted from the back porch before running to her side and kneeling beside her. "Are you all right?"

Tears streamed down her face.

I will never be all right.

If she told Travis her secret, she'd lose him and put him and Matilda in danger. If she didn't tell him, she would continue to harbor the guilt that was poisoning her insides and making her ill. Jethro had pummeled her physically and emotionally, but her deception was battering her soul.

God, show me what to do, and I'll do it. But please, don't let me hurt Travis and Matilda in the process.

"Come on, Kathryn, let's get you back inside."

Katie had lain awake all night, weighed down with despair.

She had listened to Travis' rhythmic breathing and felt the warmth of his breath on her neck but could not fall asleep.

Even though she should feel overwhelming joy, deliverance, and thanksgiving, her conscience wouldn't allow it.

The deception in her heart continued to wreak havoc on her stomach like the poison it was, and a debate—rooted deep in her soul—taunted her throughout the early-morning hours.

She had two choices.

Hide her past and allow Travis to love her.

Or love Travis enough to tell him the truth, so he could find a wife deserving of all he had to offer.

She sighed from both exhaustion and anguish.

Travis stirred, inching closer to her. "Still not feeling well?" he asked in a groggy, half-awake voice.

"I'm sure it's nothing," she whispered. "Maybe too much sun like you said."

"But now your stomach is giving you fits. Doc said if you weren't better in a few days, he wanted to take a look at you, to make sure it wasn't something more serious. Maybe we should make a trip into town to see him."

"That would be silly and a waste of everyone's time," she whispered. "Now, no more talk of me going to town. You have a farm to take care of, and I know of a certain little lady who's going to be squawking at any minute."

Katie took a deep, silent breath, swung her feet to the ground, and sat on the edge of the bed. Travis took his time, stretching and yawning before getting up.

She watched by dawn's pink light as he crossed to where his trousers hung from the hook on the wall. He slipped his legs in and fastened his belt, then stood at the washbasin and splashed a few handfuls of water on his face. Katie stared, captivated by the way Travis' muscles danced beneath his skin.

Just then, Matilda squealed, but before Katie could get to her, Travis scooped her up and cradled her against his bare chest. "How's daddy's little angel this fine day?" he asked as he smiled down at her.

Matilda cooed, her little fists punching the air.

"You're raring to go, aren't you?"

She answered with a hungry cry.

"Okay, okay, I get it. Food is more important than talking

with your pa. Besides, I have to get the milk if you're going to eat."

Travis deposited Matilda on top of the bed covers where she immediately began to fuss. He then turned to where Katie stood in nothing but her nightgown, her dress pressed against her chest. "I'll be back with the milk and eggs."

"I'm sure Matilda would appreciate that."

Travis smiled, his eyes traveling over her before he took a few steps forward and pressed a kiss to her forehead. Chills danced down Katie's spine as he gave her a wink, then was on his way.

Travis had no sooner shut the door when Matilda began to vocalize her brewing impatience.

"Now, now, little miss, you must give me time to get dressed and pull a brush through my hair."

Matilda locked eyes with Katie, all the while her fists beating the air. Katie knew her smile stretched from ear to ear, and there was nothing she could do about it. She loved Matilda and was *in* love with Travis.

She now knew what she had to do, or better yet what she *wouldn't* say.

Travis agreed to let the past be the past, so Katie was going to do the same.

She had to if she hoped to hold onto her amazing new life.

31

The week had come and gone and though Katie woke every morning hopeful she would feel better, dizziness, exhaustion, and a stomach tied in knots continued to plague her. She'd been able to hide most of her symptoms from Travis, but it was harder to mask her exhaustion and weariness in the evenings.

As she lay in bed, morning ready to break, she prepared herself physically and mentally for another day of chores and deception.

"Kathryn, you awake?" Travis whispered.

"Uh hum."

"Come to town with me today." He gently stroked her arm. "You could see Doc Hammond while I pick up the lumber."

"You're fussing over nothing, Travis," she tried to speak with upbeat certainty. "I'm just a little under the weather. A day or two more and I'll be good as new." As much as she hated the thought of Travis being gone for the day, she was looking forward to not having to pretend her symptoms were insignificant.

Travis moved closer to her, his chest brushing against her back, his hand resting on her hip. "Are you sure that's all it is? It's been almost a week."

Squeezing her eyes shut, Katie blamed herself for the

trepidation she heard in his voice. They should be enjoying these newfound moments of intimacy. But instead, Travis was worrisome, watching her like a hawk, while she spent their evenings together pretending to be fine, assuring him everything was okay.

Katie knew losing Mary to illness more than her symptoms was the reason Travis was being so over-protective.

But what could she say?

Don't worry, Travis. I'm not really sick. It's just overwhelming guilt rotting my insides, robbing me of sleep.

She reached for his hand, kissed it, then pressed his palm against her cheek. "Please don't worry, Travis. I promise. Nothing is going to happen to me."

He placed a tender kiss to her shoulder, causing her heart to race. "I'm glad, because I don't know if I could handle another . . ." He cleared his throat. "I need you here, Kathryn. God's given me . . . me *and* Matilda a second chance. I don't want anything to ruin it."

Like finding out your wife is impure?

"Kathryn, you're shaking. What is it, what's wrong?" Travis perched on his elbow and rolled her toward him.

She closed her eyes, mustering the resolve she needed, then looked up at him with what she hoped was an encouraging smile.

"What's that look for?"

"Must a wife have a reason to smile at her husband?"

She tried to sound alluring, enchanting even, anything to scuttle Travis' cause for concern. She reached for his face and stroked the morning stubble on his cheek, delighted when she saw the slightest shade of pink spread across his face. He covered her hand with his and smiled.

"Don't think tempting smiles and batting eyelashes are going to work on me, Mrs. Clark. I know a ploy when I see one. You're trying to distract me."

"Distract you?" she smiled again.

"Yes, distract me. But I'm not that easily swayed. I would feel better if Doc took another look at you, just to be on the safe side."

Katie swung her legs over the side of the bed, needing to get away from his inquisitive eyes.

"Travis, there are times during the month that a woman isn't herself. Surely you know that." Her cheeks bloom with humiliation, talking about such an intimate subject. "Some months I'm weaker than others." She got to her feet, turned, and smiled at him still lying in bed. "I promise; I'll be back to my normal self in a day or two."

Liar. Your menses have never been normal, nor have they ever made you weak.

But Travis didn't know that, and it was the only other excuse she could think of to buy her some time until she felt better.

Travis didn't say anything as he got out of bed and pulled on his pants. But he looked at her while buttoning his shirt, his scrutinizing eyes hinting that he was not completely convinced by her explanation.

"Okay. I'll give you a few more days. But if you're not better by Sunday, you *will* see the doctor first thing Monday morning. No arguments. No excuses. Understand?"

"Of course." She smiled, then quickly got dressed while Travis stoked the stove. As Katie tied her apron, Matilda made her presence known. And just like that, the three of them fell into their morning routines.

Well . . . almost.

While Travis fetched the milk and went about his other chores as usual, Katie fed Matilda. However, instead of talking and playing with Mattie while she ate, Katie spent the time pleading with God to strengthen her and take away whatever was plaguing her stomach.

When Travis returned with eggs, Katie made breakfast while he played with Matilda. She had just dished up three plates when Caleb walked in.

"Here, I'll take her," Katie said, reaching for Matilda.

"No, you go ahead." Travis positioned Mattie on his lap. "I can hold her and eat at the same time."

"Yes, but I'm sure you have a schedule you want to stick to. I can pick at my breakfast once you two have left."

Except all Katie had to do was look at the plate of scrambled eggs in front of her to know she wouldn't be able to stomach them. Taking Matilda from Travis, she pushed the eggs around on her plate, but couldn't bring herself to lift them to her lips.

"So, what time will you and Caleb head to town?"

"I'll leave just as soon as I take stock of a few things, but Caleb is going to stay here."

She looked from Travis to Caleb.

"No sense we both lose a day's work," Caleb chimed in as he shoveled a forkful of eggs into his mouth.

"Will you be home in time for dinner?" she asked Travis.

"No. Since you refuse to come with me," he said sternly but with a smile, "I'm going to ride over to Canter and pick up a few things, but I will be back in plenty of time for supper."

"Oh . . . okay."

Travis looked at her guardedly. "Is that a problem? Because if you don't want me to be gone that long, I can come—"

"Travis, I'll be fine. Really. What about you, Caleb?" She quickly changed the subject. "Will you be here for dinner?"

"Nah. I'm going to work on the fence line on the other side of the creek. I figured on starting at the farthest point and working my way back. But if you could throw a sandwich or even a couple of biscuits and an apple in a pail, that would hold me until supper."

"Okay." With Matilda on her hip, she stood.

"You don't have to do it right now," Caleb said around a mouthful of eggs. "Go ahead and finish your breakfast first."

"It's no problem." Katie moved to the stove, happy to leave her breakfast behind.

"Do you have your list ready?" Travis asked her.

"Yes." She took a slip of paper from the dresser and handed it to him.

He looked at it and frowned. "Is this it?"

"Well, yes. Why?" She looked at him, puzzled. "Is it too much? Because I can par it down some." She reached for the piece of paper, but he held it out of her grasp. When she tried again, he playfully held it over his head.

"You've only written down staples. Isn't there anything *you* would like for yourself?"

Katie hadn't thought much about it. Whenever she put a list together at home, it was understood that she only wrote down what was absolutely necessary. And of course, that never included anything for herself.

"Well, since you asked, Matilda is growing like a weed." She looked at the child on her hip and smiled. "I would like to make her some new gowns. Maybe you could pick out a fabric or two."

Caleb chuckled. "Travis? Picking out material? That alone would be worth the trip to town. Maybe I'll go after all."

Travis gave him a foolhardy slap to the back of the head along with a warning glare, then turned back to her. "I wouldn't know the first thing about picking out fabric."

"It's not that hard, Travis. Just pick out something you'd like to see Matilda in. A pretty pink or maybe a sunny yellow. Tell Mrs. Dudley I'm going to make her some gowns. She'll know what you need, but don't let her sell you a bunch of nonsense. Matilda is too young to appreciate frills and such. Just the material and some thread will do fine."

Travis shrugged, clearly unconvinced as he finished his breakfast and took the last swallow of his coffee. "But what about you? You still didn't list anything for yourself."

She smiled. "That's okay. I have all I need right here." When Travis looked at her, Katie hoped her expression conveyed exactly what she meant. When he returned a smile that sent chills down her spine, she knew she had.

Caleb took the pail she offered him and left. Travis put on his hat and coat but paused at the door. Walking back to the stove where Katie was standing with Matilda, he leaned down and placed a kiss on his baby girl's forehead then pressed another to Katie's cheek. "I'll see you at supper." He offered one last sultry smile before walking away, closing the door behind him.

Katie waited until she heard the wagon pull from the yard, then collapsed in the rocking chair with a heavy sigh. With Travis watching her every move, it took all the willpower and stamina she had not to droop in front of him and give him cause for concern.

"I've been up less than two hours, yet I feel weak as a newborn," she said to Matilda laying in her lap. "Even so, I'm not going to piddle the day away just because I'm feeling poorly. I'll simply take my time, go slow and steady, rest when I have to. I can still get a lot done without having your pa and Caleb underfoot."

Even though she felt like crawling back into bed, Katie chose instead to rock Matilda a little longer than usual and allow herself a few extra minutes rest. However, once Matilda fell asleep, Katie laid her down and looked around the cabin with a keen eye.

Since Travis and Caleb were going to be gone for the afternoon, Katie already planned on doing a little extra cleaning here and there, but now that she knew they would be gone for the entire day, she really wanted to take a heavy hand to the cabin. Even so, knowing her energy level wasn't going to be able to keep up with her expectations, she debated exactly how much she should try to do.

Looking around, she realized the place had not been given a thorough once over since she first arrived. Back then, she had nothing but time to devote to cleaning since Travis insisted she stay inside, while he spent all his days in the fields and his nights in the barn.

A lot had changed in the last few weeks, and Katie realized she had Caleb to thank for it. With his gentle nudges and strong words, he'd coaxed Travis back from a very dark place. And even though she didn't think Travis would ever get over the loss of Mary—especially with Matilda as a constant reminder of the love they once shared—she did hope, with enough time, that the tender feelings sprouting between them would take root and grow into something as deep and as meaningful as the years Travis had spent with Mary.

With a satisfying sigh and a smile, Katie looked around the cabin one more time. "I can do this," she whispered.

Slow and steady.

32

On her hands and knees, in just her slip and chemise, Katie worked the scrub water in circles on the floor.

"You wouldn't be doing this if you weren't such a klutz," she grumbled out loud.

Wanting to surprise Travis when he got home, Katie decided to do one of the more toilsome chores he took care of on Saturdays. Of course, selfishly she hoped by freeing up his afternoon, they could maybe go on a picnic, or a walk, or just spend some quality time together.

So even though she was tired and weary, she decided to tackle the ash in the stove.

Everything had gone fine until she tried carrying the heavy bucket outside. When she stumbled over the small shovel she'd been using, the bucket spilled, sending ash all over the floor.

At first, she thought she could just clean the area where the ash had spilled, but the more she scooped and shoveled the more the ash spread.

Two hours later, exhausted and overheated, Katie was almost finished with the entire floor. Due to the heat and the filth, she had decided to shed her skirt and shirtwaist at the get go. And it was a good thing she did. The knees of her slip were dark as coal, and she had taken to using the hem of her chemise to blot her sweaty brow.

All in all, she was an absolute mess, but the end was finally in sight.

Having worked her way from the front door over to Matilda, Katie waited for her to take her nap. It also gave her a chance to regain her strength. Then, with Matilda asleep, she continued working her way to the backdoor.

On her hands and knees, she looked behind her. "Three more feet," she mumbled. "Only three more—"

When the knob on the front door rattled, she panicked.

"Oh no," she whispered, knowing it had to be Caleb.

Looking down at her state of undress, she hollered, "Caleb, you can't come in right now. I'm not decent."

When the door swung open and a booted foot stepped over the threshold anyway, she gasped.

"Wade!"

He looked at her, a wicked smile on his lips, lust in his eyes. Katie felt like an animal caught in a trap. Hurrying across the still drying floor, she pulled the blanket from the foot of the bed and threw it over her shoulders.

"Modesty?" he laughed mockingly. "We both know there's no call for that."

She cleared her throat, trying to make herself sound strong and unafraid. "You need to leave, Wade. You're not welcome here, and you know it."

"I almost forgot what your voice sounded like, you being mute and stupid in the head. But I guess that was just an act."

She didn't care what he called her, as long as he left.

"Leave, Wade, before someone sees you."

"And who would that be?" he asked as he closed the door behind him and threw the bolt. "We both know it won't be

Travis. Picking up lumber was the task for today, if I heard correctly."

Katie's heart was racing so fast, her shaking turned into violent tremors. "Travis left early so he could be back early." She took a quick glance at the timepiece on the mantle. "And Caleb will be coming in for dinner at any minute. Any minute at all."

Wade took slow even steps toward her, chuckling with every footfall. "Now, we both know that's not true. I saw him sitting under a tree, eating from a pail, a spool of wire at his feet. He looked to have plenty more fencing to mend."

The room swayed as Katie clutched the quilt around her shoulders and took slow steps backwards toward the door. She batted her eyes, to clear the dancing specks of light, afraid to close them all together.

"Don't be stupid, Wade. I'm married now. I'm not just your sister; I'm someone's wife. You can't defile another man's wife and expect to get away with it. I hid the bruises from Mama and Seth, but I won't be able to hide them from Travis."

"Tell me, Katie, is Travis a good lover?" His eyes traveled over her skimpy clothing, violating her without even laying a hand on her. "Is this how Travis likes you? Barefoot and half naked?" he laughed.

She took another step backward. All she had to do is get out the door, race past the barn, and scream. Caleb was sure to hear her.

"You aren't thinking about running, are you Katie? That would leave me and that brat all alone." He glanced over to where Matilda lay sleeping. "You wouldn't want that, would you?" he sneered as he continued toward her. "I mean, anything could happen. She could tumble from her cradle, or accidentally be smothered by a blanket. Do you think Travis would keep you around then, knowing you killed his kid? It's your choice, Katie; choose wisely."

She cried out in horror but quickly covered her mouth, not wanting to wake Matilda. And just like a mountain lion springing to attack its prey, Wade lunged forward, snatched her arm, and pulled her tight against his chest. She struggled and squirmed trying to break free, but it was no use.

"Now, let's not make this more difficult than it has to be," Wade said before crushing his lips against hers.

With a fistful of her hair in one hand, and the other wrapped around her middle, he pushed her up against the wall.

Katie twisted and writhed to get her hands free from where they were pinned against his chest, but Wade's strength seemed almost superhuman, fueled by the frenzy of his lust driven hunger.

When he ripped the sleeve of her chemise from her shoulder, Katie knew her only chance to get away was to stop fighting. If Wade thought she'd given up, he might drop his guard, and then maybe she'd be able to break free.

With all the inner strength and self-discipline she could muster, Katie willed her muscles to relax.

Wade immediately reacted to her lack of fighting. Pulling back, he looked at her with crazed eyes and smiled. "Now, that's better."

When he leaned in to kiss her once again, Katie clamped her teeth down on his bottom lip. Feeling his skin tear under the pressure of her teeth, she didn't let go until he brought his forearm up under her chin and slammed her head back against the wall.

Wade spit blood in her face as he applied pressure to her neck, sneering as he cut off her air supply.

Katie grabbed at his arm and tried pushing him away, but when it was obvious she was no match for his strength, she dug her fingernails into his forearm and clawed him with all her might.

He shrilled like a wounded animal and stumbled backward. Looking at her with pure hatred, he hissed, "Why you little—"

Katie dashed toward the door but didn't get far before she felt the full force of his weight against her back. The momentum of Wade's tackle sent them crashing into the table and chairs. Falling awkwardly, oxygen rushed from Katie's lungs, leaving her with nothing to draw on.

Air.

I need air.

But Wade's weight trapped her against the floor, preventing her from taking a breath.

Moaning, he slowly rolled to one side, but Katie still couldn't breathe. Her lungs no longer seemed to function. Gasping, but feeling no relief, the pain in her gut and the lack of oxygen in her lungs caused the light around her to blur.

Then, her entire world turned to black.

33

When Katie heard Matilda fussing, she instinctively moved to get her, but a horrible pain speared her midsection, causing her to curl up and cry out in agony.

Opening her eyes, Katie saw that she was lying on the floor next to the table.

What am I doing here?

She tried to think, tried to remember, all the while fighting off nausea from the pain. Then Wade's face flashed before her eyes, and it all came back to her.

His attack.

Their struggle.

The two of them colliding into the table and chairs.

She flinched at the memory and the unbearable pain that shot through her.

I must have blacked out. But for how long?

Wrapping her arm around her middle, she pushed herself to a sitting position and glanced at the clock.

Oh no!

She'd been out for almost two hours.

Matilda!

Remembering Wade's threat, Katie pushed past the pain and got to her feet.

Please, God, not Matilda.

She stumbled to the bed, quickly sat down before her feet gave way, then looked at Matilda.

Relieved to see she was just beginning to wake from her nap, Katie cried hysterically, thanking God, knowing it had to be Him who protected her.

Startled by her outburst, Matilda looked at Katie, her little lip curling right before she let out a wail.

"Shhhh. It's all right, Matilda. Everything is going to be all right."

Katie wanted to believe that, but she wasn't so sure. She could barely stand without feeling like she was going to be sick, and the throbbing in her head was almost blinding.

Even so, the thought of Caleb or Travis walking in, demanding an explanation—Travis finding out her darkest secrets—was more terrifying than her pain.

She needed to get everything in order.

But where do I start?

Matilda was crying, wriggling around in her cradle. The bucket of dirty water was knocked over, a puddle on the floor. The table was cockeyed, the chairs laying on their sides. And when Katie looked down at herself, she sobbed.

Her chemise was filthy and torn, blood smeared all over it. And when she held up her shaking hands in front of her, she could see Wade's skin underneath her fingernails.

What do I do first?

Her head was pounding, her vision blurry, her body throbbing with pain. She could barely think, hardly walk, and kept mumbling to herself, not knowing where to start.

Finally, she blurted out, "Cleaned up. I need to get cleaned up."

An accident could account for the spilled bucket, and Matilda's crying just a show of her temper, but there was no way to explain her disheveled appearance—especially the blood.

When Katie stood, she immediately dropped back down onto the bed, the pulsing in her head nearly unbearable.

Taking a deep breath, she tried again, slower this time, and waited for the room to stop spinning before limping toward the dresser.

Removing her torn chemise and stained slip, Katie shoved them to the back of the drawer and grabbed her only other set of underthings. Carefully, she pulled them on, gasping and wincing at the pain in her middle, then frantically scrubbed her fingertips, causing herself even more pain.

Running a brush through her hair, she could only hope that she looked better on the outside than she felt on the inside.

When Katie glanced at Matilda, she was surprised to see she had stopped crying and was studying the dangling squares of material Katie had rigged to her cradle. Thankful for the reprieve, she limped to the table and righted the chairs.

Oh, no.

Seeing that a rail on one of the chairs was split explained the excruciating pain in her side.

But how am I going to explain it to Travis?

Not having time to answer her own question, she ignored it, turning instead to the puddle by the backdoor.

Slowly and with much care, she lowered herself to the floor and mopped up the water. However, when she tried to stand, her stomach cramped something fierce, the pain nearly knocking her down. Reaching out for the table, she braced herself, until the spasm passed.

After a few deep breaths, she dragged the bucket of dirty water to the backdoor, wincing and crying with every step. When she finally had it out on the stoop, she tipped it over, and watched the murky water spill between the steps. Sighing, she reveled in the tiny victory, but when she looked up, she saw Caleb rounding the barn headed her way.

Not wanting him to see her state of undress, she slipped behind the door just before he looked up and waved.

"I was just coming to tell you Travis is headed this way."

Her stomach tensed, causing her to grimace, but she tried not to show it.

"Are you all right, Kathryn? You don't look so good."

She mopped her brow. "I'm fine. Just getting some deep cleaning done while you and Travis were occupied for the afternoon. I'm not decent though," she said from where she stood behind the door, "and I just finished the floors. So, tell Travis not to come in for at least half an hour. I want to make sure they are good and dry before anyone trudges across them."

"I don't think that will be a problem. It will take us twice that long just to get everything unloaded. I wouldn't expect us much before supper."

Closing the door, Katie collapsed against it, relieved Caleb went on his way without too many questions.

I have an hour to—

Just then, Matilda let out a sharp cry, making it perfectly clear she was hungry and would not wait a minute longer.

Weary and light-headed, Katie steadied herself with a hand to the wall and slowly walked to the cradle, but when she lifted

Matilda, another agonizing pain twisted her insides.

Afraid she was going to drop her, Katie laid Matilda in the middle of the bed, where it sagged the most. Though the spongy ticking prevented Mattie from rolling over, it did nothing to silence her tantrum.

"I'm sorry, Matilda, but you are just going to have to be patient."

Ignoring the child's displeasure, Katie slowly moved to the pantry shelf and readied a bottle. When she was done, Katie clenched her teeth and held her breath, preparing herself for the pain that was sure to come.

When she picked up Matilda, she couldn't help but cry out. The stabbing pain in her belly was like no other, but she continued to the rocking chair, collapsing onto the seat.

As soon as the nipple touched Matilda's lips, she was once again her good-natured self. Katie closed her eyes in relief and wiped the tears wetting her cheeks.

What am I going to tell Travis? I can hardly stand, let alone carry on like nothing is wrong. The way he's been watching me lately, he'll notice right away.

With pain radiating from her every limb, Katie rested her head back against the rocker and looked up. When she saw the cobwebs clinging to the ceiling beam, she twisted slightly to look at the table and size up the height of the chair next to it.

That could work.

Katie knew she would have to endure a scolding from Travis, but it would explain her pain and discomfort, and a reason for the split rail of the ladder-back chair.

Feeling a small sense of relief—even though she knew Travis would be furious with her—Katie finished feeding

Matilda and held her breath as she carried her back to the cradle. Bending to lay her down was excruciating, and when Matilda proceeded to whimper and squirm, Katie felt like crying. "Please, sweetheart, you need to entertain yourself for a bit. I'm in no shap—"

Seized by a pain stronger than the last, Katie reached out for the dresser, pressed her hand to her abdomen, and tried to provide enough pressure to counteract the pain. With her eyes closed, she took slow, even breaths. When the pain finally subsided, she opened her eyes. That's when she saw the drops of blood on the floorboards by her heels.

No! Not that, too.

So angry, she let a word slip out that she didn't normally use, then slowly knelt next to the dresser and rummaged through the drawer for some rags. But then she realized this must be the reason for her cramping.

Even though her monthly situation had never affected her like this, it stood to reason between that and her fall, she was in more pain than usual.

She couldn't help but chuckle at the irony. The very reason she'd given Travis for being out of sorts, turned out to be true.

An hour later, even with several stops and starts, Katie was able to piece together a decent enough meal.

When she heard Travis and Caleb's approaching footsteps and muffled conversation, she took a deep breath—as deep as she could—and prayed she'd be able to make it through the meal.

The door swung wide, and she quickly looked up with a smile, trying to act as if it was any other day. That lasted all of two seconds. Travis immediately rushed to her side and reached for her hand. "What is it, Kathryn, what's wrong?"

She swatted his hand away with a chuckle and turned back to the pot on the stove. "Who says anything is wrong?"

"You're white as a sheet, and I can tell you've been crying. What's wrong?" His voice was firm, letting her know he was not the least bit fooled by her performance.

Glancing over his shoulder at Caleb, then back to the stove, she whispered, "we can discuss it after dinner."

"Why can't we discuss it now?" he insisted.

"Because," she continued in a low voice, "it's of a private nature." Katie looked at him with a raised brow, waiting for him to get her point.

When understanding finally flashed in his eyes, he blushed slightly and lowered his lips next to her ear. "I'm sorry. That was thoughtless of me."

She shooed him away from the stove as if nothing was wrong, then turned. "Not there, Travis!" Katie barked just as he was ready to take a seat.

He jumped to attention, startled. "Why not?"

"I . . . uhh . . . had a little mishap today, and the rail on that chair split. I'm sure it can hold my weight, but I don't know if it's sturdy enough to hold yours."

He squatted in front of the chair, examining it. Running his hand down the split in the rail, he turned to her. "How on earth did you manage to do this?"

Carrying one plate at a time to the table, with her other hand pressed firmly against her stomach, Katie ignored Travis' question completely.

"I'll just get the biscuits, and then we can start." At the stove, she bent to pull the hot tray from the oven, a whimper escaping her lips. She quickly started humming a tune, hoping to disguise her soft cry as just a sour note.

Knowing the pain would slowly subside, Katie took her time placing the biscuits in the basket. When she finally took a seat in the damaged chair, she immediately felt Travis' glare. When she chanced a look at him, his sullen expression told her he was not happy.

Not in the least.

Travis and Caleb covered a great many subjects during the meal, and though he didn't press her for more information, Katie could feel the weight of Travis' displeasure.

Caleb caught on pretty fast that something was going on between the two of them, because once his plate was empty, he feigned exhaustion and excused himself for the night.

He was barely out the door before Travis pounced on her like a fox on a hen. "Okay, I made it through dinner without causing a scene, but you better explain what's going on, and fast." He crossed his arms against his broad chest, his stance that of a man who would not be challenged.

She looked at Travis, and even though she knew he was angry, she saw deep concern in his eyes, making what she had to do even harder.

I hate lying. But what choice do I have?

"If you must know, I fell today. Pretty hard in fact. I was careless and stupid, and now I'm paying the price."

Travis dropped his arms and cocked his head with sympathy. He stepped forward and caressed her cheek with the back of his hand. "Are you okay?"

She looked up at him, tears welling in her eyes, not so much from the pain but from the lie she was about to tell. "No. But I will be."

He continued to stroke her cheek. "You're so pale, and I can see you're in a lot of pain. Tell me what happened."

She placed her hand over his, wishing she could do just that. Wishing she could tell him the whole truth and finally be free of it. But that would be selfish. Though it might rid her of her demons, it would only serve to endanger him and Matilda.

Please, God, forgive me for my lies. It's the only way to keep them safe.

She carefully pointed above the table. "See those cobwebs on the ceiling?"

"Yeah."

"I thought I could reach them if I . . ." She took a slow measured breath. "If I put one of the chairs on top of the table."

"You didn't!" he snapped, clearly exasperated.

She looked at him, then quickly turned away. "I was doing fine until I swung at a cluster that was just out of reach. The chair shifted, and the leg slipped right off the edge of the table. The chair and I landed in a heap. That's how the spindle got broken, and why I feel so poorly."

He reached for her shoulders and gave them the slightest shake. She took another deep breath before looking up into eyes of disappointment.

"Do I even have to tell you how dangerous that was?"

She was going to answer, but he didn't give her a chance to.

"And what if you weren't okay? What if you were lying there seriously hurt while I was gone half the day? And what about Matilda? What would she have done without someone to care for her?"

He released her shoulders and paced to the fireplace. There he stood, staring at the mantel, his shoulders taunt, his back stiff. "I thought you had more common sense than that, really I did."

The disappointment in his tone hurt Katie more than Wade ever could. He and Jethro were brutal, but the soft tone of Travis' displeasure hurt far more than any physical blow.

"I'm so sorry. I know now how careless it was."

He turned back to her. Though his posture was still rigid with irritation, his words were heavy with concern. "Where are you hurt?"

She brushed her hand across her stomach. "Here, mostly. My muscles keep knotting on me."

He moved forward, tipping her chin up. "What about this bruising on your neck?"

Katie reached for her neck, remembering the pain of Wade's forearm pinning her to the wall, depriving her of air. "I don't know. I must have hit it on something."

Travis shook his head, clearly frustrated. "How could you have been so reckless, Kathryn?"

"I'm sorry, Travis, really I am." She started to cry, no longer able to hold back her tears. "I never intended for this to happen."

"Well, of course you didn't." He reached out and wrapped her in a gentle hug. "That's why it's called an accident." He stroked her back as he held her close. "But please, don't let there be a next time. You need to be more careful. If not for your sake, do it for us. Matilda and I are counting on you to be around for a very long time."

34

Though Travis let her know how disappointed he was with her poor judgment, he was sympathetic as well, making Katie feel even more guilty for lying.

The way he assured her he could take care of Matilda's needs and insisted she turn in early for the night, was like heaping coals on her head. But since she was in too much pain to argue, she thanked Travis for his understanding, and readied herself for bed.

However, when it came time to see to her nightly ablutions, she was surprised at the amount of blood loss she'd experienced. Though she tried not to worry, and mentally listed off several reasons why her flow could've changed, her conscience was telling her it was something more.

Arguing with her inner voice, she finally came to a compromise. *If it's still bad on Monday, I'll tell Travis and go see the doctor.*

Katie had been in bed for hours, but sleep continued to elude her. Even though she was exhausted and would drift off for a few minutes at a time, her muscles would seize, waking her, and her stomach would twist and knot. She tried to remain still and silent, not wanting Travis to know the amount of discomfort she was in, but once he turned down the lamp and crawled into bed next to her, it was harder to disguise the pain.

Curled up on her side, Katie gritted through another spasm. With her eyes squeezed shut, she pressed her clenched fist into her stomach and waited for the pain to subside. When her muscles finally released, she sighed with relief, but it sounded more like a whimper.

Travis rolled over and gently rested his hand on her hip. "You haven't slept at all, have you?"

She shook her head, knowing if she spoke, he would hear her tears.

"Kathryn, say something."

"I can't," she sobbed.

Immediately, Travis propped himself up on his elbow and stroked her arm. "Why didn't you tell me it had gotten worse?"

She just shrugged, while stifling her cry.

Travis threw back the covers and got out of bed. She heard him rustling around, clinking the jars and cans on the pantry shelf before he appeared on her side of the bed.

"You need to sit up."

She looked up at him, standing before her in nothing but his underwear, an amber bottle in one hand and a spoon in the other.

"It's laudanum." He answered her question before she could even ask. "It will help with the pain."

It took what little strength she had to swivel her legs over the side of the bed and slowly sit up. "I need to go to the privy first."

"Then I'll help you." He placed the bottle and spoon on the dresser and with his hand under her elbow, he gently pulled her to her feet.

"I'll be fine," she said as she stepped around him, grabbed some cloth strips from the dresser drawer, and made her way out the backdoor. She tried to hurry, wanting to make it to the privy before the cramping returned, but the light-headed feeling forced her to slow down in order to stay on her feet.

With the moon lighting her way, Katie made it to the outhouse just as another pain pierced her belly. Squeezing her eyes shut, she held her breath and waited for her muscles to relax. But when she opened her eyes, she gasped at the amount of blood she had passed.

It was not normal.

It wasn't anywhere *near* normal.

A wave of nausea rocked her, and for the first time since her altercation with Wade, she was truly scared.

It took all the inner strength she had to control the panic rising inside her.

It will do me no good if I fall apart. I just need to get back to the cabin and make it through the night.

After the initial shock wore off, Katie took care of her needs, slipped the soiled rags in the burlap sack she'd placed in the privy, and took slow measured steps back to the cabin. Travis was waiting for her when she got to the door, worry framing his eyes.

"You're going to see Doc Hammond tomorrow, and there's nothing you can say to convince me differently."

"Okay." She had no intention of arguing with him. She just hoped she could hold on until morning.

Walking slowly to the bed, Katie took the laudanum Travis offered, and steeled herself for a very long night.

35

Travis sat in the rocking chair, listening to Kathryn's steady breathing, thankful the laudanum had allowed her to get some rest.

Unfortunately, sleep eluded him.

Between feeding Matilda and his concerns for Kathryn, he'd stayed up most the night, replaying their conversations in his mind, his feelings teetering between frustration, guilt, and worry.

He was frustrated with Kathryn for her lack of judgment, still not believing she actually put a chair on top of the table.

What was she thinking?

He'd asked himself a thousand times, imagining her falling, realizing she could've broken her arm, her leg, or worse.

But he was also struggling with guilt.

I should have noticed the pain she was in, especially when she agreed to go to bed early.

Then, when he put his foot down about seeing the doctor, and she didn't even bother to argue with him, that's when real worry set in.

Turning to the mantel, he squinted to see the clock, but the moon was already on its descent, so there wasn't enough light. Getting up, he struck a match against the hearth, and held it up to the timepiece.

Three hours.

Thankful Kathryn had gotten some sleep, Travis sighed with relief, feeling the worst had passed. Even so, he would take Kathryn to see the doctor in the morning, just as a precaution.

Now, if I can get just a few hours of sleep myself.

Carefully, he slipped into bed, trying not to disturb Kathryn, but his weight made the ticking shift, causing her to roll back against him.

That's when he realized she was burning up.

Quickly, he pulled the sheet back from her shoulder and reached for her arm, her cheek.

Heat radiated from her entire body, and her nightgown was drenched with sweat.

"Kathryn?" He shook her shoulder gently.

She moaned but didn't wake up.

"Kathryn!" He firmly patted her cheek but couldn't arouse her.

Jumping from the bed, Travis hurried to turn up the lamp, then rushed back to Kathryn's side. That's when he saw the blood staining her nightgown, and the pool she was lying in.

"Oh, God, please, no!"

Travis jammed his legs into his trousers and threw open the front door. In his bare feet, he raced to the barn, yelling for Caleb. When he got there, Caleb was already on his feet, staggering toward him.

"What is it? What's wrong?"

Travis slumped over, hands on his knees, panting. "You need . . . to ride to town. Get . . . Doc Hammond. Something is wrong . . . with Kathryn. She's . . . bleeding."

"What do you mean? What happened?"

"She fell . . . earlier today. She . . . I . . . I don't know. I don't have time to explain. I just need you to get the doc!"

Travis ran back to the cabin and saw that Kathryn hadn't moved. Grabbing the cloth hanging on the side of the water basin, he dunked it and rung it out, then hurried to Kathryn's side of the bed.

"Kathryn?" He sat on the edge, ran the cloth across her forehead and blotted her cheeks. He watched the rise and fall of her chest, thankful her breathing seemed normal. "Come on, Kathryn, I need you to wake up." He shook her briskly, but he didn't care. When her eyelashes fluttered, he shook her again. "Kathryn, look at me!"

"Please stop shaking me." Her words were barely more than a whisper.

"No!" Travis shouted, so terrified, he was angry. "I'm going to keep shaking you until you open your eyes and look at me."

Her lids separated, and he watched as her eyes rolled back in her head before she squeezed them shut. "Then I'm going to throw up on you."

He stopped shaking her but continued to stroke her face. "Kathryn, what's wrong? What's happening?"

"I thought it was my menses," she said, licking her lips, her breathing labored. "But I think it's the fall. It hurts so much more than—"

She winced, pain cutting off her words. "Laudanum . . . please. It helped before."

"Kathryn, I can't. The doctor is on his way, and I don't want to give you anything before he gets here." He mopped her brow as she struggled to open her eyes again.

"But it made it so much better." Her eyes pled with him to

do something. To help her.

He shook his head. "I can't. You're bleeding too much, and I need you to stay awake."

Again, she winced, but this time she grabbed her stomach, doubled over, and cried out in pain. "Please, Travis. It hurts so bad."

He watched as tears ran down her cheeks, causing his own eyes to pool. He hated seeing her in such pain, but he was afraid it was the laudanum that had numbed her to what was happening, and he couldn't take the chance of her lapsing back into unconsciousness before the doctor got there. "Kathryn, I need you to keep talking to me."

Her eyes squeezed tight into little slits as another pain tensed her entire body. She clutched his arm and cried out in utter anguish, this time waking Matilda.

Travis didn't know what to do. Kathryn needed him, but so did Matilda. But Matilda was just startled while Kathryn was in pain.

"Go to her, Travis," Kathryn whimpered as she let go of his arm. "There's nothing you can do for me."

"No. She'll be fine. She's just—"

Kathryn went completely still, her arms limp at her side.

"Kathryn? Kathryn!"

36

By the time Caleb showed up with Doc Hammond, Travis was beside himself with panic.

"What's going on, Travis?" the doctor asked as he crossed the room with no-nonsense steps.

"I don't know."

Travis knew the second Doc saw Kathryn's bloodied gown, because he quickly pulled off his jacket and started rolling up his sleeves. "Caleb said something about a fall?" he asked calmly as he approached the bed.

"Kathryn said she was knocking down cobwebs and lost her balance. She fell off the table and landed on a chair, but she also said something about her menses. I gave her laudanum earlier this evening, but when I couldn't wake her, that's when I saw the blood."

Doc sat on the edge of the bed and pressed his fingers to her neck. "How long has she been out?"

Travis turned to the clock, feeling like it had been an eternity. "She's been in and out since Caleb left."

Doc looked at Travis, then to Caleb. "Caleb, why don't you see to Matilda, while I get some more information from Travis?"

"Uh . . . yeah. Sure." He reached for Matilda and pulled her to his chest, then clutched Travis' shoulder in reassurance. "She'll be fine, Travis. Kathryn's too stubborn to let anything keep her down."

Travis didn't say anything. He just shook his head, praying Caleb was right.

As soon as Caleb was gone, Doc Hammond removed the bloodied cloths and began examining Kathryn. Travis immediately turned away, feeling ill at ease. It didn't matter that he was her husband. They hadn't been intimate, and to look on her this way felt wrong.

"Travis, you okay?"

"I don't know." He leaned on the table and took a deep breath.

"I don't mean to be insensitive, Travis, but I can't take care of both you and Kathryn. So, if you think you're going to pass out, I'm going to ask you to wait outside."

Travis took another deep breath, and without turning around, he asked, "Do you need my help?"

"If I do, I'll call you. Just go outside and get some fresh air. I'll let you know when I have some answers."

Travis stepped outside feeling more like a coward than a gentleman. He should be inside, helping the doctor see to Kathryn—his wife.

But he couldn't.

Travis paced on the stoop, wanting to be close in case the doctor needed his help. "Come on, Kathryn, you've got to be okay," he mumbled as his stride lengthened.

"Why would You do this, God? Why would You allow Kathryn to come . . . for us to get attached to her, just to take her away? This can't be Your plan. We need her here. You can't take her away."

"Travis?"

He looked up to see Caleb holding Matilda, just as she began to wail. "I came back to see if I could get Matilda's bottle. She keeps sucking on my finger but is getting pretty upset nothing is coming out."

"Here." Travis reached for Matilda, held her to his shoulder, and began to sway. Immediately, Matilda nuzzled up against him and stopped her whining.

"Wow, look at you. You're a miracle worker."

"Kathryn showed me. She said Matilda likes swaying over bouncing." Travis buried his tear-filled eyes into his baby girl's shoulder. "I can't lose her, Caleb. I just can't. She needs to be okay. Matilda needs her." He looked at Caleb. "I need her."

He stared at his friend, looking for reassurance, but all he saw was solemnity. Travis squeezed his eyes shut, not wanting his tears to fall.

Please, God. Don't do this to me again. Don't take Kathryn away from me too.

Travis lulled Matilda to sleep as the three of them waited just outside the cabin. He paced in silence, stopping each time to stare at the door, knowing with every passing minute that something was horribly wrong. "It's taking too long. She's not going to make it."

"Travis! Don't say that! Just go in and see what's going on."

"It wouldn't be right."

"You're her husband. You have every—"

The door creaked open, and a haggard Doc Hammond step outside. He raised tired eyes to Travis, and with a heavy sigh, he said, "She's going to be okay."

Travis squeezed his eyes tight, but the tears still came. "Thank you, God." He kissed the top of Matilda's head and held her a little tighter.

"Caleb, could you take Matilda again?" Doc asked. "I'd like to talk with Travis for a moment."

"Sure."

Travis carefully handed over Matilda, waiting to see if she would stay asleep. "Remember, swaying not bouncing."

Caleb nodded. "Got it."

Travis wiped the tears from his face with the heels of his hands and let out the deep breath he didn't know he was holding. But the look on Doc's face told him something wasn't right. "She's not okay, is she?"

"No, she'll be okay. Kathryn just needs some time to heal." Doc rubbed his chin as he walked in a circle.

"Come on, Doc, what aren't you telling me?"

Doc's eyes held heartbreak. "I hate to tell you this, Travis, especially with all you've been through. And since you haven't asked, I'm assuming you didn't even know."

"Know what?"

"Travis," again, Doc sighed as if the weight of the world was on his shoulders. "The fall Kathryn took cracked a few ribs, but also caused her to . . ." He looked like he was trying to find the right words.

"Caused her to what?"

"Travis, Kathryn was pregnant."

"Pregnant?"

"The fall caused her to miscarry. I'm so sorry."

"What . . . wait . . . no, that can't be." Travis tried to digest what the doctor was telling him, but it didn't make any sense.

"I'm sorry, Travis."

He could feel the color draining from his face and had to

lean against the cabin to keep from falling down.

"Kathryn will need bed rest for at least a week, maybe more. After that she'll . . ."

Travis heard the doctor giving him instructions, but he couldn't concentrate on anything he said.

Kathryn was pregnant?

It was more than he could comprehend.

Travis thought back to the day he'd been approached by Mrs. James. She offered her condolences then told him about Kathryn. It was Mrs. James who thought he should consider taking a wife.

It was all a setup.

Mrs. James didn't care about my well-being or Matilda's. She just wanted to save face and salvage her daughter's reputation . . . to make sure someone provided for the unwanted child since it was obvious the father was nowhere around.

Thinking back, Travis mentally replayed conversations he'd had with Kathryn, acknowledging her inexperience.

What a fool I've been.

"Travis, maybe you should sit down." Doc reached for his arm, but he pulled away.

"I'm fine." His words were laced with anger.

"No one expects you to be fine, Travis. You've experienced another devastating loss. You have every right to mourn."

"I'm fine!" He balled his fists at his side, trying to rein in the anger building inside him. "Now, tell me again what Kathryn has to do to get better."

37

As the doctor pulled out of the yard, Travis heard the telltale sign that Matilda was awake once again.

"Okay, Travis, I don't think she'll be put off any longer." Caleb walked up with an inconsolable Matilda.

When Travis swung around, Caleb took a step back. "Travis what is it, what's wrong?"

He looked to the sky, wanting to do nothing more than get on his horse and ride away. Ride hard and fast and leave the pain and the lies behind.

"Travis, you're scaring me. What's wrong?"

"It's Kathryn. She's had a miscarriage."

"A miscarriage?" Caleb muttered, clearly confused. "But I thought you said you two hadn't—"

Travis' slicing stare cut into Caleb's words, giving him all the explanation he needed.

"Oh."

Travis paced with pounding steps, flexing his fingers at his sides. "She lied to me, Caleb. Every day that I thought we were growing closer, she was actually lying to me."

Matilda continued to cry, and when Travis reached for her, Caleb stepped away.

"No. Just get me Matilda's bottle; I will take care of her.

You need time to cool down."

"What . . . you think I would hurt my own child?" he snapped.

"No. But feeding her is the last thing you need to be doing right now. Just get me her bottle. I'll see to Matilda."

Travis shook his head. "I don't know if I can go in there right now. Kathryn is the last person I want to see."

"But should she be left alone?"

"Doc said she was resting and would probably sleep what's left of the night."

"And then what?"

"She'll need bed rest for a week."

Matilda let out another doozie of a wail.

"Okay, sweetheart. I'll get it."

Travis glanced at Caleb, then at the door. It took him a few seconds to gather his nerve before stepping inside the cabin.

He quickly walked to the pantry, refusing to look at the bed where Kathryn lay. His hands were shaking when he poured the milk and measured the mixture. Once the bottle was prepared, he walked out, never looking at Kathryn.

"Here." He handed the bottle to Caleb. "Shake it really good before you feed it to her," he explained, then took a few steps back.

"Hey, where are you going?" Caleb asked.

"For a walk. I just need some time to sort things out."

Travis started walking, but his gate soon turned to an all-out sprint. He ran until his lungs burned. And when he found he couldn't run any longer, he doubled over, panting for the air his lungs so desperately craved. Then, with the guttural cry, like that of a wounded animal, he yelled and argued with the God who had betrayed him once again.

38

As the tinted sky turned from deep blue to pink, Travis stood and walked away from the weathered tree where he'd sought refuge overnight.

It was time to go back home.

He had wrestled all night with what he would do. And in the end, he decided he wouldn't throw Kathryn out right away. He would be civil, let her heal, but once she could ride, he would take her back to her despicable family. Then he and Matilda would return to his family home, and he would never have to set eyes on Kathryn again.

Standing before the cabin door, he reached for the handle, but could not bring himself to open it. He thought he had his anger under control, but he could feel it churning inside his stomach and beating in his chest.

He had come to care for Kathryn, had wanted to protect her from her father, had even convinced himself he could love her. But she had manipulated him from the very start.

Playing the part of the wallflower.

Acting timid. Naive.

Pretending to be embarrassed when she undressed in front of him.

Acting awkward being in bed with him when she had bedded another man—maybe even more than one.

Travis' gut twisted at the thought.

One. Two. Ten. It doesn't matter. She lied to me from the start. She is not the woman I thought I was falling in love with.

Turning the knob, he walked into the cabin, surprised to see Caleb sitting in the rocking chair. "What are you doing here?" Travis whispered angrily.

"I didn't think she should be left alone."

Travis quickly glanced at his sleeping daughter but refused to look at Kathryn. "How's Matilda doing?"

"She's fine," Caleb answered, "but that's not who I was talking about. Don't you want to know how Kathryn's doing?"

Travis bristled, angered that Caleb was offering compassion to Kathryn when all he felt for her was disgust and betrayal. "No."

"Then you don't want to know she spent the night crying in her sleep?"

"Why should that matter to me?"

Caleb stood. "Come on, Travis, I know you're hurt, but think about what she's gone through."

"No! She's getting what she deserves. It's called reaping what you sow." Travis' voice raised an octave. "She used me and Matilda to protect her own reputation. She's nothing but a two-bit whore who was stupid enough to get pregnant."

"Travis, you don't know that!"

"Don't I? Well, her mother knew exactly what she was doing. She didn't come to me because she was concerned for Matilda's well-being. She wanted me to marry her tramp daughter to save her family from humiliation."

"Come on, Travis, Kathryn has just lost a child. Surely

you're not so calloused that you can't understand how difficult that must be for her?"

"A bastard child! It's better off in the arms of God than in a world where cruel, ruthless people will mock and ridicule him."

"Travis!" Caleb snapped, but quickly lowered his voice. "Listen to yourself. What gives you the right to be so cruel and heartless?"

"Because she lied to me!" he hollered.

"Keep your voice down. You're going to wake—"

"It's all right, Caleb."

Both men turned to see Kathryn's red, sunken eyes staring back at them. "Travis has every right to be angry."

39

Katie looked at Travis. Seeing the utter anguish and torment in his eyes brought fresh tears to her own. "Travis, I know you hate me, and you have every right to, but you have to believe me; I didn't know I was pregnant. If I had, I never would've married you."

Travis' laugh was caustic and bitter. "And you expect me to believe that? You must think I'm some kind of fool. Or better yet, maybe you know exactly who I am. Is that it, Kathryn? Did your father find out about the money?"

Katie was more confused than ever. "I don't know what you're talking about, Travis. What money?"

An odd look settled over his face; one she couldn't read.

"He probably thought he struck a goldmine. And why not? He could easily kill two birds with one stone. Find a husband for his wayward daughter and have her marry into money. Jethro's smooth, I'll give him that. He knew if he tipped his hand when we were bartering for land, I would get suspicious. So, he decided to wait. He banked on the fact that once a child was involved, I wouldn't turn my back on you."

Travis shook his head and let out a haughty laugh. "But what he didn't figure into his little scheme is the fact that I was still grieving, so I didn't bed you right away. Otherwise, I never would've found out."

Katie's head was spinning. Travis was talking in circles, none of it making any sense.

"I don't know what you're talking about, Travis, but please believe me. I never would've expected you to raise another man's child."

He ignored her as he sauntered back and forth like an angry bull, disdain twisting his expression.

"Come on, Travis," Caleb cleared his throat. "Let's take Matilda outside, give Kathryn time to rest."

Spinning around, Travis darted an angry finger at Caleb. "Not until I find out who it is!"

Turning back to her, his face beet red, Travis looked at her with contempt. "Who is it, Kathryn? Someone I know? Someone from Milford? Was I going to ride into town one day and have a man come up to me and tell me how good my wife was in bed? Or maybe he was just someone passing through."

As Travis' voice grew louder, Katie looked at Matilda, knowing she would wake soon from the noise. But Travis continued.

"Did he fill your head with empty promises? Is that it? Did he say he would come back and marry you? Did you think if you let him have his way with you, he would make good on his promise? Tell me, Kathryn! Tell me who it is!"

"It wasn't like that, Travis!" She shook her head, her voice a fevered pitch. "It wasn't like that at all!"

Matilda let out a wail, no longer able to sleep through the shouting. Katie slowly swiveled her legs over the side of the bed, but before she could stand, Travis loomed over her, blocking her way, his fisted hands clenched at his sides.

"Tell me who it was, Kathryn!"

"I need to see to Matilda; she's frightened." Katie tried to stand, but with Travis in the way, she fell back to the bed.

"Answer me, Kathryn! Who is it?"

She looked up at him, her chin jutted out, trying to exude strength she didn't have. "What does it matter? It doesn't change the outcome. The child is dead, and as soon as I'm able, I'll be gone. But Matilda still needs someone to care for her until then. Let me see to her, Travis."

"After you tell me who it is." His tone was cold, barely controlled.

"No," she whispered.

Travis grabbed her by the forearms and shook her. "Tell me who, Kathryn!"

Caleb took a step forward. "Travis, stop!"

But with a quick and deadly stare he looked at Caleb. "Step back; this doesn't concern you." Turning to her, venom in his eyes, he glared. "You owe me the truth, Kathryn! Tell me who it is!"

"I can't! Don't you see? I can't!"

"You can't?" He let go of her arms and nearly stumbled backwards, horror coloring his face. "So, I was right? There wasn't just one man. The reason you *can't* tell me is because you've been with more than one man."

She hung her head, wishing she could tell him the truth. Wishing she could explain to Travis the years of abuse and terror she had endured, but she couldn't.

Jethro's threat was very real.

If Travis found out, she would put everyone she loved in danger. After all this time, after sacrificing herself for so many years, she could not allow that to happen.

Not now. Not ever.

Katie lay in the quiet of the cabin, wrestling with what she had to do.

After her shouting match with Travis, he packed up his things as well as Matilda's and moved them out to the barn. He told her he couldn't stand to be in the same room with her, that the very sight of her made him sick.

So, she'd spent the last few hours crying, hating herself, for what she'd done, for what she'd become.

Hating the very breath that gave her life.

Travis said he would give her the week to heal before taking her back home to the depravity she thought she had escaped.

But Katie had already decided she wouldn't go back.

She would end her life before she let anyone hurt her again.

With her hands over her face, she sobbed.

Why God? What did I do that was so bad? Am I so horrible that You would curse me with a man like Jethro James, then have Travis come along only so You could snatch him away? I started to hope again. I wanted so much to believe You really hadn't abandoned me.

But here I am again.

Without hope.

I dreamed of deliverance but know now that it's Your judgment I will face.

She sighed, her last ounce of will power gone.

You showed me no mercy in this lifetime.

I pray You show me mercy in death.

40

When the door slowly creaked open, Katie looked up from where she sat in the rocker, hoping it would be Travis, but just like the last three days, it was Caleb.

Sheepishly, he walked in and closed the door, then gathered a few items from the pantry. "How are you feeling?"

He asked the same question every day, and each time that he did, she turned toward the window without saying a word.

"The eggs and milk I brought yesterday are still sitting here. You need to eat if you want to regain your strength."

She could feel his stare but ignored him, knowing she didn't need much strength for what she was going to do.

"Kathryn, look at me."

She continued to stare out the window.

"I'm not leaving until you look at me."

She sighed, knowing it was futile to ignore him. Caleb was stubborn, and a man of his word, so she slowly turned toward him and met his eyes.

"There wasn't another man, was there? At least not the way Travis thinks."

She quickly turned away.

"Talk to me, Kathryn."

"There's nothing to talk about. Please, just leave me be."

"Clearly someone hurt you. But what I don't understand is why you're choosing to protect that person instead of telling Travis the truth."

It took all the inner strength she had not to react to his words. "You don't know what you're talking about, Caleb. In fact, you don't know me at all. But I'm sure we agree that Travis deserves better."

"Then why did you marry him?"

"I had no choice. I was told, not asked."

"Travis gave you a choice. He told me himself."

"I was selfish, okay!" she lashed out, sounding cold and calloused. "I wanted something more out of life, and I thought Travis could give it to me. And it would've worked. It was only a matter of time before Travis and I . . ."

Blush crept into her cheeks, but she shrugged it off with a cavalier tone. "If I hadn't miscarried, no one would've known. I took a chance. Who can blame a girl for trying, right?"

She stared at Caleb emotionless, hoping she sounded cynical enough to be convincing.

He picked up the pitcher of spoiled milk and walked toward the door.

She closed her eyes and hung her head, exhausted from their exchange.

"You know . . . I've been meaning to ask you something," Caleb said as he turned back around. "What was your brother doing here the other day?"

"What?" She snapped her head up, her heart nearly leaping from her chest.

"I saw him leaving the day of your accident, but in all the commotion, I forgot to ask you why he was here."

She stuttered, feeling as if a noose was strangling her words. "He . . . he was just . . . um . . . checking in on me, making sure I was doing okay."

"That's strange; I got the impression you two weren't that close."

"Wh . . . why would you say that?" She chuckled, as if his comment was preposterous.

"Oh, I don't know, maybe because the few times we've gone to church together, you've never once spoken with him. In fact, it always looked like you were trying to avoid him."

"Well, uh, actually, that's why he was here. Wade and I parted on bad terms. He came by to patch things up."

Caleb nodded, but Katie could tell he didn't believe her.

"And why were you on bad terms, if you don't mind me asking?"

Katie swallowed hard, trying to think of something to say when she blurted out, "He knew about the other man."

She regretted her words the minute they left her lips, but there was nothing she could do about it now.

"The day I married Travis, Wade cursed me, said I wasn't fit to be any man's wife."

"And now?"

She shrugged. "What does it matter? Travis hates me."

"So tell him the truth. Why let him believe a lie?"

She turned away. *Because the truth will get him killed.*

"Talk to him, Kathryn. Let him decide."

"Don't you see, Caleb," she yelled in frustration. "Nothing I say will change the facts. I lied to him. I'm used and spoiled. Travis wants someone who will raise Matilda in a godly fashion. I'm not that person."

"Yeah, you're right. Travis could never abide a woman like

you."

Caleb's words hit her like a ton of bricks. Even though it's what she'd thought all along, to hear Caleb say it made it hurt even more.

He opened the door and swung it wide, then turned back to where she sat in the chair. "Just so you know, Kathryn, Travis would forgive you anything. Any action. Any deed. But deceit is the one thing he will not tolerate."

41

"You're wrong about Kathryn, Travis; I'm sure of it," Caleb hollered as he marched into the barn.

Travis was changing Matilda on the makeshift table he'd made from a long piece of board and two sawhorses.

"Kathryn's a liar," Travis bristled. "You can't believe anything she says."

"She didn't tell me, Travis, I told her."

"What are you talking about?"

"Her timidity, her apprehension, her shyness, those aren't things someone can pretend to be."

"Well, she did a pretty good job of it."

"Come on, Travis, can you picture Kathryn lurking around, having a secret rendezvous with a man no one has ever seen?"

"Who said we haven't seen him? It could be anyone in town."

"I don't believe that. Milford hums with gossip. Surely such a torrid affair would have been rumored about. Come on, think about it, did you ever see Kathryn in town alone? Without an escort? Or better yet, with someone other than her kin?"

Travis ignored him, picked up Matilda and lay her on the blanket he'd nestled between two hay bales.

"Answer me, Travis," Caleb demanded.

"What do you want me to say? I didn't spend my time studying Kathryn. All I knew was that she was mute, and some thought she was even dumb."

"But they were wrong, weren't they? Kathryn isn't mute *or* dumb."

Travis whirled around, exasperated. "What does that have to do with anything?"

"It proves that the townspeople talk about everything under the sun. Real or imagined. If that's the case, how did Kathryn have an affair without anyone finding out?"

With hands fixed to his waist, Travis stared at Caleb, clearly angered. "She played me for a fool, Caleb. Why can't you see that? Better yet, you're supposed to be my friend, yet here you stand defending her. Why is that? Is there something you're not telling me? Maybe you're sweet on Kathryn just like you were sweet on Mary."

Caleb's punch was quick and sure, knocking Travis to the ground. "How dare you insinuate such a thing!" Caleb hovered over him.

Travis made no attempt to get to his feet, he just rubbed his jaw and stared at the ceiling, tears welling in his eyes.

After a prolonged silence, Travis groaned. "I'm sorry, Caleb. I had no right accusing you of such a thing. My mind just keeps thinking the darkest and vilest thoughts."

The broken expression on Travis' face turned Caleb's anger to compassion. He offered him a hand up and pulled him to his feet.

In silence, Travis walked from the barn and headed for the pasture.

Caleb watched his friend, seeing the sag in his shoulders, his head hung in grief. It was obvious Travis had genuinely fallen for Kathryn. Yet once again, he would be left abandoned and alone.

Caleb decided if Kathryn wouldn't talk to him, he would speak with the only other person who seemed to know the truth.

To be fair, he would give Kathryn a few more days to come to her senses, but if she still chose to say nothing, he would ride out to the James' property and have a little talk with her brother.

42

Caleb did his best to talk some sense into Kathryn. He knew she was hiding the truth; he just couldn't figure out why.

With his patience gone, Caleb decided to visit the James farm after breakfast and have a talk with Wade. One way or another, he would find out the truth. However, he feared even the truth would not be enough to heal Travis and Kathryn's shattered relationship.

Travis ignored anything Caleb said about the situation, and absolutely refused to speak with Kathryn. And whenever Caleb tried to talk to her, she would just turn to the wall and close her eyes.

Well, enough was enough!

"Kathryn, I think you should know . . ." Caleb barged into the cabin with a full head of steam, but when he saw Kathryn's deteriorating condition, he stopped.

Lying motionless, she looked like a shell of a person. Her skin held no color, her eyes sunken. She'd gone another day without eating and drinking, and the stench in the cabin spoke of an unwashed body.

She was giving up, plain and simple.

He pulled a chair next to her bedside and sat down.

"Kathryn," he whispered.

When she didn't answer, he lightly patted her cheek.

Nothing.

"Kathryn, this is not the answer. You can't give up."

Her eyes rolled back in her head before focusing on him. Licking her cracked lips, she closed her eyes. "Please, just let me be," her scratchy whisper was barely discernable, her throat obviously parched. "I won't go back, and I can't stay here."

"Who did this to you, Kathryn? And why are you letting them get away with it?"

"It's of little importance now." She looked at him again, reached for his hand, and squeezed it with what little strength she had. "Please believe me when I say I love Travis and Matilda, much more than I have ever loved anyone before. That is why I must go. I don't want them to live with my shame."

"No! I will not let you do this!" He backed toward the door. "I'm going to find out the truth, for both yours and Travis' sake."

Caleb ran to the barn and quickly saddled Gent. When he charged out of the double doors, he nearly plowed into Travis.

"Where are you going?" Travis yelled, Matilda snug in his arms.

Caleb reigned in Gent and spun around. "To find the truth. And if you have even one ounce of decency, you will go see to your wife before it's too late."

Travis watched as Caleb took off in a cloud of dust. He had no idea where he was going or what he meant. Had Kathryn finally told him who her lover was? And if so, what did Caleb think he would accomplish by confronting the man? And what did he mean 'before it's too late?'

Travis made several starts and stops toward the cabin before he mustered enough courage to see his way in.

The second he opened the door, he was assaulted by a pungent odor.

"It reeks in here!"

Disgusted, he stormed across the cabin and opened the backdoor. However, when he glanced at Kathryn for the first time in several days, his breath caught.

If it were not for the fresh tears rolling down Kathryn's cheeks, Travis would assume he was looking at a body already expired.

Kathryn's complexion was a deathly shade of gray, the dark circles under her eyes her skin's only color. And her already petite body seemed to all but disappeared under the quilt that rested beneath her chin.

Travis now realized what Caleb meant. Though the doctor assured Travis that Kathryn would make a full recovery, he failed to mention it would depend largely on her desire to want to.

Clearly, she did not.

Travis ached for Kathryn, but at the same time he felt the sting of betrayal. Concern and anger warred inside him. He hated seeing her this way but had no intention of going back on his word. As soon as she could travel, he would send Kathryn home to her family.

However, in order for that day to come, she would have to get stronger.

Travis pulled a blanket from the shelf, spread it out on the floor, then laid Matilda on it with a few things to entertain her.

After dipping a cup into the water bucket on the table, he walked over to the bed and sat on the wood frame.

"You need to drink something."

He placed his hand behind Kathryn's neck and forced her head up. Pressing the cup to her lips, he watched as she took a few small sips.

"More," he demanded, his tone void of any emotion.

She did as he asked until the cup was empty.

When Travis stood, he tugged back the covers surrounding her, unleashing a fresh wave of foulness. Coughing at the strong odor, he looked at the stains on her nightgown and bed sheets. "For heaven's sake, Kathryn, you're filthy."

"You've already made that clear."

Though her words were barely discernible, her inference was evident. But Kathryn's condemnation only fueled Travis' ire.

Pulling her nightgown from her shoulders, he easily slid it down her rail-thin body until it lay in a heap at her feet. Kathryn quickly crossed her arms to hide her nakedness, causing Travis to laugh, disdainfully.

"Come now, surely you're not embarrassed. You needn't keep up the charade any longer."

He tugged at the bed covers beneath her, gathered them into a ball, then hurled everything she'd soiled out the backdoor and shut it with a hearty slam.

Rifling through the dresser drawers, Travis was unable to produce another nightgown, so he flung one of his own shirts at her. "Before you put this on, you need to get washed up." With pail in hand, he stomped out the backdoor.

Travis made four trips in order to fill the wash tub with a

decent amount of water while Kathryn sat on the edge of the bed, clutching his shirt to her chest.

"Come on, Matilda," Travis said as he reached down and picked up his daughter. "Let's give Kathryn her *privacy*."

On shaking limbs, Katie moved to the washtub and carefully stepped inside.

Though she drank at Travis' insistence, and bathed at his command, she had not changed her mind. She only did these things so when the end came, Travis would not blame himself. He would be able to reason that he'd done for her what she wasn't even willing to do for herself. That, paired with his obvious hatred, should be enough to soothe him from any guilt.

The water was cold and soon tinged pink. Katie cleaned herself with as much care as she could muster, then stepped from the tub and slowly dried off.

Feeling exhausted and numb, as if the body she touched wasn't even her own, she took a seat on the bed frame, then slipped Travis' shirt over her head.

Without permission, her emotions gave way to a torrent of tears. She held the collar of Travis' shirt against her nose, inhaling the masculine scent that was uniquely his.

She'd wanted a life with Travis and Matilda.

Wanted it with all her heart.

But she should have known nothing good would come from her deception.

Drying her face, she haphazardly tossed a bed sheet over the ticking, so she wouldn't soil anything else of Travis'.

After putting on her undergarments, she took the last blanket from the shelf and pulled it over her body.

By the time Travis returned with a sleeping Matilda on his shoulder, Katie was weak and spent from her exertion.

Travis put down the bucket he was carrying, then carefully laid Matilda on the quilt still spread out on the floor.

Crossing to the stove, he glanced her way. "You need to eat something. You can't expect to get better if you don't take care of yourself."

"Maybe that's the idea," she mumbled.

He turned to her and scowled. "What did you . . . forget it," he said as he cracked two eggs against the side of the pan. "It matters little."

Her thoughts exactly.

Travis dumped the scrambled eggs onto a plate, then held it out to her. But when Katie reached for it with shaky hands, he snatched it back and pulled up a chair.

"I'll do it, but only because I have no intention of cleaning up after you for a second time."

He fed her forkfuls of eggs, barely giving her time to swallow. When she could stand no more, she raised her hand and turned her head.

"You need to finish," he insisted. "A few more bites aren't going to kill you."

"I don't think you will feel the same way if you have to clean them up off the floor."

He glared at her. "Fine."

Tossing the fork and tin plate into the frying pan, he pushed it to the back of the stove.

Even though Katie felt tired, and Travis was being unkind, she willed her heavy eyelids to stay open, not wanting to miss a single moment with him and Matilda.

Straining, she looked at the little girl who had captured her heart. She was fast asleep on the blanket, her face angelic, the picture of contentment.

However, when Katie turned to Travis, she found him staring back at her, his eyes filled with regret. She couldn't help but look away, her heart breaking for what might have been.

With her energy spent, Katie finally allowed her head to fall back against the pillow. "Where did Caleb go?" she asked.

"Who says he went anywhere?"

"You wouldn't be here if he was around."

Travis didn't deny it; he just shrugged. "I have no idea, but maybe *you* can tell me." He crossed his arms against his chest.

"How would I know?"

"Because he said something about finding out the truth. I thought maybe you told him who your lover was."

Katie's mind whirled and spun, trying to remember what they had talked about. Her thoughts were cloudy and disjointed, a jumble of fuzziness. Then it hit her.

Wade.

She felt her stomach heave, but quickly fought to keep its contents in check.

I told Caleb that Wade knew the other man.

God, no!

Please don't let Caleb question Wade.

If Wade thought she'd said anything about him and Jethro, Travis and Matilda would be in terrible danger.

43

The James' property wasn't much to look at. The barn needed a new roof, and the size of the house was much smaller than Caleb expected for a family of five.

Approaching slowly, he wasn't sure how he was going to get information out of Wade, especially if Kathryn's folks didn't know what was going on. Caleb certainly didn't want to make things worse for Kathryn; he simply wanted to get to the bottom of this whole mess so Travis could know the truth.

As Caleb rode closer, he saw Mrs. James step out onto the porch, a rug snapping in the breeze. When she saw him, she stopped and shaded her eyes.

"Good morning, Mrs. James."

"Mornin'."

"Sorry to come unannounced. I'm Caleb, a friend of Travis and Kathryn's.

She nodded. "I've seen you at church."

"I was wondering, could you tell me where I might find Wade?"

She shrugged. "He's around, but I can't say exactly where." Her eyes thinned as she took a step forward. "What are you wantin' with Wade?"

"I just need to talk to him about something."

She stepped off the porch and closed one eye against the sun. "Why? What has Katie done?"

Not exactly the reaction I expected from a loving mother.

Caleb sidestepped her question. "Actually, Wade came to visit Kathryn the other day. I just wanted to ask him about their conversation."

Mrs. James took hurried steps forward, clutching the rag rug to her chest. He couldn't tell if her expression was worry or exasperation.

"Has Katie run off? Is that what this is about?"

"No ma'am. Kathryn is home. Why would you think she ran off?"

"Because otherwise you'd be askin' her about their conversation, instead of lookin' for Wade."

Realizing he was getting nowhere, Caleb decided to tell her a version of the truth. "Actually, Mrs. James, Kathryn is ill."

The woman dropped the rug as all color drained from her face.

"She's going to be fine." Caleb quickly assured her. "I just thought maybe Wade might know something about her condition."

"Her condition? What do you mean by that?"

He considered what he should say.

What does it matter? It will come out eventually. Doc Hammond seems nice and all, but nothing says he'll keep this information from Kathryn's family. Besides, this will give me a chance to see if she knew about Kathryn's pregnancy.

"Mrs. James, Kathryn has suffered a miscarriage."

The woman gasped, clutching the neck of her high collar

dress, her eyes immediately welling with tears. "My Katie was with . . . with chi—" Her guttural sob cut off her words. She mumbled and stuttered, then spun on her heels and dashed toward the porch. "I need to go to her."

"Mrs. James!" Caleb shouted to get her attention.

She turned around, tears rolling down her face.

"Kathryn is quite distraught and isn't well enough to see anyone right now."

"But I'm her mama."

"And Travis is her husband. You need to leave them be, give them time to figure things out."

Her shoulders wilted as she brought her apron up to blot her eyes. "Poor Travis. He's already lost a wife, now to lose a child. He must be devastated."

Either Mrs. James was an amazing performer, or she had known nothing about Kathryn's pregnancy. Though Travis was certain he'd been tricked into marrying their wayward daughter, Caleb wasn't so sure.

"Is Travis gonna turn her out?"

"Ma'am?"

"I mean, if he thinks Katie is too damaged to carry a child, is he gonna end the marriage?"

Damaged. Why would she say such a thing?

"That's an interesting choice of words, Mrs. James," Caleb said, his tone frigid.

"Well . . . I just mean . . . or what I was trying to say is . . . ahh . . . having a wife who can't bear babies is difficult for some men to accept. I just hope Travis will give Katie another chance."

"I guess that's for him to decide."

It took every ounce of self-control to swallow the words of

211

contempt Caleb wanted to pour out on this woman. Instead, he watched silently as Mrs. James fidgeted with the hem of her apron, waiting for her to say something more.

"So why is it you want to talk to Wade?" she finally asked.

"He was the last person with Kathryn before her collapse. I wanted to see if he could shed some light on what happened. Perhaps Wade noticed she was feeling poorly or maybe Kathryn confided in him about her condition."

Mrs. James shook her head. "I can't imagine her confiding in Wade about anything. They aren't close. In fact, he's never had much use for her."

If Caleb and Kathryn didn't get along, why was he visiting her? Maybe it did have something to do with the other man.

"Well, Mrs. James, if it's all the same to you, I would still like to talk to Wade."

She lowered her head, continuing her fidgeting.

Is she contemplating or scheming?

Leaning on the pommel of his saddle, Caleb waited for Mrs. James to say something. Finally, she looked up at him, squinting against the sun.

"I think Wade and my husband are working the soil on the new parcel Travis gave us."

"Travis gave you property?" Caleb asked, baffled.

"Yes. In exchange for Kat—"

She didn't finish, noticeably ashamed.

"Well then," Caleb did nothing to hide his disgust. "I guess you got the better end of the deal."

He pulled the reigns to one side, turning Gent around, but Mrs. James reached out and grabbed his leg, forcing him to stop.

"Please don't say anything about Katie's condition in front of my husband."

"Why?"

"Jethro is a . . . well . . . he's easily angered. If he thinks Katie has been hurt in any way, he might take matters into his own hands."

"Why do you assume somebody has hurt Kathryn?"

Mrs. James twisted her hands together, her eyes downcast. "I . . . I don't, but Jethro might think bad things and blame Travis for her condition. He's a drinking man, Mr. . . . ."

"Marshall."

"Mr. Marshall. And when he drinks, he's ugly. Don't rile him. If you really want to help Travis and Katie, you'll steer clear of my husband."

Caleb's jaw twitched as he bit back his rising anger. "And what about Wade? What if I talk to him and he tells your husband about our conversation?"

"Wade is a smart boy. He knows what his pa is capable of. Jethro will be furious if he finds out Wade went to see Katie without him knowing. Wade won't chance upsetting his pa."

Caleb turned around to leave.

"Mr. Marshall?"

He glanced back.

"I won't come to see Katie. I don't want to cause any strife between her and Travis. But when she's ready for visitors, will you send word to me?"

"I'll let Kathryn know you asked about her. It'll be her choice if she wants you to visit or not."

When Mrs. James walked away, Caleb headed to where Travis' and the James' property would naturally intersect, a revelation so vile, he felt ill just thinking about it.

But it all added up.

The scars Travis spoke about on Kathryn's back.

Her refusal to name the man she'd been with.

Mrs. James' obvious fear of her husband.

Her warning not to talk with Jethro about Kathryn's condition.

Could Jethro actually be the one responsible for Kathryn's pregnancy?

It was too sickening to consider but nevertheless, Caleb couldn't shake the notion.

Finally, it all made sense.

Kathryn's silence, her wasting away, not caring if she lived or died. She knew if Travis forced her to return to her family, she'd suffer who knows what kind of abuse. It also made Caleb realize just how dangerous it might be to question Wade and run the risk of Mr. James finding out.

Help me, Lord. Show me what to do. All I want is the truth, but not at the expense of Kathryn's safety.

And what about Matilda and Travis? What danger would they be in if Caleb exposed Jethro's secret? What lengths would a desperate man go to, to keep his abominations hidden?

It was a question Caleb pondered as he rode.

Finally, he spied someone in the distance. The figure was large, swinging an ax with ease. As he rode closer, he realized it was Wade.

Glancing from side to side, he strained to see if Jethro was anywhere around. When Caleb was convinced Wade was alone, he took a deep breath and prayed.

Tell me what to do, Lord.

44

Katie couldn't stop her heart from racing. She felt every pulse of blood whoosh through her veins. Her chest, her temple, her neck, her every limb throbbed with fear.

What would Wade say if Caleb confronted him? Would he lie? Would he blame everything on his pa?

Worse yet, what would Jethro do if Caleb tried to force a confession out of him? He was not a man to be backed into a corner and bullied. In fact, Katie was sure he wasn't a man at all; he was evil incarnate. He took pleasure in the pain he inflicted and thrived on the wickedness in his heart.

The thought made her wretch and reach for the bowl Travis had left near the bed. Leaning over the side rail, she heaved several times, the pain in her side excruciating, then wiped the foul taste from her lips.

Resting her head back on the pillow, perspiration spotting her forehead and upper lip, she closed her eyes and pleaded with God.

Only you can protect Caleb. Stop him, Lord. Stop him from doing something that can't be undone.

Katie wasn't sure how long she'd been resting, but the creaking front door immediately pulled her from her sleep.

She turned, thinking she'd see Travis, but instead it was Caleb who walked across the room and sat in the chair pulled up alongside the bed. With his elbows resting on his knees and his expression matter-of-fact, he looked at her.

"It was your stepfather."

She cringed, absolutely terrified.

"Caleb, please, I don't know what Wade told you, but you have to let this go. No good can come from confronting Jethro."

"So, I'm right?" Caleb sat back and let out a deep breath, looking like he'd just been sucker punched.

Katie was confused. Hadn't he just named Jethro as her attacker? Why was he looking so devastated?

"I don't understand. What did Wade tell you?"

"I never talked to Wade. I was going to, but something told me to stop."

Did God really hear my plea?

"Then how did you find out about my stepfather?"

"I put two and two together; but I wasn't sure." He leaned in closer. "Not until I saw the reaction on your face."

She closed her eyes. *What have I done?*

Caleb shot to his feet, his hands fisted at his sides as he paced the cabin.

"You can't say anything, Caleb," she sobbed. "Not to Travis, not to anybody. You can never let anyone know the truth."

"Why, Kathryn?" He walked over to her and hovered like an animal ready to pounce. "Why are you willing to throw away everything you have with Travis and Matilda to protect a piece of trash like Jethro James?"

"Because he'll kill Travis and Matilda if I say anything!

He told me if I ever spoke a word of it, he wouldn't just come after me . . . he would go after them."

Caleb shook his head, resuming his pacing. "No! I don't believe you. This isn't a onetime thing. I'm betting this has gone on for a while, long before Travis and Matilda came into the picture. Those scars on your back are old. Why, Kathryn?" He turned and looked at her. "Why have you protected him for so long?"

She wilted against the headboard. "Because before Travis and Matilda, he threatened Mama and Seth. Jethro warned me over and over again, that if I ever told a single soul, he would burn our house down with them in it. Don't you see? I had no choice. If I didn't do what he said, he would kill my family."

"I can understand being scared as a little girl, but you're an adult now. Travis is an adult. Jethro would never get away with it."

"But he already did!" she shouted.

Caleb stopped in his tracks. "What are you talking about?"

"Mr. Burrows, the old schoolmaster, he knew something was wrong. He asked me questions all the time, weird questions, and he would stare at Jethro during Sunday services. When I stopped talking all together, he met with Mama and Jethro. I listened as Mr. Burrows explained to them elective mutism was most likely brought on by a traumatic event—that I was scared into silence. He then asked if they could shed some light on what that might be."

"What did they say?"

"Mama just sat there; she didn't say a thing. But Jethro told Mr. Burrows I almost drowned. That I was lucky to be alive."

"Was that true?"

She nodded.

"Then what happened?"

"Five days later, Mr. Burrows' house mysteriously caught fire in the middle of the night. It burned to the ground with him inside. Just like Jethro threatened to do to Mama and Seth."

"But what about Wade? You said he knew. Why didn't he do something to help you, to stop his father?"

Katie turned away unable to look Caleb in the eye.

"Kathryn, no!" He sank into the chair next to her. "Him too?"

She stared at the wall across from her, recalling the first time it happened, as clear as if it were yesterday.

"One day, after Jethro had been particularly rough with me, Wade found me in the barn. My dress was torn and disheveled, and I was crying hysterically. He sat down next to me and pulled me close. I told him everything; the threats, the late-night visits, all of it. Wade assured me everything was going to be all right. I cried tears of relief, thinking my torment would finally come to an end, that somehow Wade would be able to make things right."

She closed her eyes, remembering how she felt in that instant, thinking her ordeal was over.

"What happened?" Caleb whispered.

She glanced at him, then down at her hands. "He leaned in and kissed me. I tried pushing him away, but his hold was too strong. I kicked and clawed, but it was no use. Wade pinned me to the ground and told me the only way Mama and Seth would ever be safe is if I kept my mouth shut."

"How long, Kathryn?"

"Years," she whispered, feeling like she was going to be sick.

Caleb looked away.

Katie didn't blame him. She couldn't even stand to look at herself.

"Now do you understand why Travis must never know. Jethro James is an extremely dangerous man. If he feels cornered, he will kill someone. I can't be responsible for that. I've already suffered too much, telling myself I was protecting the people I love. Travis and Matilda are better off without me."

"But he loves you, and you love him."

"No, Travis could never love me knowing what I've done."

"But Kathryn this isn't your fault. Something horrible was done *to* you."

"It doesn't matter. I can't put Travis and Matilda in danger. I love them too much to stay."

"But where will you go that Jethro won't find you, where Wade will leave you alone? You're in no condition to travel, and even if you were, a woman on her own isn't safe. You'll be easy prey wherever you end up."

"That's not true," she said softly as she closed her eyes and rested against the pillow. "Where I plan to go, no one will be able to hurt me."

"Where is that?"

"Caleb, the less you know, the better off you'll be. But promise me, if Travis ever finds out the truth, you'll warn him of Jethro's threats. Travis is not to seek vengeance."

She reached for Caleb's hand and gave it a squeeze.

"And after I go, please tell Travis how very much I loved him and Matilda. And whatever choices I made, I did it to protect them."

45

When Travis walked into the cabin with Matilda, and saw Caleb and Kathryn sitting together, he didn't know what to think. He'd already accused Caleb of being seduced by Kathryn—even though he knew in his heart of hearts his friend would never betray him that way. However, the way Caleb refused to meet his stare was very unsettling.

Pulling the blanket from his shoulder, Travis tossed it on the floor and bent to place Matilda on it.

"Can I hold her, Travis? Please."

Not wanting Matilda anywhere near Kathryn, he lay her on the blanket and placed a few toys around her. "She's fine on the floor; it helps to get her squirming out."

Standing, he looked at the pair of them and watched as Caleb whispered something to Kathryn, but she just closed her eyes.

"So, Caleb," Travis crossed his arms against his chest. "Did your little expedition lead you to the truth?"

He watched as Kathryn and Caleb exchanged glances, an unspoken conversation transpiring between them.

"No." Caleb shook his head. "I thought if I talked to Kathryn's family, I would find the truth, but they didn't tell me anything."

"Of course they didn't. Do you really think a family of schemers is going to turn on their own?"

"Travis! Stop being so ugly! You might not think much of Kathryn at the moment, but that doesn't minimize the fact that she's very ill and has experienced a tremendous loss. Your caustic remarks are not necessary."

"Necessary or not, they're true. And for the record, I have no sympathy for liars." He looked at Kathryn, cutting her with an icy stare. "Especially when they've lied to me."

Moving to the stove, he poured himself a cup of coffee. "So, what did they say when you told them their precious daughter fouled up their plans and would be moving back home soon?"

"I didn't. I was hoping you might have a change of heart."

He slammed his coffee cup down, shattering it, making Kathryn jump, and Caleb spring to his feet.

"A change of heart! Are you insane?" Travis shouted. "Listen to yourself, Caleb. I don't know what kind of spell Kathryn has cast on you, but I'm not going to change my mind. She is a liar and has manipulated me since the day she arrived. Why can't you get that through your thick head?"

"And you're a jackass who hasn't got a clue what he's talking about."

"Oh, I am, am I? Well, you know what . . . there is no reason to wait until next week. Why drag this out any longer than we need to. If Kathryn can sit up and carry on a conversation with you, she can sit in a wagon and make her way home. And since you're all fired up about her well-being, you can be the one to take her."

"That's it, Travis. I'm not going to let you do this. You think you know what's going on here, but you haven't the slightest clue. Kathryn hasn't been unfaithful; she's been—"

"Caleb, stop!" Kathryn yelled. "Stop it right now! Travis is right. I betrayed his trust. I lied to him. No matter what you say, you cannot change the truth."

Travis watched as Kathryn glared at Caleb, surprised how easily she would turn on her only ally. Then she looked at him.

"You're right, Travis. There's no reason to drag this out any longer. I'll be ready to leave in the morning." Tears glistened on her cheeks, but she flicked them away. "I would ask just one indulgence. Even though I don't deserve even an ounce of your favor, could I hold Ma—"

Emotion cut off her words and her head sunk to her chest.

He quickly looked away, reminding himself of the depths of her immorality. *I will not be manipulated by her tears or her words!*

"Travis . . ."

He turned back to her, Kathryn's emotion-filled eyes nearly his undoing.

"Could I hold Matilda just one more time? Because of my choices, I fear I'll never have a child of my own. I just want to feel again what it's like to hold one so precious."

What was it about her? How was it that Kathryn stirred such emotion inside him? In his mind, he knew she didn't deserve to hold his beautiful little girl, but in his heart, he saw the woman who cared for his daughter without reservation. He didn't answer her request; he just moved to where Matilda was lying on the floor, picked her up, and carried her to Kathryn. He gently placed Matilda in her outstretched arms then took a step back.

Kathryn pulled Matilda close. "Goodbye, little miss," she whispered, unrestrained tears wetting Matilda's fingers as

Kathryn brought them to her lips. "You take good care of your pa. He is a fine man, and he loves you something fierce. I know you won't remember me, but I will never forget you."

Travis watched as Kathryn gently kissed Matilda's brow, her lips lingering like she was committing the moment to memory. She then turned to him, surrendering Matilda into his waiting arms.

"Thank you, Travis." She looked at him through glossy eyes. "I will never forget your kindness."

He hurried out the door, Matilda in his arms. Then he began to weep, though he didn't know why. Returning to the barn, he laid Matilda in her cradle, and with fisted hands against his eyes, he tried to stop the tears that flowed.

How can I have feelings for her after all she's done?

Kathryn's betrayal was beyond pardon. Yet, his heart was telling him to run back to the cabin, beg forgiveness for his cruel and uncaring words, and ask if they could start again.

But that was just it, they couldn't start again. Travis would never know when Kathryn was being truthful or telling a lie. He didn't even know if what he felt between them was real, or just a part of Kathryn's well-orchestrated scheme.

And what about her family? If Jethro dabbled in other forms of deception, Matilda could be in harm's way because of Kathryn's family ties.

No . . . I already made my decision.

They would move back to his family home.

Putting several states between Matilda and Kathryn—her kin included—was his only choice.

I'm doing this for Matilda. She's all I have left. I will not jeopardize our future.

Lying down on his makeshift bed, bone tired, feeling

physically and emotionally exhausted, Travis rested his forearm over his closed eyes.

Tomorrow this will all be behind us. After Kathryn is gone, I'll start making arrangements for our move back home.

Unfortunately, Travis realized it was a very real possibility that he would lose Caleb's friendship for a second time. But it was a sacrifice he was willing to make if it meant keeping Matilda safe from harm.

He would not allow her little heart to be broken like his had been.

Twice.

———— • ————

Caleb didn't know what to do.

He'd promised Kathryn he wouldn't divulge her secret, but watching Travis treat her with such ill contempt—after all she'd been through—had almost brought them to blows.

He wanted to blurt out the truth, his promise be damned, but Kathryn's pleading eyes prevented him from doing so.

She slept now; her strength completely gone.

Looking so weak and fragile, Caleb found himself concentrating on the rise and fall of Kathryn's chest, afraid she was slipping away.

Sitting in the rocking chair, weighing all he knew, Caleb decided to do the only thing that made sense.

"I'll take care of you," he whispered.

He would take Kathryn tomorrow like Travis said, but he had no intention of returning her to the prison of her family home.

They would go someplace safe, for the time being, but once she felt well enough to travel, they would head east to a convent he knew of on the Carolina Coast.

There, Kathryn would be able to heal physically, and hopefully emotionally, and in time, be strong enough to strike out on her own.

Caleb stared at Kathryn, his heart breaking for all she'd endured.

You deserve so much more than you've been given.

I'm going to do my best to make sure you get it.

46

It was still dark when Katie made her way to the table. She lit the lantern and turned down the wick, giving her just enough light to see the parchment in front of her. Sitting, and with her hand shaking, she wrote,

My dearest Travis,

I am sorry I have brought such heartache into your life. But please believe me when I say, I meant you no harm.

These last few months spent with you and Matilda have been the happiest days of my life. You gave me such a special gift. You allowed me to be a wife and mother, if even for a short time. It is something I never would have experienced if it had not been for you.

I know I have hurt you something terrible. For that I am without excuse. Just know that what I did or did not tell you was for your own good. Please do not be angry with Caleb. You could have no truer friend. He loves you like a brother and loves Matilda like his own.

Matilda is sturdy now. I have no doubt you will be able to raise her into a beautiful, God-fearing woman. You were so right to hold onto your faith. It has served you well, and I know it will help you get through this trial I have caused you.

Do not be afraid to love again. You deserve to be happy and receive love only a wife can give. I am so much better for knowing you. You showed me the ways of a real man. You treated me like a real woman. It will be yours and Matilda's face I take with me into eternity.

Forever grateful, Kathryn

When Katie stood, she saw through the window the first streaks of sunrise coloring the horizon. Knowing her time was short, she placed the letter under the lantern, then snuffed out the wick. Dressed only in her nightgown, she slipped quietly from the cabin and allowed the thin bands of pink to light her way.

She was surprised that she didn't feel afraid, knowing what she was about to do. In fact, she actually felt relieved because the pain, hurt, and guilt she had struggled with for so long would soon be gone.

Standing next to the deepest part of the creek, she touched her toe to the water. Though it was frigid, she found the cold to be inviting . . . cleansing even.

With a backward glance at the barn, and the realization she would never see Travis or Matilda again, she felt a moment's regret.

But this is what's best for them.

She struggled, wishing there was some other way, but knowing as long as she was around, Travis and Matilda would be in danger.

With tears running down her cheeks, Katie slowly waded into the crystal-clear water, careful not to splash or cause any noise. Lowering herself into the slow-moving current, she leaned back until the water reached just under her chin, then closed her eyes and prayed.

God, I know I have lived a life of sin. I am ashamed that I have done things Your Word speaks against, and I know I am not worthy of Your love. Even so, I ask Your forgiveness. I want to be washed clean. I want to be free from the pain. Please forgive me, God, and allow me to live in Your kingdom.

When she opened her eyes, dawn was just breaking through the clouds. It had long been her favorite part of the day because it always seemed to offer her hope.

However, today she desired something more.

Anxious to know what true freedom felt like, Katie allowed her head to sink below the surface and watched as the water flowed over her face.

Closing her eyes, she smiled, because in the distance, she could hear God calling her home.

47

"Wake up, Travis. It's time you know the truth."

Travis felt Caleb's boot connect with his own, one, two, three times.

He wasn't asleep. In fact, he hadn't slept all night because he'd spent it wrestling with his unexplainable feelings for Kathryn. He was angry with his heart because—much like Caleb—it had betrayed him.

"Get up, Travis," Caleb yelled. "You need to hear what I have to say."

"I'm not asleep, so you can stop your yelling. And as for listening to what you have to say, I'm not the least bit interested."

"I don't care if you're interested or not. You have to listen to me before you make the biggest mistake of your life."

"I already did that, Caleb. I allowed my grief to cloud my judgment. I'm not about to do that again."

"Kathryn was never with another man, Travis. She's telling you the truth."

Travis jumped to his feet, feeling like he wanted to punch something, or *someone*. "How can you stand there and say that!" he shouted as he backed Caleb against the barn door.

"Kathryn miscarried! We never had relations! She had to be with another man! Even *you* can't explain away the basics of science."

Caleb grabbed him by the collar and drove him backwards into the middle beam of the barn. "She was raped, you jackass! Her stepfather and stepbrother have been violating her for years!"

All the oxygen in the room was suddenly sucked out.

Travis couldn't breathe. His vision blurred, and his ears began to ring. He broke loose from Caleb's hold and bent over, hands to his knees, doing what he could to not pass out.

"No. No, she's lying. It's another one of her tricks."

"And the scars on her back, are those tricks too?"

Travis shoved Caleb, sending him to the straw. "Then why didn't she just tell me?"

"Because Jethro threatened her."

"So, to save herself, she lied to me?" Travis stood over Caleb, not letting him get up.

"No. Jethro threatened to kill you and Matilda."

Dropping to his knees, Travis straddled Caleb and reached for his collar. Twisting it in his left hand, he pulled back his right, wanting to pummel him.

Caleb shielded his face but kept talking. "Jethro warned Kathryn that if she ever told anyone what he had done, he would go after you and Matilda. She was terrified he would follow through, so she stayed silent. She would rather have you hate her than put you and Matilda in danger."

Travis tightened his fist, wanting to hit Caleb.

"Kathryn loves you; can't you see that? She's lived through hell but was willing to go back to her family in order to protect you and Matilda."

Jumping to his feet, Travis charged out of the barn, the first hint of dawn breaking on the horizon.

"Kathryn!" he yelled as he stormed across the yard and threw open the cabin door. "Why didn't you—"

Travis stopped in the middle of the cabin.

It was empty.

When he heard the hinge on the back-door moan, he turned and saw the light morning breeze swinging it to and fro.

Travis started for the door, but something caught his attention. A piece of parchment lay under the lantern on the table. He moved the lamp, feeling its warmth as he snatched up the paper and began to read.

My dearest Travis—

As he continued to read, he realized it was a goodbye letter.

What did you expect? You threw her out, called her unspeakable things. Of course it's a goodbye letter.

But when he read the last line, a horrifying chill coursed through his body. It wasn't just a goodbye letter. If the sinking feeling in his gut proved to be right, Kathryn was planning to take her own life.

"Kathryn," he yelled as he burst out the backdoor, his thoughts tumbling over in his mind.

She couldn't have gone far. She's too weak, and the wagon and horses are still in the barn.

"Kathryn!" he shouted at the top of his lungs.

"Travis, what's wrong?" Caleb ran around the side of the barn. "Where's Kathryn?"

"I don't know, but we have to find her. I think she's going to hurt herself."

"What? I don't understand."

"A letter!" he shouted. "She left me a letter! And I'm afraid she's going to . . ." He couldn't even bring himself to say it.

"Ride toward town while I search the property. If you find her, fire a shot. She couldn't have gotten far; she's still too weak."

Both Travis and Caleb rushed to the barn. Travis scooped up Matilda, grabbed his revolver from his holster hanging on a peg, and ran to the house. Making a nest out of blankets, he lay Matilda down and made sure both doors were shut tight.

Be with her, Lord. Keep my little girl safe.

He heard Caleb gallop out of the yard as he checked the privy.

Empty.

"Kathryn!" he yelled at the top of his lungs, emotion causing a tremor to shake his voice. He focused on the horizon in front of him as he walked alongside the creek.

She couldn't have gotten far, he kept telling himself. It had only been light for a few minutes, and the lantern was still warm to the touch.

"Kathryn, don't go! I love you!"

There . . . he'd said it. He yelled it for all to hear.

He would no longer deny what he had been feeling. But what if he was too late? What if he never got the chance to tell Kathryn?

When Travis came upon the place where he'd first spied Kathryn bathing, the memory was so sweet, so real, it nearly drove him to his knees.

God, please, don't let me be too late.

He watched as the dawning sun reflected off the creek, causing it to shimmer and shine. But when he saw Kathryn's reflection in the water, he quickly spun around, expecting to see her standing there.

But she wasn't.

Realizing it was just his mind and his eyes playing a cruel trick on him, Travis turned back to the water, but Kathryn's reflection was still there.

God . . . no. That's not a reflection.

48

"Kathryn!"

Travis threw down his weapon and leapt into the water, but his boots slipped on the rocky bottom, causing him to go under. He came up sputtering, with Kathryn in his arms, but she was limp as a rag doll.

Holding her head above water, Travis patted her face. "Kathryn, can you hear me? Come on, Kathryn, say something."

His gentle pats quickly turned to brisk slaps, and even though he was afraid he was going to hurt her, he was more afraid she couldn't feel anything at all.

She's got to be okay, Lord. Please spare her. Even though I don't deserve an ounce of your mercy after the way I've treated her, please don't take Kathryn away from me.

He carefully navigated the uneven creek bed, then laid Kathryn on the grassy bank. Crawling out next to her, Travis fired a quick shot into the air, tossed his revolver aside, then draped her across his lap, noticing her lips were a faint shade of blue.

"I'm sorry, Kathryn. I am so, so sorry," he sobbed, pressing her to his chest, rocking her like a child.

Tell me what to do, Lord. Tell me what to do.

Then he remembered watching a man save a boy from drowning after he'd fallen into a river during a church picnic.

Laying Kathryn on her back, Travis raised her arms over her head, then brought them down and pressed them to her chest. He repeated this action several times, but nothing happened.

Come on . . . come on . . . breathe, cry, anything.

"Travis!"

He looked up and saw Caleb running toward him, but he continued to work on Kathryn.

"What happened," Caleb asked, dropping to his knees beside him.

"I found her in the creek," he said, lifting Kathryn's arms over her head and then back to her chest. "I don't know how long she was under, but she's still not breathing."

Travis quickened his motions out of sheer desperation. "Come on, Kathryn!" he yelled. "Fight for me! Fight for Matilda! We need you! Do you hear me? We need—"

Kathryn lurched forward, water spewing from her mouth.

"Yes!" Travis shouted. "That's it, Kathryn! Breathe!"

But when she started to choke violently and gasp for air, Travis quickly turned her on her side and pounded on her back.

After a few frantic moments, Kathryn's choking turned to deep coughing, and though he could tell it was painful and rattled her entire body, a hint of color slowly brightened her complexion.

"Kathryn . . ."

She had yet to open her eyes or acknowledge him, but

when she started to tremble, Travis scooped her up and carried her toward the cabin.

"Caleb, get the door for me, then check on Matilda."

Travis hurried through the backdoor and laid Kathryn on the bed. But as he tucked the quilt up around her shoulders, he glanced over to where Matilda was lying in a cocoon of blankets, fast asleep.

"She's fine, Travis," Caleb said, smiling down at Matilda. "Everything is going to be fine."

Travis could feel emotion welling inside him. He was so undeserving of God's grace, especially after the way he'd behaved the last few days, yet God continued to show up for him.

It was truly humbling.

Taking a deep breath, he turned his focus back to Kathryn, concerned that her eyes were still shut, and she had yet to say anything.

Sitting on the edge of the bed, he brushed her wet hair back from her face. "Kathryn . . ."

Her eyes fluttered, but she turned away from him, tears wetting her face.

"Kathryn, please look at me."

She shook her head and sobbed. "Why, Travis? Why didn't you just let me go? It would be better for everyone."

"No . . . don't say that. This is my fault. I said horrible things to you, things you didn't deserve."

"But you're right. I'm a liar and a—"

"No. Stop." He stroked her cheek with his thumb. "I love you, Kathryn, and I don't care about your past. I don't care about any of it. I just want you here with Matilda and me. I don't know what I would've done if you had . . . if something had happened to you."

"You know . . . don't you?" she asked, anguish in her whisper.

"Yes. But it doesn't change the way I feel about you."

"How can you say that?" she cried, then started to cough.

"Because I love you."

"Please . . . stop." She covered her face, her cough deepening.

Travis pulled her hands down, but she turned away.

"Look at me, Kathryn."

"I can't. I'm so ashamed." She continued to cough as she stared at the wall. "I need to go. I don't belong here. You and Matilda deserve so much more."

Travis framed her face with his hands, forcing her to look at him, but she squeezed her eyes shut.

He waited.

When she finally looked at him, he stared at her, hoping she could see the love he felt for her in his eyes. "Do you love me, Kathryn?"

She closed her eyes again. "Please don't ask me that. Please don't make this any harder than it is. I can't stay." She began to cough again, but this time, she couldn't catch her breath.

"Caleb, go for the doctor!"

Kathryn shook her head as she continued to choke and sputter. "No!" she said between coughs. "I'll be fine."

"You don't know that. You were underwater for who knows how long. You weren't even breathing when I found you."

"I don't need a doctor . . . to tell me what I . . . already know." She pushed herself up to a sitting position, trying to catch her breath. "My chest will burn . . . for a while. . . the cough . . . will last a little longer."

Travis was surprised Kathryn was so calm, so sure, but like a punch to the gut his surprise turned to shock. Sitting back, he raked his wet hair away from his face. "You've done this before, haven't you?"

"No." She looked at him briefly, then down at her hands. "But I have nearly drowned before."

Rage thundered in his chest, her point clear. "What else, Kathryn?" he exploded, startling Matilda. "What else have they done to you?"

When Matilda wailed, Caleb quickly picked her up and comforted her. "I think Matilda and I are going to have breakfast in the barn."

Caleb gathered a few things from the stovetop and pantry, then stacked them in the frying pan. "You two have a lot of talking to do, so I think Matilda and I are going to spend the day together." He walked out the door, but before he closed it, he looked at Travis. "Call me if you need me to ride out for the doc."

He nodded, then closed the door and turned to Kathryn. He watched her shoulders shake under the quilt and heard her teeth chattering. "Kathryn, you're still shaking."

"So are you."

Forgetting he was soaked from head to toe, Travis looked at his hands and watched them shake. "But I'm only chilled on the outside. You're cold clear through to the bone."

He moved to the stove and gathered the large cooking pots. "I need to heat some water, so you can take a hot bath." Walking toward the backdoor, he hesitated. "Are you going to be okay while I fetch some water?"

She closed her eyes without answering.

"Kathryn . . ."

She looked at him.

"Promise me you're not going to hurt yourself."

With tears and a defeated sigh, she whispered, "I promise."

Travis returned to the cabin in a matter of minutes, setting the heavy kettles on to boil, then watched as Kathryn laid with her eyes closed, her body shaking, coughing on and off.

Stripping out of his waterlogged clothes, Travis quickly pulled on his warmest dungarees and a flannel shirt, then dragged in the washtub from outside. Running to the barn, he rushed past Caleb and gathered up the blankets he had used to fashion Matilda's makeshift bed.

"How's she doing?" Caleb asked.

"She's freezing and can't stop coughing."

"Should I go get the doc?"

Travis stopped and looked at Matilda, content in Caleb's arms. "Not yet. But if I can't get her warmed up, I'll let you know."

Hurrying back to the cabin, Travis dropped the blankets near the bed, then touched the water on the stove.

Almost there.

After a few more trips to the creek, Travis had water in the tub, on the stove, and sitting nearby in case the tub was too hot.

Though Kathryn's coughing continued, and sounded quite painful, he actually preferred it over the silence. Twice, when he returned to the cabin, she was so quiet, he stopped what he was doing, and watch the bed quilt, thankful when he saw it move.

With the water hot, Travis poured one more pot into the tub then sat on the edge of the bed. Placing his hand on Kathryn's shoulder, he whispered, "It's ready."

She was curled up in a ball, facing the wall, her teeth chattering. "But I'm so cold."

"I know; we'll make it quick." He pulled the quilt down from around her chin, causing her to tremble even more. Carrying her to the tub, he slowly lowered her into the warm water, gown and all.

"It stings," she whimpered.

"I know it does, sweetheart, but only for a minute."

Sitting in the center of the tub, her legs pulled up against her chest, her forehead resting on her knees, Kathryn continued to shake.

Travis knelt beside the tub, and with repeated handfuls of water, bathed her back with the warm liquid.

"Kathryn," he whispered, "you need to take off your gown."

She didn't put up a fight, but slowly moved until the gown was loose, its hem drifting to the water's surface. Gathering it up, Travis gently lifted the material over her head, and slid it down her arms. Kathryn held her arms out until her gown pulled free, then quickly hugged her legs back to her chest.

Travis could not help but stare at the massive bruising coloring her side and the scars that crisscrossed her back. They screamed of the pain she had suffered, sacrificing herself for years in order to keep her mother and brother safe.

Quietly, he continued to bathe her back until he finally saw her body relax into the water.

"Is the stinging gone?"

She nodded.

After a few more handfuls, he gently brushed his fingers across the raised marks on her back, knowing he too had caused her tremendous pain. Pain so deep, she tried to take her own life. "I'm so sorry, Kathryn, for everything."

She lifted her head and looked at him over her shoulder. "It's not your fault, Travis."

"Yes, it is. I said ugly things to you, accused you of horrific acts. I should have known. The way you jump when I raise my voice, and the way you flinch when I move too quickly. All the signs were right in front of me. I should have trusted you."

She turned away. "I didn't want you to know. Somehow, I convinced myself if no one knew, I could pretend it never happened."

"Well, I know now. And so help me God, Jethro and Wade are going to pay for every wicked thing they've ever done to you."

"No, Travis." She shook her head, a frantic look on her face. "You can't. You mustn't do anything. Jethro is a dangerous man. If you try to expose him, he'll make good on his threats. You have to let this go."

"I can't do that," he said as he watched another handful of water run down her back. "You're my wife, and it's my job to protect you. And the only way I can be sure you're safe is if Jethro and Wade are behind bars."

She pressed her forehead to her knees, her shoulders shaking.

"Please don't cry, Kathryn." He gently massaged her neck. "We'll talk about this later when you're feeling stronger. Right now, you need to put on some dry clothes and get back into bed."

Travis held up a towel as Kathryn slowly stepped out of the tub. Wrapping it around her, he held her close, pressing his face against her wet and tangled hair. He held her tight, never wanting to let her go, but knowing she needed to get into bed before she got chilled again.

Stepping back, he tipped her chin up and looked into her eyes. "I'm going to give you some privacy while you get dressed, all right?"

She ducked her head and nodded.

"You're sure you'll be okay? I mean . . . you won't try to hurt—"

Shaking her head, she stepped back into his embrace. "I'll be fine, Travis. I promise."

49

When Travis entered the barn, Caleb jumped to his feet. "How is she?"

"I think she's going to be okay."

"Is it safe . . . you know, to leave her alone?"

"Yes." At least he prayed it was.

Travis looked at Matilda laying in the straw, a horse blanket beneath her. She was smiling and cooing, blissfully unaware of all that had happened.

How he wished he could say the same.

Pacing silently, it was some time before Travis had enough control over his anger to speak. When he did, his words were cold and measured.

"I don't know what I'm going to do, Caleb. Kathryn is terrified of Jethro, and what he'll do if word gets out about the . . . about what he . . ." Travis could not even put words to what it was Jethro had done to her. "But I'm not going to let him get away with it, him or Wade. Kathryn deserves justice for the pain and suffering she's endured."

Caleb watched him pace. "Were you able to talk at all?"

"If you're asking if she gave me the gruesome details, no."

"So, what are you going to do?"

Travis shook his head. "I don't know. Kathryn wants me to let it go, but I can't do that. I just can't stand by and do nothing. But right now, Kathryn is my first concern. As long as her family keeps their distance, I'll keep mine. At least until I figure out what I'm going to do."

"Travis . . ."

He turned to face Caleb and watched as he fidgeted. "What is it? What's wrong?"

Caleb took a deep breath. "Wade was here the day Kathryn miscarried."

"What!" Travis felt like he'd been gut-punched. Again.

"I saw him riding off . . . but when I asked Kathryn about it, she . . ." Caleb shook his head. "What she said, it didn't add up. I think he had something to do with her accident. I don't think she fell off a chair."

Travis felt sick to his stomach. The thought of Wade coming onto *his* property and attacking *his* wife, made him shake with anger. It proved his point. Kathryn would not be safe until Jethro and Wade were behind bars.

"There's something else, Travis."

He looked at Caleb, not knowing how much more he could handle.

"I'm pretty sure Kathryn's mom knew what was going on. She as much as warned me not to mention Kathryn's condition in front of her husband."

"What did she say?"

"Well . . . it's more how she acted. Though she was clearly upset Kathryn had miscarried, she seemed more worried about what her husband would do if he found out."

Travis' heart quickened. "What if she talks to her husband or Wade? What if they think we know what they did and try to make good on their threats?"

Caleb shook his head. "Kathryn's mom is not going to say a thing. Believe me, she'll wait for them to say something first. And since I never spoke to Wade or Jethro, that's not going to happen."

"But what if she wants to see Kathryn, and Jethro decides to tag along? I don't think I could control myself if I saw either one of them. It's taking all the self-control I have not to grab my shotgun and go after the whole lot of them."

"I told Mrs. James I would send for her as soon as Kathryn was up for visitors, and I don't think she'll do anything to raise suspicion with her husband. I'm telling you, Travis, she was scared."

50

When Katie woke, she felt disoriented. She looked around, straining, hoping to see Travis, but the cabin was dark and still.

"You okay?"

Katie jumped at the sound of his whispered words so close to her ear, then she felt the bed sway slightly as he rolled toward her.

"Kathryn?"

"I'm . . . I'm fine." A shiver raced through her. "I was just confused. Sorry I woke you."

He lay back on the pillow and sighed. "Don't be sorry. You fell asleep on my side of the bed, and I didn't want to wake you. That's probably what confused you. Try to go back to sleep; you need your rest."

She pulled the quilt up to her chin and closed her eyes. Laying there for what felt like an eternity, she was unable to fall asleep. "Are you still awake?" she finally whispered.

"Uh huh. Am I making you feel uncomfortable?"

"No!" She cringed, not meaning to sound so abrupt. The truth was, she did feel uncomfortable, but it wasn't because Travis was lying next to her. It was because it felt like they were starting all over again.

Two strangers.

Laying in the same bed.

Wondering what the other was thinking.

But this time, she wouldn't wonder. She would be brave enough to ask.

"What are you thinking?" She held her breath, waiting for him to answer.

"You didn't fall off the chair, did you?"

She let out the breath she was holding and swallowed. "No."

"Did Wade ra—"

"No! No . . . he didn't do that."

"Would you tell me if he did?"

Hearing the doubt in Travis' tone made her realize how much her lies had hurt him.

"Kathryn, I need to know the truth."

"I know. And I promise to tell you everything from now on, but you have to promise me something in return."

"What?"

"That you won't go after Jethro or Wade."

"I can't do that, Kathryn."

She felt him tense beside her.

"They deserve to be punished. And so help me, I plan to see that they are."

"But Travis, Jethro is a dangerous man without a conscience. If he feels cornered, he'll make good on his threat; he already did once. If anyone else gets hurt because of me, I won't be able to live with myself. Especially if it's you and Matilda. You have to let this go. You can't—"

First it was tears, then coughing silenced her plea. She sat up, the fire in her chest burning.

Slipping his arm behind her, Travis rubbed her back until

the coughing subsided, then gently pulled her close.

"Don't get worked up about this, Kathryn. It's going to be all right. We'll figure it out together."

With her head tucked in the crook of his arm, she lay her hand on Travis' bare chest, the thunder of his beating heart pounding beneath her palm. She melted, lulled by the way he gently stroked her arm. Though she wished they could fall asleep together and pretend today never happened, the accelerated rhythm thumping in Travis' chest assured her he was nowhere near falling asleep.

"Kathryn, what did you mean when you said, he already did?"

She closed her eyes, wishing they could lay together without all the pain and fear of her past stealing their time.

"Kathryn . . ."

"He killed Mr. Burrows," she blurted out.

"What? Wait, who's Mr. Burrows?"

"He was the schoolmaster before Miss Brown."

"What happened?"

"He died in a house fire. Everyone said it was a tragic accident, but I knew it wasn't. Jethro killed him because Mr. Burrows suspected the truth."

"Are you sure?"

"Yes. A few days after it happened, Mama and I went to the Barker's for lunch. Usually, I would just sit by her side when she went calling, but Mrs. Barkers' sister was paying them a visit and had a daughter my age. Maisy. We played together that afternoon, and Maisy didn't seem the least bit bothered that I didn't talk. I actually felt like I had made a new friend."

Katie closed her eyes, revisiting the memory. It was the most fun she could remember having as a little girl.

Travis gave her a gentle squeeze. "Are you okay?"

She nodded against his chest. "Just remembering," she said before continuing. "During supper that evening, Mama told Jethro how well Maisy and I got along, said we were thick as thieves the whole day. That night, when Jethro came to my room, he was rougher than usual."

When she felt Travis tense again, she stopped, knowing he was getting angry.

"I'm sorry," he said, stroking her arm.

"It can wait until tomorrow."

"No . . . please, tell me what happened."

She didn't want to, but she'd promised to be honest with him. So, she took a minute to gather her thoughts, then continued.

"When Jethro . . . got up to leave, he told me he was glad I had such a good time with Maisy, but that I had better not tell her our secret. And then, I'll never forget what he did. He pulled me close and made me look him in the eye and said, 'Isn't it a tragedy what happened to Mr. Burrows? It would be a shame if something happened to the Barkers' as well. But that's what happens when people stick their noses where they don't belong.' That's when I knew for sure he was responsible for Mr. Burrows' death."

Katie pressed her hand against Travis' chest and winced as she pushed back so she could look him in the eye. "Jethro's a murderer, Travis, plain and simple."

"All the more reason he needs to pay," he said defiantly.

"Then you leave me no choice." She rolled away from him, clenching at the pain in her side. "I won't stand by and watch you get yourself killed." Katie swiped at the tears wetting her lips, feeling such anger she wanted to scream.

Travis rolled over behind her. "And what's that supposed to mean?"

"I'm going to get our marriage annulled."

"You're what?" He sat up like a shot.

"You heard me," she coughed. "I'm going to confess to getting myself pregnant by a drifter and tricking you into marrying me. I'll explain we never consummated our marriage so when I miscarried, you became aware of my charade. Of course, being the honorable man you are, you decided to go on with the marriage, but the guilt was too great for me. I'll tell the circuit judge that I went home to my family and begged their forgiveness. And out of the goodness of their hearts, they took me back in."

"You can't mean that, Kathryn! You can't go back there!"

Katie didn't know what hurt more, the pain in her throat from talking or the desperation in Travis' tone.

"I do and I will! So help me, if you refuse to protect yourself and Matilda, that's exactly what I'll do. And if you even try to hint at Jethro or Wade's abuses, I will refute anything you say and show my disgust that you would spread such vicious rumors about my family just because you can't deal with my rejection. I will ruin your reputation if I have to, Travis. I will do anything to keep you and Matilda safe."

51

Travis flung himself back against the pillow, his hands pressed to his forehead, utterly perplexed. One minute they're talking, the next, Kathryn's threatening to get an annulment. "I don't understand . . . what just happened?"

She didn't answer.

"Kathryn, talk to me."

"I can't!" she cried. "Not when you're being so unreasonable."

Travis tossed back the covers, jumped to his feet, and marched around to the other side of the bed. "*I'm* being unreasonable?" he snapped, stabbing his chest with his finger. "You're talking about returning to hell on earth if I try to seek justice. How is that being reasonable?"

Back and forth he paced. "No! I won't let you do it. We'll leave Milford. I have enough money for us to move wherever we want. You're not going anywhere near your family."

Cradling her side, Kathryn slowly sat on the edge of the bed and looked up at him. "If you love me, Travis, you'll let me do this my way."

He knelt in front of her and framed her tear sodden face with his hands. "It's *because* I love you, Kathryn, that I want those men to pay for what they've done. Why can't you see that?"

"They will pay, Travis. We just have to be patient."

"Patient for what?"

"For Jethro and Wade to turn on each other."

He shrugged. "I don't understand."

"Whenever Wade would . . . umm . . . hurt me . . ." Kathryn looked down, twisting her fingers in her lap, "he would make sure Jethro wasn't around. But one time, when Jethro came home early from Ripley, Wade had me pinned in the barn. As soon as he heard the wagon pull into the yard, he covered my mouth and told me to keep it shut. Then he met Jethro at the door and helped him unload the supplies."

Travis was trying to follow Kathryn, but she wasn't making any sense.

"Don't you see," she looked at him. "Jethro doesn't know what Wade was doing. And if he found out, he wouldn't take kindly to it. Jethro's not the sharing type."

"So why didn't you tell Jethro?" he asked, still confused.

"I was afraid of what he would do. After all, Wade is his son."

Travis reached for her hands and gave them a gentle squeeze. "Then what do we do?"

"Nothing for now. We just need to wait."

He kissed the palm of her hand then brought it up to his face. "But no more talk about going back there, understand? I will bind and gag you and ship you off to England before I let you go anywhere near Jethro or Wade."

She smiled, then leaned forward just enough to allow her lips to brush against his. Her kiss was timid, and Travis could feel her shaking. She pulled away and looked deep into his eyes.

"I love you, Travis."

Returning Kathryn's affection, he realized an instant too late that his kiss was so full of emotion, he might be scaring her. Pulling back, he stroked the side of her face, then leaned his forehead against hers and whispered, "I'm sorry. I didn't mean to be so . . . enthusiastic."

"Please don't ever apologize for loving me, Travis. Just come back to bed and hold me. Things will look better in the morning."

52

The next morning, as Travis approached the barn, he heard moaning. When he walked through the double doors, he saw Caleb down on all fours, lumbering and mooing, lumbering and mooing, entertaining a smiling Matilda.

"What are you doing?"

Caleb jumped to his feet, looking like a kid caught playing with matches. "I was just showing Matilda the difference between a cow and a horse."

"Really? What a relief," Travis said while mockingly wiping his brow. "Now I don't have to worry about her trying to saddle a steer or milk a plow horse. He cracked a smile causing Caleb to roll his eyes.

"Very funny, Travis. Ha ha." Caleb crouched and picked up Matilda.

Travis stepped forward and put a sturdy hand on his friend's shoulder. "Come on, I'm just giving you a hard time."

"Yeah . . . well, you're lucky I'm in love with this little lady," Caleb said as he tickled Matilda. "Or else I'd make you pay for that snippy comment."

Travis reached for Mattie, his heart melting at the smile she gave him.

"How's Kathryn doing?" Caleb asked, clearly concerned.

Travis sighed as he massaged his forehead. "She's doing okay. We had our ups and downs last night. She even threatened to have our marriage annulled."

"She what?"

"Yep. She told me if I went after Jethro and Wade, she'd file for an annulment, confess to having relations with another man, and ruin my reputation."

"She wasn't serious, was she?"

"You're darn right she was serious. She also thinks Jethro is guilty of murder. He all but admitted to Kathryn that he was responsible for the previous schoolmaster's death."

Caleb nodded.

"You knew?" Travis was shocked. Hurt. Angry, even.

"Only because I forced her hand. Kathryn told me what happened so I would know the lengths Jethro would go to. It's the leverage he's used all these years to guarantee her silence. She was afraid you and Matilda would be next."

A chill shook Travis at the thought of anyone hurting Matilda. He looked down into her big, soulful eyes. *I will never let anyone hurt you. I promise.*

"So, what are you going to do?" Caleb asked.

"I don't know." Travis started to pace. "Kathryn wants to wait, but I'm not sure I can."

"Wait for what?"

"For Jethro and Wade to turn on each other."

"Why would they do that? If they haven't turned on each other yet . . ."

"Kathryn doesn't think Jethro knows Wade's been . . ." Travis swallowed back the bile creeping up his throat and tried again. "Jethro doesn't know about Wade. Kathryn thinks he will turn on him if he finds out. She also thinks Wade will run scared if he's cornered. So, we have to come up with a plan that makes them think their backs are up against the wall."

"Like what?"

"I don't know. But I don't want Kathryn anywhere near—"

When Matilda squawked and started to squirm in his arms, Travis turned to her and smiled. "Okay, little darlin', let's get you something to eat."

He picked up the pail that Caleb had already filled with milk and headed for the house, but Travis noticed Caleb didn't make any move toward the barn door. "You comin'?"

"Naw. I think I'll stay here. You three need your family time."

"You're right; we do. And that includes you. Now, do me a favor and bring those eggs," Travis nodded toward the basket Caleb had already gathered, "and get some ham from the smoke house. We're going to have ourselves a morning feast."

53

When Katie saw Travis walk into the cabin with Matilda in his arms, unexpected tears clouded her eyes. She felt such a rush of emotion, she could hardly contain it.

Lifting the bucket onto the table, Travis walked over to the edge of the bed and sat down. "Are you okay?" he asked her.

"Yes." She quickly brushed away her tears and smiled into Matilda's beautiful blue eyes—eyes that mirrored Travis' perfectly. "Hey there, little miss, I've missed you."

When she reached for Matilda, Travis gently laid his daughter in her arms. Even though she whimpered and squirmed, letting everyone know she was hungry, it was music to Katie's ears.

"Hold your horses, missy," Travis said as he got up and walked over to the bucket. "I'll have your bottle ready in two shakes of a lamb's tail."

When Caleb walked in a few minutes later, Katie felt embarrassment warm her cheeks, knowing he knew such intimate details about her life. Even so, her gratitude outweighed her shame. If it wasn't for Caleb's fierce protectiveness of Travis, and his determination to get to the truth, she might be dead . . . or worse, back under Jethro's roof.

"Good morning, Caleb."

"Mornin', Kathryn." He smiled at her. "I'm glad to hear you're doing better."

"Thank you." She coughed, getting Travis' attention. She waved off his look of concern and turned to back to Caleb. "Travis told me you talked to Mama about my miscarriage."

He nodded. "I did. And she seemed genuinely concerned. She wanted to come right over and tend to you yourself. But I told her, you and Travis needed some time alone. I said I would send for her when you felt up to visitors."

Katie didn't know how to feel. It angered her that Mama acted concerned when she did nothing to protect her or care for her when she was under her own roof.

Matilda cried out, pulling Katie from her tangled thoughts. Travis took a seat alongside her and pressed the bottle to Matilda's lips. "Here you go, sweetheart. No need to throw a tantrum."

Katie looked from Matilda to Travis and back again. This was all she wanted; her every dream come true. A husband, a child, someone to love her.

God, You have granted my dreams. I don't need You to mete out Your punishments or Your justice. Your favor is a far greater gift.

She glanced at Travis sitting next to her and smiled, then remembered something he had said the night before.

"Travis, what did you mean when you said you had the *means* to ship me off to England?"

Travis smirked. "So, you *were* listening."

"Yes, I was. But I know it takes a great deal of money to travel that far." She waited for him to look at her. "More money than a field of wheat brings in."

Travis got up from the bed and moved to the stove. "I never said I didn't have money."

"But you never said you did."

"Maybe that's because I don't think it's as important as other people do."

"But I don't understand. If you have *means,* why didn't you just hire a nanny for Matilda? Why did you marry me?"

Travis struggled to answer. Combing his fingers roughly through his hair, he turned to Caleb.

"Travis, are you a criminal? Are you running from the law?" she whispered, fearing saying it out loud would somehow make it true.

Both Travis and Caleb chuckled. "No," he answered assuredly. "I'm not a criminal running from the law."

"Then, what?"

Travis pulled up a chair alongside the bed. He leaned forward, elbows to his knees, hands tightly clasped. "I come from a wealthy family, Kathryn. The Clark's have been influential on the east coast for more than a hundred years," he said sheepishly with his eyes cast down.

"But I don't understand. You say it like it's an embarrassment. And I know that's not the case because you told me how much you loved and respected your father, and how he taught you the importance of faith and family."

"You're right; he did. My father was the most honorable man I've ever known. He stood against those who thought the privilege of money bought them the right to live above the law. It angered him when he watched men of wealth act like they were better than those less fortunate and thought they answered to a different set of rules—rules manipulated to serve their own purpose. People like my grandfather."

Katie carefully shifted Matilda to her shoulder, wincing slightly, then gently patted Mattie's back while she waited for Travis to continue.

"It's hard to explain," he said as he wrung his hands in frustration.

"No, it's not!" Caleb said as he shot up out of his chair. "Bartholomew Clark—Travis' grandfather—was the poorest excuse for a man if ever there was one. He was corrupt, and a swindler, and involved himself in all sorts of illegal practices. He lined his pockets with dirty money and ruined reputable men all for the sake of the almighty dollar. The man had no conscience."

Katie looked at Travis, surprised he wasn't coming to his grandfather's defense. Instead, he slowly dragged his hand down a line-weary face and massaged his jaw.

She coughed quietly, holding her ribs as she did, then resettled Matilda in her arms. "We don't have to talk about this, Travis. It's really none of my business."

"Of course it's your business," he looked at her. "It's part of who I am. It's just not a part that I'm proud of." He wrung his hands, sat in the rocking chair, and sighed.

"My father worked for my grandfather since he was a little boy. He looked up to him, was proud of him, and followed him into the family business. Slowly, my grandfather gave him more responsibility, more decision-making power. My father learned to be a good businessman in his own right. However, it wasn't until he brought me into the company that we realized something was terribly wrong."

"Like what?"

"Well, even though Clark Trade & Company was a very

lucrative business, the wealth it acquired didn't add up."

Katie watched as anguish washed over Travis' face. "I don't understand."

"On the surface, everything Clark Trade & Company did looked reputable. At least the business dealings my father handled. But, one day, when my grandfather was on a business trip, I was looking through some papers and found something."

Travis took a deep breath, as if the weight of the world had settled on his shoulders. His pain was so tangible, it made Katie tear up. "What is it, Travis? What did you find?"

"I discovered my grandfather's trade of choice." He shook his head. "Human flesh."

"You mean . . . slaves?" she whispered.

He looked at her, his complexion void of color. "Slaves, orphaned boys, orphaned girls, women who were widowed and unable to pay their debts, anyone who would bring him a price."

Katie gasped in horror, jarring Matilda from her sleep. Her little hands flexed but Katie quickly swayed and shushed her back to sleep. Once Matilda was calm, Katie looked at Travis, almost afraid to ask. "What did you do?" she whispered.

"At first, we didn't know what to do. My father was devastated, and it took a while for the information to sink in. This was his hero after all, the man he respected above anyone else. We knew we needed to be careful and discreet before we did or said anything. So, I quietly reviewed business transactions that were handled solely by my grandfather. Unfortunately, what we found out was even more heinous than we first thought."

Katie watched as Travis paced, no longer able to sit as he spoke.

"My grandfather was involved in every illegal business imaginable: gambling, corruption, extortion, pirating of cargo, and human trade. And even though we had no real evidence, we were fairly sure he was even involved with a man known to be a hired gun."

Katie sat still, not knowing what to say. She just waited for Travis to continue in his own time.

"Once my father realized the extent of my grandfather's crimes, he feared for our safety and our security. So, he slowly started separating our holdings from my grandfather's. It wasn't that difficult since my grandfather had turned over the bookkeeping to me."

"Weren't you afraid he would find out?"

"I was more concerned about my father. It took months to examine all the journal entries and trace them back to their origins. During that time, my father started feeling poorly. He attributed it to the stress of what we were doing, and the despair he felt realizing the father he worshiped was a criminal. However, I was worried that it was something more. As it turned out, I was right. Within weeks, both my mother and father were dead from Cholera."

She ached for him, seeing the pain on his face. "Travis, I'm so sorry."

He moved to the stovetop and poured some coffee. Katie watched as a tear roll down his cheek.

"Is that when you moved here?" she asked.

"Not right away. During the time we were gathering information on my grandfather, I started courting Mary. My parents loved her from the start, but my grandfather was not at all pleased with my choice."

Travis turned to Katie. "You see, Mary didn't come from a family of wealth or influence, so grandfather refused to acknowledge our relationship. He told me it was fine if I wanted to take her as a mistress, but she was socially unacceptable as a wife. In fact, he threatened to disinherit me if I insisted on marrying her."

Travis chuckled but did not smile. "That threat meant nothing to me since I didn't want his dirty money. So, after Mary and I were wed, I decided I wanted a clean slate, to make a way for Mary and me without the need of the Clark name. We left town a week after we were married, right after I tipped off the county auditor to look into Clark Trade & Company's business practices."

Katie was stunned. What Travis was telling her sounded like a melodrama or the plot of a clandestine novel. But to think, it was his life. "What did the auditor do?"

"It turned out that the auditor was in business with my grandfather. And I'm quite sure he wasn't the only official my grandfather had in his hip pocket. As far as I knew, nothing was ever done."

"And your grandfather never sent someone to look for you? Or did he not know it was you who tipped them off?"

Travis shrugged. "He knew. I was the only one with access to that kind of information, and the auditor worked for him. But I guess he didn't think I was worth chasing after. I'm sure he just bought off the officials he didn't already own."

"And he's never tried to contact you?"

"Not until now." Travis walked over to the dresser and pulled out an envelope from between two books. "He sent this with Caleb." He extended the swollen envelope to her. She reached for it, never taking her eye off Travis. "What does it say?"

Travis bent down and took Matilda from her arms. "Read it," he said while he situated Matilda in her cradle.

Katie carefully pushed herself up to a sitting position against the headboard, glanced at Travis one more time, then silently read to herself.

Travis,

I've asked Caleb to deliver this to you because I knew you would never accept a letter from me. By the time you get this, I probably will be gone. I am dying. and the doctors say I don't have much time left. But. I could not leave this earth without trying to make amends with my only grandchild.

You were right to turn me in. Yes, I knew it was you. I had never felt more betrayed in my life then to know it was my own grandson who had turned on me.

In fact. I had planned to send someone after you. to make sure you paid for your disloyalty. But in the end. I could not do it. You're my own flesh and blood. And thankfully, even I had a line I would not cross.

But ever since that day, I have been haunted by the realization of what I had become. I paid a dear price for my greed. Your father passed hating me. and you left town wanting nothing to do with me or the Clark name.

It took some time for me to realize how truly poor I was. I want you to know that even though there was no way I could amend for all my sins, I've tried to leave behind a Clark legacy you would be proud of.

Enclosed you will find a list of institutions I have erected in the Clark name. You are their benefactor, along with the family property. A board of directors is in place to keep things going in my absence.

If within a year of my death, you do not come forward to claim what is rightfully yours, ownership will be given to the board with a stipulation that nothing can be liquidated, and these institutions are to continue as they are now, but the family property will always be yours. That will never change. You are a Clark, and Golden Oaks is to be passed down to each generation. If you decide not to return to the property, the current caretaker will be in charge until a Clark heir comes to claim it.

Travis, I know none of this makes up for what I've done to you or to your father and mother, or to the many lives I've destroyed in the name of greed. I do not deserve your forgiveness, but I am asking that you make sure the Clark name continues on with a reputation that honors you and your father. Please know how much I love you, and how much I have grieved these last years over losing you.

I was sorry to hear about Mary's passing. I wish I had taken the time to get to know her. I also know I have a great-granddaughter, and I think that might be my greatest regret—not ever holding her.

You were always strong, Travis, so I know you will survive your loss. Cling to God. He will always be there for you. I am thankful I can say I realized this before it was too late for me.

        With much love and regret, Grandpa

Katie flipped through several sheets of paper as her tears blotted each one. They were all deeds. *Clark Home for Widows, The Clark Foundation, Travis House for Men, The Mary Clark Home for Orphans.* Included was a list of bank accounts and holdings. Katie could tell that even though the accounts spoke of wealth, the likes of which she had never known, it was modest compared to what Travis had told her.

She looked up at him dumbfounded, then to Caleb. "Is he still a—"

Caleb shook his head. "Mr. Clark had an agent from the Pinkerton National Detective Agency locate me. There was a note for me as well, begging me to find Travis and get this information to him. The agent explained briefly what the envelope contained and told me Mr. Clark passed away two days prior to him finding me."

She looked at Travis, his eyes swollen with unshed tears.

"Are you all right?"

He nodded. "When Caleb first gave me the letter, I was angry. My grandfather could've hunted me down at any time and explained all this to me. But he was right, I probably would not have listened." He let out a deep breath. "I'm grateful he tried to make things right, but more than that, I'm just thankful he got things right with God. Because of that, I'll see him again."

The rest of the evening was quiet, the mood reflective, words unnecessary.

Caleb excused himself early, so once Matilda finished her night feeding, he and Kathryn turned in early as well.

Although Kathryn fell right to sleep, she continued to cough.

And as Travis lay awake listening to her, he stared at the ceiling, his hands tucked beneath his head.

The whole evening spoke of the power of forgiveness and the will to make things better, but somehow, he couldn't let go of his anger toward Jethro and Wade.

Rolling onto his side, Travis saw the scars on Kathryn's back peeking out from the neckline of her gown, evidence of the pain and suffering she'd been forced to endure.

They are beyond forgiveness!

He clenched his hands, feeling his boiling blood rushing through his veins.

So help me, justice will be done.

Jethro and Wade will pay for every contemptible act Kathryn has suffered.

54

The next morning, as they all gathered for breakfast, Katie entertained Matilda while Travis worked at the stove. He insisted on making the meal, not wanting her to overdo it, and she conceded knowing there was no use arguing. Besides, she wanted to talk to him about something, and needed him to remain in a good mood.

"You know, Travis," Caleb said as he carefully balanced on the chair with the split rail, "food doesn't have to be burnt to be done."

"Very funny!" he said while waving his hand over the stovetop, clearing some smoke. "The skillet just got a little hot."

When Travis placed the sizzling skillet of ham on the table, Katie carefully laid Matilda in the cradle, then sat opposite Caleb. Travis dished up her plate and his, but let Caleb fend for himself.

When they bowed for prayer, Travis not only blessed the food, but listed all the things he was grateful for, her included. Katie couldn't help but tear up, especially when Travis reached for her hand and gave it a squeeze.

The rest of the meal included the usual banter. She listened as the men discussed the crop, the building project they were anxious to get started, and a list of other chores. She debated saying anything, not wanting to spoil Travis' good mood, but fear for the future spurred her on.

Here goes nothing.

"Travis, I got to thinking last night . . ."

"About what?" he said around a mouthful of eggs.

"About us."

He glanced at her, waiting for her to say more.

"I was thinking . . . uhm, maybe we could . . . I mean . . . why don't we leave Milford, start somewhere new?"

Travis stopped, his fork halfway to his mouth. Even though his eyes said no, Katie kept talking.

"I know you've worked hard on the land and the crops, and I'm not saying you have to go back home if you're not ready. I just think it would be easier if we left. I'm sure you and Caleb could find a place you could work on together and—"

"I'm not running, Kathryn."

"I'm not asking you to run. I just think if we start over some—"

Travis sat up straight as a pole, his shoulders raised, his jaw clenched. "I'm not leaving until I know Jethro and Wade are behind bars or dangling from a rope." He turned to her, reaching for her hand. "I'll send you away to some place safe if you're afraid to stay, but I'm not leaving until justice is served."

"And what if something happens to you?" She stood, her eyes immediately filling with tears. "What will I do then? Go back to living under the same roof with that man, me *and* Matilda?"

"No. You'll go to North Carolina. You will take those deeds and our marriage certificate and show them that you are the surviving Clark. You'll have everything you and Matilda will ever need."

"Everything but you!" She turned and walked to the backdoor.

"Don't leave, Kathryn. You're not strong enough."

"I just need a minute, some air. I won't go far. I promise."

———————————————— • ————————————————

Travis set down his coffee cup and tipped his head back. "What am I going to do, Caleb? I just can't let Jethro and Wade get away with all they've done, especially if Jethro is guilty of murder. But Kathryn won't even listen to me. Her solution is to say nothing . . . do nothing. And now she wants to up and leave. Why can't she understand I'm doing this for her?"

"Are you?" Caleb asked dryly.

"Of course I am!" Travis cut his piece of ham even though he'd lost his appetite. "Kathryn has been brutally assaulted for years. I just can't walk away knowing what I do. Jethro and Wade need to answer for their actions."

"But are you seeking justice for Kathryn? Or for yourself?"

Travis dropped his fork. "It's the same thing, Caleb! Justice is justice. Why are you acting like such a jackass?"

"I'm not. I just want you to understand full well what you're doing and why. Because Kathryn has been through enough already. She has suffered horrible acts, least of which being impregnated by her stepfather only to miscarry. She just wants it all to stop. Bringing those men to justice is not going to take away her pain or her nightmares or her loss. It will only serve your purpose of revenge."

Calmly, Travis answered. "It's not revenge—it's justice."

"Fine. Then leave Milford with Kathryn. Go to Golden Oaks. Once there, you can contact the authorities and let them handle it."

He shook his head. "No. I want to see them hung. That's the only way I will know Kathryn is truly safe."

"And it's the only way you will get your revenge."

"Fine!" He jumped to his feet. "You're right! I want revenge!" Travis spun around, threw his coffee cup against the wall, and watched as the brown stain slithered down the wood planks.

Picking up the dented cup, he leaned against the wall with his outstretched arms, his head hung low.

"They've touched my wife in ways only a husband should," he whispered, unable to hide his anguish. "Kathryn and I haven't even been intimate yet, and now I'm not sure we ever will. She jumps when I raise my voice and flinches when I move too fast. And there have been times when I've touched her . . . I felt her body tense. I know she doesn't mean it, that it's a reflex, but what if it never goes away? What if Kathryn sees Jethro instead of me when we lie together at night? What if she mistakes my acts of love for their acts of violence?"

"I would never do that, Travis."

He turned to see Kathryn standing just inside the doorway.

"I could never mistake you for them. Ever." She walked the length of the room, wrapped her arms around his waist, and pressed her head to his chest. "Please don't ever think those things, Travis."

He wrapped her in his arms and lay his cheek against her head. Caleb quietly slipped from the room while they held each other.

"How can I not, Kathryn? I lay beside you last night, afraid to touch you, worried I'd startle you or churn up horrible memories."

"Then talk to me, Travis. Don't be afraid of me . . . of us. Don't give Jethro or Wade that kind of power. We can get through this; I know we can. I just need a little time."

As they held each other, Travis silently prayed she was right.

"You know . . . you're lucky Matilda didn't wake from your little tantrum," she teased, staring at the coffee running down the wall, trying to lighten the mood.

"Sorry about that." He scrunched up his face. "I'll clean it up. I was just so—"

"I know." She pressed a finger to his lips and smiled. "You don't have to apologize. You want justice, and so do I. We just have to wait for the right time, to make sure no one else gets hurt."

———— • ————

Travis spent the afternoon splitting wood. It helped him get out his aggression while thinking about what to do next.

Leaving Milford without seeing Jethro and Wade punished was out of the question, even though taking action would mean upsetting Kathryn.

He understood her fear, at least he thought he did. However, fear wasn't a good enough reason for not seeking justice.

I just need to convince her of that.

55

The next few days were much the same as the ones before. Travis saw to Matilda during mealtimes, allowing Katie to rest, and after supper, Caleb took Matilda on little adventures, so she and Travis could have some quality time together before they fell into bed at the end of the day.

Her strength was returning slowly, and she was moving around without as much pain. Her appetite was almost back to normal, at least on the days Travis didn't talk about Jethro or Wade. But she continued to cough from time to time, and no matter how many times she reassured Travis she was fine, he still worried.

"Please, Travis, don't say anything to Doc Hammond. It's just a cough. It will go away soon enough. There's nothing he can do for it, so there's no reason to tell him what happened."

He pondered for a moment. "Okay, how about this? I won't tell Doc what happened, but I will mention that you've been coughing. If he shows little concern, I'll let it go. However," he raised a playful finger, smirking as he scolded, "if he gets inquisitive, we'll explain that you took a spill in the creek and swallowed quite a bit of water. How's that?"

Figuring that was the best compromise she was going to get, she sighed. "Fine."

"Okay, I have only one more stipulation," he added.

"And what is that?"

"I want to be present during your exam."

"Travis, you can't mean that?" She took a step back, horrified he would even suggest such a thing.

"Oh, yes I do." He crossed his arms against his chest in his *this is not open for discussion* stance.

She walked to the corner of the room, too embarrassed to look at him. "Please, Travis, you have to understand, the doctor's exam will be quite . . . intrusive." Katie could feel heat pouring into her cheeks. "And even though you're my husband . . . and have every right to be present, I will be humiliated beyond words for you to see me in such a . . . well, such an immodest way."

Travis walked up behind her and gently wrapped his arms around her shoulders. She immediately latched onto his wrists as he brought his lips down next to her ear. "I said I wanted to be present, Kathryn. I didn't say I was going to watch."

She turned to face him. "Then why?"

He looked at her, seriousness creasing his brow. "Because I want to hear for myself what the doctor has to say, not your sugarcoated interpretation. If he says you need more bed rest, I'm going to ask him how much. If he says you're still too weak for chores, I will ask him exactly what you can or cannot do."

"But Travis—"

"Uh, uh, uh . . . let me finish."

She crossed her arms and waited.

"And . . ." he continued with a grin, "if the doctor gives you a clean bill of health, I promise not to coddle you any longer.

So you see, this works out for both of us. If Doc says you're as good as you keep telling me you feel, I won't argue with you anymore."

"That'll be the day," she mumbled under her breath.

"I'm sorry, Mrs. Clark, did you say something?" He bent down, looking at her directly, mischief dancing in his eyes. But to Katie, his ultimatum no longer mattered. He called her Mrs. Clark. He might as well have called her 'Queen of the world' because that's how he made her feel.

If only he would give up his need for justice; let the past be the past.

But she knew Travis; his sense of honor wouldn't allow for it. He would not settle for anything less than Jethro and Wade behind bars.

No matter how long it took.

56

Katie waited until Travis and the doctor stepped outside before melting to the edge of the bed. The look she'd seen in Travis' eyes nearly scorched her. Her heart had never beat so fast or her blood run so hot. If she read his expression correctly, he too was concentrating on the one restriction the doctor had given them.

Reaching for a book on the shelf, she began to fan herself, hoping to cool her skin and her racing thoughts. Then, out of nowhere, a Bible verse came to mind.

Your desire will be for your husband.

Where had that come from? And why all of a sudden was her mind and body acting without her permission?

Fresh air. That's what she needed. Fresh air and something to occupy her thoughts.

Something other than the look in Travis' eyes.

Katie was placing the basket of biscuits on the table when Travis and Caleb came in for supper. They were discussing cattle as they hung their hats by the door, but when Travis turned and looked at her, it was obvious cattle were no longer on his mind.

Immediately, her heart skipped into double time.

"Supper is ready," she said, trying to steady the tremor in her voice.

"Looks good." Travis grinned, his eyes never leaving hers.

Why is he doing that? He's purposely trying to make me feel all jittery and off-balance. Well, it's not going to work, Mr. Clark.

Travis' behavior did not improve during supper. He continued to offer her hooded smiles, sideway glances, and mischievous grins. By the time she had Matilda bedded down and Caleb called it a night, Katie was seeing red—and it wasn't just the blush Travis kept bringing to her cheeks.

As soon as he latched the door, Katie said what she'd been thinking all evening. "It's not going to work, you know."

Travis turned around, a beguiling look on his face. "Whatever do you mean?"

"Your plan . . . to make me feel . . . I don't know . . . nervous or unsteady, or both."

Without a word, Travis walked over to where she stood by the stove. He slipped his arm behind her back and gently tugged her toward him. "Actually, I was just thinking there's been something missing between us from the start."

She cleared her incredibly parched throat, her body tingling where Travis' hand rested at the small of her back. "But Doc Hammond said we should wait another week before we . . ." She couldn't even say it.

Blushing, he chuckled. "I'm not talking about that."

"Oh?"

"No, ma'am. You see, we went straight to marrying and skipped courting all together."

"Courting? Is that what you were doing?"

"No, ma'am. I was flirting. Everyone knows flirting comes before courting."

She was speechless. Something Travis took full advantage of. He bent down, moving in for a kiss. But a split second before his lips touched hers, she pressed her hands to his chest and pushed him away. "And *everyone knows* flirting doesn't involve kissing."

"Well now, Mrs. Clark, you would be correct. But seeing as we're already married, I figured we could probably move things along at a little faster clip."

This time when he leaned in for a kiss, she welcomed it.

Wholeheartedly.

57

It had been three glorious days since Travis started *courting* her. Glorious because he never once brought up the subject of Jethro and Wade, or the need to bring them to justice.

During the mornings and afternoons, he *flirted* with her relentlessly, even in front of Caleb. And in the evenings, he wooed her like only a married man could.

Lying on her side of the bed, Katie watched as Travis went about his nightly routine. He stoked the stove to keep the chill away until morning, then stared at Matilda by lamplight before extinguishing the lantern for the night. She listened as his boots hit the floor, and his buckle jangled as he hung his dungarees from the post on the wall. Her heart fluttered as he slid into bed next to her, and all but stopped when he rested his hand on her hip.

"Supper was very good tonight," he whispered softly.

"It was just stew."

"But it was mighty fine stew."

She smiled to herself. "I think you and Caleb would've been happy with shoe leather and gravy after all the work you put in today."

"Maybe so, but knowing we always have a hearty meal

waiting for us is motivation to do the job right." He nuzzled closer. "That and the fact that I have a beautiful wife and child counting on me to take good care of them."

She rolled closer to him and looked into his eyes. "Is that enough for you, Travis? Is that really enough?"

He stared at her, and she saw the moment he understood what she was asking. He sighed as he slipped a wayward strand of hair behind her ear. "You and Matilda are all that matter to me, Kathryn."

She smiled with overwhelming relief, but when he didn't smile back, she knew there was more. "You're not going to let it go, are you? No matter what I say?"

"I can't."

She tensed. "Yes you can. You're just choosing not to."

"I'm *choosing* to do what's right for my family."

Family. Her *own* family. Something she thought she'd never have.

"Speaking of family, your mother is going to want to come look after you. Caleb told her he would send word when you were ready, but I don't know if she's going to be able to wait much longer. And I'd rather have Caleb get her than take the chance of Jethro or Wade bringing her here. Because if either one of them sets foot on my property, I'll drop them where they stand."

Katie could hear the hate and anger in Travis' voice, and it frightened her. She struggled with the thought of Travis killing someone in cold blood. She wanted to think he was too honorable of a man to do something so violent, but if he thought Matilda's safety was on the line . . .

Like when Wade barged into the cabin and assaulted me. What if he hadn't left after pushing me around? What if he had taken Matilda . . . or worse? Katie's thoughts were spinning out of control, her heart racing.

"Kathryn, what's wrong?"

"Nothing."

"Don't tell me, nothing," he said as he stroked her arm. "One minute we're talking, and the next you're shaking like a leaf."

Katie took a second to calm herself enough to speak. "I can't lose you, Travis. I just can't."

He pulled her close. "You're not going to lose me, Kathryn. Why would you say such a thing?"

"Your talk. You scare me when you talk that way." She pushed away from him and swung her legs over the side of the bed. "All your talk about vengeance and getting even. You could go to prison. You could hang for murder. Why would you do that? Why would you take the chance of Matilda and me being left all alone?" She tried to stand, but Travis reached for her elbow and wouldn't let her go.

"Kathryn, I'm sorry. I didn't mean to upset you."

"But it does upset me." She turned to face him. "It scares me to the point I can barely breathe."

"Come here." He pulled back the bedcovers and held out his arm.

She willingly lay down beside him and allowed Travis to pull her close.

"I'm sorry I scared you," he spoke quietly as he stroked her arm. "It's just whenever I think of Jethro and Wade, I immediately see red. It's only because of you and Matilda that I haven't already ridden to Jethro's place and filled him and Wade full of lead. Though if I did, I think the law would see things my way."

"The law does not condone vigilantism, and you know it."

"Protecting my family is *not* vigilantism."

"But riding onto someone else's property and killing them in cold-blood is murder." Completely frustrated, she tried to roll away from him, but Travis held her tight.

"I'm sorry, okay? I'm sorry I upset you." He pressed a kiss to the top of her head. "Let's not talk about it anymore."

"You can't do anything foolish," she whispered, her arm draped across his chest, feeling every beat of his heart. "Matilda and I need you too much."

"And I plan on being here for both of you, for a very long time."

Long after Katie heard the even breaths of Travis' slumber, she lay awake thinking, worrying, and wondering.

There has to be a way to make Jethro and Wade pay for their sins, but how?

She couldn't just waltz into the sheriff's office with her story and expect him to lock them up, no questions asked. Sheriff Chambers would give Jethro and Wade a chance to defend themselves. And given that time, Jethro would make her pay. Once he knew she had talked, he would make good on his threats.

But if I told the sheriff about Jethro's threats, maybe he would handle things differently. Understand the danger they were in.

Even so, knowing the sheriff and Jethro were longtime friends, Katie was afraid Jethro would be given the benefit of the doubt.

Maybe Doc Hammond could confirm my injuries.

She thought about it, knowing he'd treated her a fair number of times. But whenever he did, Katie had a ready story to explain away her injuries. He never asked her probing questions like Mr. Burrows did. Doc Hammond was just gullible enough to believe she was a child prone to mishaps.

I should have killed him myself.

That's it!

That's how I can make sure Travis and Matilda don't get hurt.

She was the one with the injuries. She was the one who had suffered the abuse. If there was anyone the law would grant leniency to, it would be the victim. And if they didn't, Matilda would at least still have her father.

Now all I have to do is come up with a plan . . . some way to lure Jethro and Wade to me. It's the only way I can convince the authorities that they're guilty. If I kill them on Jethro's land, it would be obvious I hunted them down, even if I told the sheriff the reason why. But, if they were on Travis' property, I could tell the sheriff that they were planning on killing me, and I had no choice but to defend myself.

Katie lay awake the rest of the night sorting out ideas, trying to come up with the perfect plan. It would be hard enough to figure out a way to get both Jethro and Wade to come to her, but it would be harder still to figure out how to get Travis and Caleb to leave her alone on the ranch.

By daybreak, Katie had a plan, but she would need her mama's help.

I guess I'll find out if she's as sorry as she claims to be.

58

When Travis and Caleb came in for breakfast, Katie tried to give her best smile without looking like she was hiding something.

"Hey," Travis said, obviously surprised. "What's all this?" He motioned toward the twisted sweet rolls on the table, and the sizzling ham in the skillet. "You're supposed to be taking it easy."

"Travis, you can't keep saying that. The doctor said I can do anything I want."

"Well . . . not anything," he grinned.

Katie's chin dropped as her complexion flashed red. She cut him an '*I can't believe you just said that*' look as she snatched the egg basket out of his hand. "Just sit down . . . both of you, while I fry up some eggs."

After working quickly at the stove, she slid eggs onto two plates, then set them in front of Caleb and Travis. She waited while Travis said grace before moving back to the stove to scramble some eggs for herself. As she tossed them around in the skillet, she silently practiced what she was going to say. "So Travis, I was thinking about our conversation last night."

"Last night?"

"Yeah . . . about Mama." She scooped up the eggs and took

a seat next to him.

"And?"

"I'm ready to see her."

"Okay then," Caleb chimed in. "I can go get her today or at least ride out and see if she can come."

"But don't pressure her." Katie hurried to say. "Because if today isn't a good day, she doesn't have to come. I don't want her here because she feels guilty or thinks it's the right thing to do. She has to want to come."

"Oh, she'll want to. Believe me, if you could've seen the look on her face when I spoke with her, she wanted to be here in the worst way."

She shrugged. "If you say so."

Travis and Caleb continued to talk over breakfast while Katie saw to Matilda. When they were through, Caleb made his way outside while Travis crossed the room and placed a gentle kiss on her cheek.

"Are you sure you want to do this? Seeing your mother, I mean?"

She nodded. "She's a victim too. I have to remember that." *And I need her if my plan is going to work.*

He gave her a squeeze. "Okay, but if you decide differently, that's okay too."

Katie paced the cabin, debating if she could go through with her plan. But she didn't see that she had a choice. The only way to make sure Travis didn't do something reckless to Jethro and Wade, was to kill them both before he got the chance.

Katie knew the minute the wagon pulled into the yard.

With Matilda tucked against her shoulder, she closed her eyes and took a deep breath.

I have to do this before Travis does something that can't be undone. Hopefully, Mama will see, this is the only way.

The rap on the door made her jump, even though she was expecting it. Opening the door, she looked at Mama standing on the stoop, a smile on her face and tears in her eyes. Stepping forward, she wrapped Katie in a hug. "Thank you for letting me come."

Katie pulled back, then put Matilda down on a blanket with her colored blocks to occupy her. Moving to the stove, Katie nervously poured two cups of tea while Mama gazed around the cabin.

"This place is very cozy."

"Cozy, as in small," Katie said defensively.

"No. Cozy as in warm, like a home should be." She stood and watched Matilda play. "She's growing fast, isn't she?"

"Yes. Very fast. She's rolling from side to side and trying to get up on her knees."

See. I can do this. Pleasant conversation. Two adults talking about everyday things.

She turned and placed the cups on the table.

Then why does my heart hurt so much?

Her mama sat across from her and stirred her tea. "How are you doing, Katie?"

"Don't you mean, *Kathryn?*" she snapped.

Her mama looked down, continuing to stir. "Is that what you prefer?"

Rage immediately bubbled inside Katie. What she *preferred*, was to lash out, scream and holler, berate the woman who dared to call herself a mother.

But she had a plan and needed her mama's help in order for it to work.

"Yes. I prefer Kathryn. As far as I'm concerned, Katie no longer exists."

Her mama nodded, then took a sip of tea. "How are you doing, *Kathryn?*"

Katie cleared her throat and gained control of her emotions. "It depends on what you're asking me. How am I doing as a wife, as a mother, as a woman who just miscarried, or as a girl who spent her entire childhood terrorized in her own home?"

Mama looked away, a tear slipping down her cheek. "I guess if you're up and about, you must be faring pretty well."

So, she's going to ignore what happened.

More tears fell, and the silence grew louder.

"I'm sorry about the baby, Kathryn. I'm sure that was real hard on you and Travis. I mean, he's already lost a wife, and struggled to take care of his little girl."

Katie clenched her fists in her lap, trying to hold back her anger but the more Mama carried on, the harder it got.

"He's sure been through a lot these past few—"

"It wasn't Travis' baby!" Katie shouted then lowered her voice. "Do you understand what I'm saying? I didn't get pregnant by Travis; I got pregnant by *your* husband or *his* son."

She turned ashen. "Wade?"

"Yes, Mama." Katie stood and moved to the far side of the cabin. "Jethro wasn't the only one hurting me. And you would've known that if you had cared about me at all. If you hadn't turned a blind eye." She started to cry and hated herself for it.

"Kathryn . . . I . . . I don't know what to say."

Katie wiped her face and sat back down. "I don't want you to say anything, especially that you're sorry. Because what you allowed is unforgivable. And you know how I know that? That little girl right there." Katie pointed to Matilda as she played on her blanket. "She's not even my own flesh and blood, but I would do anything, and I mean anything, to protect her. Because she depends on me. Because that's what a *mother* is supposed to do."

"But Kathryn I—"

"No, Mama." Katie put up her hand. "I don't want to hear your excuses. I don't want to hear that you had no choice. Because the truth is, a *real* mother never would have allowed her child to go through what I did."

Mama sat for a moment, silently drying her tears. After a deep breath, she stood and walked toward the door.

"So, that's it? You're just going to leave?" Katie asked, a tremor in her voice.

Mama stopped but didn't turn around. "What can I say, Kathryn? I am truly ashamed of what I've done. What I *didn't* do. And I know there is nothing I can do or say to prove to you otherwise."

"And if there was, would you do it?"

She turned. "What do you mean?"

"If there was something you could do to prove to me how sorry you are, would you do it?"

She rushed toward Katie but stopped just short of embracing her. "Anything! Anything at all! I no longer care what happens to me. As long as you and Seth are safe, that's all that matters."

"Then I need your help."

After a long conversation with Mama, insisting what had to be done, Katie sent her on her way.

Standing on the porch, she watched as Caleb pulled out of the yard. Mama glanced over her shoulder before the wagon crested the hill and gave her a slight wave.

Travis stood next to her, his arm around her waist. "You okay?" he asked.

She nodded.

"You're sure?"

"I'm fine, Travis." Katie turned and walked back into the cabin.

He followed. "I guess I just figured she would stay longer."

"She was afraid Jethro would find out. Mama didn't want any trouble." Katie bent to pick up Matilda.

"But she told Caleb he wasn't expected back until afternoon."

"Well . . . yeah, um . . . he wasn't. But she told me he and Wade are going to Ripley next week. Overnight. She said she would like to come back then and have a nice long visit."

"That's good, right?"

"Yeah. Good." Katie hitched Matilda up on her hip and turned to the pantry. "I know it's a little late, but would you like me to make you a sandwich or something?"

"No. Caleb and I already ate."

She could feel Travis staring at her, but she didn't dare look at him. "Okay, well, Matilda and I are going to pick some vegetables for supper." She grabbed a basket from the pantry shelf and hurried out the door.

It didn't take long for Katie to realize how weak she still was. By the time she dug up some carrots and potatoes, and carried Matilda back to the cabin, she was winded, and her body ached. Though she felt weak physically, Katie's mind would not rest. She kept replaying the conversation she had with Mama, as she outlined her idea.

Katie made it clear upfront that her forgiveness could not be bartered but helping with her plan was one way Mama could prove she was truly sorry. After hearing the details, Mama was almost hysterical at the thought of crossing Jethro, but she still agreed to help.

Of course, none of it will matter if I can't convince Travis and Caleb to leave for the day.

She thought about her plan, a chill causing her to tremble.

But if they do decide to leave, every step will have to be flawless.

———— • ————

When Caleb returned from taking Mrs. James home, Travis met up with him and helped unhitch the wagon. "No trouble at Kathryn's house?"

"Nope."

"Did Mrs. James have much to say about her visit?"

"Nope. She was quiet as a church mouse. I asked if she was okay, and if she was glad she visited, but all I got was a whispered yes and a nod." Caleb led the horse to its stall as he continued. "It's funny . . . she wasn't silent for one second on the trip over here. But going home, she just sat with her hands twisting in her lap and her eyes focused straight ahead."

Caleb took the tack and hung it up, while Travis tossed some oats in the trough. "So, what did Kathryn say?" Caleb asked.

"That her mother was afraid Jethro would find out she'd

visited. So, Kathryn invited her to come back next week. I guess Jethro and Wade are planning a trip to Ripley. Since that's more than a day's ride, her mother can come without worrying about being found out."

"Maybe that would be a good time to plan our trip to Quincy," Caleb said.

Travis turned to him. "I don't know. I'm not sure it's a good time to leave Kathryn. She's still recovering."

"But just think about it for a moment. Jethro and Wade will be out of town, and her mother would be visiting. This would be the perfect time. You wouldn't have to worry about Jethro and Wade causing problems, and I'm sure Mrs. James would love the chance to do some mothering."

"Yeah, but will Kathryn let her? She's still struggling with the fact that her mother knew what was happening and did nothing. I don't know if she'll allow her to fawn all over her."

"Well, think about it. You wanted to get the trusses for the addition in place before the first snow. It seems this would be the perfect opportunity to get the extra supplies we need."

Travis gave Caleb's idea some thought. He was looking forward to expanding the cabin. And it was because of the additional rooms he planned to add that they needed to get their lumber from Quincy instead of Milford.

"Travis?"

He turned to where Caleb was standing, a couple of buckets in his hands. "What?"

"I asked if you wanted one bucket or two?"

"Two."

"It was just a suggestion, Travis. If you don't feel

comfortable leaving Kathryn just yet, we can do it another time."

Caleb walked away with the buckets while Travis gave the idea some more thought.

59

A strange silence accompanied supper. Katie felt Travis' glances, and watched as Caleb pushed his food around on his plate.

"Okay, what do you want to know?" Katie put down her fork and dropped her hands into her lap.

Both men looked up, at each other, and then at her. "What do you mean?" Travis asked.

"I mean, the silence in here is worse than getting the third degree. If you want to know what happened between me and Mama, just ask."

Travis shrugged. "I figured if you wanted us to know, you'd say something."

"It was awkward . . . and hurtful. Mama acted like nothing had happened. She talked about Matilda, our home, the weather, the garden, anything but the past. She said it was exciting to think she had a granddaughter."

Katie glanced at Travis, then down at her lap.

"It upset me, and I yelled at her. I told her she had no right to consider Matilda her kin . . . or me for that matter. As far as I'm concerned, I don't have a mama. I told her she lost that right the first night Jethro came to my bed instead of hers."

Caleb looked everywhere but at her, and Travis' complexion turned an angry shade of red.

"I'm sorry. That was inappropriate."

"Don't be sorry," Caleb said. "You should never apologize for the things done *to you*," He waited for her to look at him, sincerity evident in his eyes.

"Thank you, Caleb."

Travis cleared his throat, obviously trying to swallow back his anger. "If you had such cross words with her, why would you want her to come back next week?"

"Because . . ." Katie had to think fast. "If I'm going to put my past behind me, I need to resolve things with Mama, and that wasn't going to happen with a quick conversation filled with apologies. I need to hear her side, but I wasn't ready to listen, at least not today. I told her if she came back next week, I would be civil and give her a chance to speak."

"I think that's a good idea, Kathryn. I'll gladly sit with you when—"

"No!" she said abruptly. "I mean . . . this is something I have to do by myself. I think if it's just Mama and me, we will be able to talk honestly."

"Are you sure you want to face all that on your own?"

"I'm sure."

Caleb looked at Travis and arched his brow.

"What?" she asked, feeling as if they were keeping something from her. "Is something wrong? Do you not want her here?" She looked at Travis.

"No. Nothing like that. It's just . . ."

The two men shared another glance.

"If nothing is wrong, why do you two keep looking at each other that way?"

Travis pushed his fork around on his plate. "I need to go to Quincy to pick up supplies for the addition. Caleb thought next week would be a good time. You could visit with your mother, and I'd feel better knowing Jethro and Wade are out of town."

Katie couldn't believe her luck. The hardest part of her plan was going to be getting rid of Travis and Caleb for the day. But they did it for her. "I think that's a good idea, Travis."

"I don't know." He leaned back in his chair. "I don't like the idea of being that far away. You're not completely healed yet. What if something happens while I'm gone?"

"Nothing is going to happen, Travis. The doctor said I'm fine. But I promise, if I feel peaked, I'll sit. If I get weary, I'll lay down. Besides, with Mama here, you wouldn't be leaving me alone."

Travis shook his head but stopped when she gently laid her hand on top of his and looked into his eyes.

"I need to do this Travis. I have to put the past behind me once and for all."

He looked at her, concern etched on his face.

"Under one condition," he finally said, sandwiching her hand between his. "Once you get things settled with your mother," his looked turned from concern to determination. "I get to settle things *my* way with Jethro, Wade, and the sheriff."

Her gut twisted, knowing if everything went as planned, he wouldn't get the chance. But if her plan failed, she was giving Travis permission to cross an extremely dangerous line. "Okay," she whispered, feeling like she was going to be sick.

"Okay?" Travis repeated, clearly surprised.

"As long as you involve the sheriff from the start. No going after them without the law on your side."

"I can do that," he said stoically.

Getting up from the table, Katie slipped her plate into the wash water, unable to look at Travis in light of what she was planning. Clutching the basin, she felt weak and queasy. She had promised Travis there would be no more lies, yet what she was planning went far beyond lying.

But it has to be done.

There was only one way to keep Travis and Matilda safe from Jethro.

And I'm the only person who can do it.

"You sure were quiet after supper tonight," Travis said once Katie crawled into bed and pulled the quilt up to her chest.

"Was I?"

"Yeah, you were." He rolled toward her, planting his elbow on his pillow, and bracing his head with his hand. "You okay?"

"Yeah," she mustered a smile. "I'm fine."

"Yes, ma'am, you are." He flashed her a handsome, beguiling smirk. "You might just be the finest thing in all of Danforth County."

She felt heat rise from her chest and bloom across her face, thankful their only light was what the moon was willing to share. "Have you always been this charming, Mr. Clark?"

He muffled a chuckle but couldn't hide his smile. "So, you find me charming? That's nice to hear."

She reached up and brushed her fingers across the shadow of whiskers on his cheek. Travis' expression turned serious as he captured her hand and pressed a sensuous kiss to her wrist. The look in his eyes was charged with passion. Possessiveness even. When he leaned in for a kiss, he used his whole body. His lips were firm and searching as his bare chest pressed gently against her flimsy nightgown.

Katie's heart nearly exploded with emotion. She wrapped her arm around his neck and pulled him even closer.

"Be careful of your ribs," he whispered against her lips.

But she didn't want to be careful. She didn't care about the pain. Katie wanted to stay in this moment forever. She wanted to feel Travis' love. Soak up every kiss, every touch, every caress.

God had granted the prayer of her heart.

To know the love of a man.

One incredible, amazing man.

A love strong enough to wipe away every ugly, tawdry detail of her life. She would cherish the next few days and nights with Travis and Matilda, because come Wednesday—one way or another—her life would change forever.

60

Clara James could not stop shaking.

She was terrified.

But Katie was counting on her to do what she had promised.

She jumped when the door swung wide, Jethro and Wade tromping into the house.

This is it, God. Give me the courage to do this for Katie.

Jethro and Wade lumbered to the table and plopped in their chairs. She placed the stew pot in the center of the table while Seth took his seat without making a sound. Setting down the basket of biscuits, she drew a deep measured breath, then slipped into her chair.

Supper was always a noisy affair, even if there wasn't much talking. Jethro and Wade ate their meal with unbridled gusto, accompanied by loud moans and smacking lips.

Just listening to them, Clara lost what little appetite she had.

Seth, on the other hand, was always quiet. Well mannered. Because Katie taught him to be. They had sat on the same side of the table since Seth was just a toddler. Katie would correct him whenever his eating habits were inappropriate. All she had to do is look at him sideways or squeeze his knee under the table, for him to know his behavior was unsuitable. Luckily, it instilled good habits in Seth. Because even now, though Katie was gone, his manners remained intact.

As the meal dwindled, Clara's nerves began to falter. If she didn't handle this right, things could go horribly wrong. She didn't worry for herself, but Katie and her family would be in danger, and so would Seth.

But you have to do this! Clara's conscience insisted. *This is your only way to make amends for all the years you turned your back on Katie's plight.*

Seeing that Seth was done, Clara cleared her throat. "Seth, why don't you run along and do your evening chores. I have a matter I need to discuss with your pa and brother."

He set his fork down and took a final swig of milk. "Okay, but if I get them all done real quick like, can I work some more on my squirrel traps?"

"Sure," Clara said with a smile.

"But," Jethro chimed in, his tone harsh. "If you go messin' with them traps, and your chores aren't done right, I'll be takin' a switch to your backside, you hear?"

"Yes, sir." Seth answered with fear in his voice.

Clara watched as he took his bowl and cup and placed them on the counter, then disappeared out the door. When she turned back to the table, Jethro and Wade were staring at her.

"What's this all about?" Jethro asked gruffly.

Clara fiddled with her spoon handle and took a deep breath. "I went to see Katie today."

"Don't you mean Kathryn," Wade said with a sneer and a cackle.

Clara looked at him, seeing Jethro's evil in his eyes. *How did I not know? How did I not see that he was just like his pa?*

"She will always be Katie to me," Clara answered Wade.

"Yeah . . . well, she'll always be mute and stupid to me," he laughed.

"Shut up boy," Jethro barked, then turned to her. "What'd you go see her for?"

"Because she was ailing and sent for me."

"Don't surprise me none," Jethro huffed as he swallowed a spoonful of gravy. "The girl was always weak. But why is she sendin' for you? She's Travis' problem now."

"She had a miscarriage, Jethro."

He laughed sardonically. "She really *is* good for nothin', ain't she? Can't even do the one thing women are meant for."

"It's more than that, Jethro."

"It always is with her, ain't it? What? Let me guess. Travis wants to go back on our deal. Now that he knows Katie really is a half-wit, and can't even carry his seed, he wants to renege. Well, that ain't happenin'. He can send Katie back if he wants, but he ain't gettin' his land back. A deal is a deal."

Clara cleared her throat. "That's not the problem, Jethro. The fact of the matter is the baby she was carryin' . . . well . . . it wasn't Travis'."

Both Jethro and Wade snapped their heads up and looked at her with guilty eyes. She stared at Wade for a labored moment, then turned to Jethro.

"You see, Travis and Katie haven't consummated their marriage yet. He was serious when he said he was just lookin' for a mama for Matilda. So, there's no way the baby could be his." Clara turned and looked at Wade. "Do you have something to tell us, son?"

He dropped his spoon and coughed out a mouthful of stew. "What are you talkin' about?" he said as he ran the sleeve of his shirt across his gravy-splattered face.

"Why didn't you tell us you went to visit Katie the other day?" Clara asked.

"What?!" Jethro hollered as he shoved his chair out with the back of his knees and lunged toward Wade. He grabbed his son by the collar and twisted tight. "What is your mama talkin' 'bout, boy?"

Wade grappled with Jethro's hands. "It's not what you think."

Jethro twisted harder. "And what is it I'm thinkin'?"

"She seduced me, Pa," Wade hollered. "*Katie* seduced *me.*"

Jethro yanked him up out of his chair and slammed him against the kitchen wall. "I don't believe you, boy." Pulling back his fist, he planted it in Wade's gut.

Wade doubled over, coughing and gasping, but when he came to stand up right again, his demeanor had changed.

Clara said a quick prayer. Her entire plan hinged on Wade being too fearful of his pa to say anything, at least anything in front of her, but the look in Wade's eyes told her something different.

"I wasn't the only one, *Pa.*" Wade glared at Jethro.

It was the way he said '*Pa*' that chilled Clara. She watched as a silent conversation transpired between father and son.

"Just let me go and I'll explain."

Jethro waited a beat, slammed Wade against the wall one more time, then released him. "Sit down and explain, but I'm warnin' you, boy," Jethro shook an angry finger in his face. "You be careful what you say. You're in enough trouble as it is. You understand me?"

Wade nodded at his pa's veiled warning.

Jethro took a slow step back.

"I admit it. I had . . ." Wade looked from Jethro to Clara, then mumbled under his breath, "I had relations with Katie."

Clara gasped.

She was worried she wouldn't be able to pull off this charade but listening and watching as Jethro and Wade sparred was enough to make her stomach twist.

Swallowing back her emotions, Clara chanced a look at Jethro and saw the barely contained rage tensing his body. He really hadn't known what Wade was doing. And now that he did, he looked like he was ready to kill his own son.

"She seduced me, Pa. I swear. She seduced me to keep me quiet, so I wouldn't tell you she was beddin' someone else."

"And who is this someone else?" Clara asked with tear-filled eyes.

Wade turned to Jethro but didn't say a word.

"Your mama asked you a question, *boy.* Are you gonna answer her?"

Clara watched as the fury in Jethro intensified. His face was beet red, his knuckles white as he clenched his hands together. His jaw clamped tight. She held her breath, knowing if Jethro and Wade came to blows, there would be nothing she could do.

Wade turned to Clara, even though he flicked a glance at Jethro over his shoulder. "I don't know. I never saw him."

Okay. Step one, done.

Clara had gotten Wade to admit to Jethro he had relations with Katie, even if he'd lied about another man.

Now to let them know Katie is going to be all by herself on Wednesday.

"No wonder Travis is leaving for a few days." Clara blurted

out as she wiped tears from her cheeks.

Jethro snapped around and looked at her. "What did you say?"

"I . . . I said Travis is leaving for Quincy on Wednesday. He and his friend are going for supplies. Well, that's the excuse he gave, but I know it's because he's upset with Katie and doesn't trust her."

"You mean because he found out his wife's a whore?"

Clara bit back her retort. She wanted to lash out at Jethro, to smack the horrid comment from his filthy lips. But she couldn't. She had to stick to the plan.

I have to do this for Katie.

"Travis is upset because he found out Wade was at the house."

Jethro turned to Wade. "Explain yourself, *son*. What were you doin' there?"

"Ah . . . ah, I didn't go to see Katie; I went to see Travis. I was gonna tell him what she'd done. I figured he was a decent enough man and should know what kind of woman he married."

Jethro crossed his arms against his chest, the tapping of his boot the only sound in the room. "Well, there you go, Clara, you have your answer. The boy was there to see Travis."

"But he's not—"

"Woman!" Jethro shouted. "You got your answer, now leave it be! The way I see it, you best talk to that daughter of yours. She's the problem here, not my boy. I suggest you make good of your time when you go see that . . . that Jezebel. We wouldn't want her spreadin' any nasty rumors about our family, now, would we?"

———■ ● ■———

Wade could not get out of the house fast enough. He sauntered around the barn, hands on his head, trying to come up with a plan.

He had to leave.

He didn't know where he'd go, but he couldn't stay here.

Now that Pa knew he'd been with Katie, *and* knew his ugly secret as well, he had to get out of there.

And Fast.

With a plan forming in his mind, Wade hurried toward the door, but stopped when Pa filled the doorway.

"Going somewhere, son?" Pa said as he slowly stepped toward him.

"I . . . I was just going to check on Seth."

"But we need to talk, boy. We have a bit of a problem to discuss. Wouldn't you agree?"

For every step Pa made toward him, Wade took a slow step back.

"I'm disappointed in you, boy. I never took you for stupid." Pa grabbed a shovel resting against one of the stalls and bounced it against the palm of his hand. "But what you done, with your sister, thinkin' no one would find out, well . . . that was just plain foolishness."

"Oh really!" Wade said, his fear turning into anger. "How does that saying go? Like father, like so—"

Pa swung the shovel, connecting with Wade's jaw, sending him to the ground.

Lying face down on the dirt floor, the acrid taste of blood in his mouth, Wade rolled to his back and saw Pa with the shovel raised high overhead. He brought it down so quick, Wade barely had time to roll to his left. The shovel thudded on the dirt floor so near to his head, he heard the vibration of the metal ringing in his ear.

Wade scrambled to his knees as Pa pulled back the shovel again, and with a thundering roar, swung at Wade, connecting with his ribs, knocking him flat on his back.

Throwing down the shovel, Pa straddled him, grabbed his collar, and shook him violently. "You stupid boy! What did you think you were doing? Katie wasn't yours. She was mine!"

"Yours?" Wade sneered, as he turned his head and spit blood. "She was supposed to be your daughter, not your woman. You already had a woman in your bed, but one wasn't enough for you, was it?"

"Why you son-of-a . . ."

Pa pulled back his balled-up fist.

"Go ahead! Hit me again!" Wade yelled. "Hit me all you want! But it ain't gonna change nothin'. I know you've been forcing yourself on Katie for years, and I ain't got no reason to keep that information to myself anymore. So, if you're gonna shut me up, you better do a real good job of it. Otherwise, I'm going to the sheriff."

Pa looked down at him, veins popping out on his neck and forehead, his face purple with rage. Wade braced himself for a final blow.

But it never came.

Pa let go of his shirt, got to his feet, and roared like a wounded bear. Wade didn't move, he just lay there. Then Pa looked at him, pure evil reflected in his eyes. "Get up!"

Slowly, Wade got to his feet, fighting dizziness and pain. He leaned on a nearby post, clutching his side, not trusting his legs to hold him.

When Pa came at him from across the barn, Wade braced himself—sure he was going to do him in—but Pa just darted his finger in his face. "There's no way I'm lettin' that . . . that stupid girl come between me and my boy. She's the problem here. So . . . you and me are gonna pay Mrs. Clark a little visit on Wednesday. And when we're done, all this bad blood will be behind us. You hear what I'm sayin'?"

Wade spit out another stream of blood. "Yes, sir."

61

It was Tuesday night, and Katie was a bundle of nerves. She had no way of knowing if Mama had done what she promised she would. But if she had, Katie knew what she needed to do, even if it meant sacrificing a life with Travis and Matilda.

She watched as Travis went about his nightly routine, then dimmed the light and climbed into bed. When she rolled toward him, he draped his arm around her shoulders. She loved the way she fit in the crook of his arm. It made her feel truly safe, a feeling she wished could go on forever.

Timidly, she rested her hand atop his bare chest and stroked at the dusting of hair that covered his upper body. She felt the rhythmic beating of his heart increase at her ministrations, and it made her smile.

"Are you sure you're going to be okay tomorrow?" he asked as he gently caressed her arm.

"You don't have to worry; I'll be fine." She pressed against his chest, lifting up so she could look into his eyes. "I love you, Travis, you know that don't you? I mean, no matter what happens in life, even if something pulls us apart, you know I love you and would do anything for you and Matilda, right?"

"Of course I do." He looked at her with knitted brows. "But why would you say such a thing? I'm not going to let anything pull us apart."

"I just wanted to make sure you knew is all."

Concern still creased his brow. "Are you sure nothing is wrong? Because if there is, I don't have to go tomorrow. I can stay home."

"No. I'll be fine. It's just that . . . well . . . this is the first time you'll be gone overnight since we've been married, and I want to make sure you know how I feel, that's all."

She leaned in close, allowing their lips to touch. Travis responded immediately, kissing her with unrestrained fervor. He pressed his hand to the back of her head, not allowing the contact between them to end. His kisses became passionate and searching, and she followed in suit. When she finally pulled back enough to allow herself room to breathe, she looked into Travis' eyes. "You know . . . it's been more than a week since the doctor was here."

"I know. Why?" Suddenly, Travis scooted back against the headboard and sat up. "Is something wrong? Are you feeling poorly again? Is that what this talk is all about?"

"No. Nothing is wrong. I was just thinking about the restrictions the doctor gave me . . . us."

"Well, there was only one," he said with a smirk.

"I know. But like I said, it's been more than a week. So . . ." She could feel her cheeks heat up, and the look on Travis' face made her blush even more.

"Are . . . are you sure? I don't want to rush you or make any demands of you. Especially if you're not read—"

She pressed her finger against his lips, stopping him from speaking. "You're not rushing me, Travis. I just think I'd like to know how it feels to be Mrs. Travis Clark . . . if that's all right with you?"

He grinned, and Katie was pretty sure he was blushing.

"Yes, ma'am," Travis said, swagger in his tone, looking more handsome than ever. "I'm happy to oblige."

Katie sat in the rocker, Matilda on her lap. She had fallen right back to sleep after her bottle, but Katie couldn't bring herself to put her down.

Not just yet.

She wanted to stretch out this moment for as long as she could.

Staring into Matilda's tiny angelic face, Katie studied her heart-shaped lips, her feather-soft eyelashes, and her rosy cheeks. Everything about her, Katie wanted to commit to memory.

Then she looked at Travis as he slept, tears immediately flooding her eyes.

Their night together had not been without its awkward moments, but Travis had been so patient . . . so loving. He whispered to her throughout their exploration, assuring her there was no right or wrong way. Though he was experienced, she could tell he was still nervous.

Closing her eyes, she remembered what he had whispered to her. "We'll have the rest of our lives to share our love with each other."

If only that were true.

After taking a few more minutes to bask in the memory, she nestled Matilda in her cradle and slipped back into bed. Travis stirred, wrapping his arms around her.

"You're shaking," he said in a groggy whisper as he pulled her closer.

"I just got a little chilled. Go back to sleep," she said quietly. "You have a busy day ahead of you tomorrow."

It didn't take long before Katie heard Travis' slow even breaths of slumber. She clenched her eyes shut and pulled the quilt up over her mouth, trying to silence her cries.

I love them, God. That's the only reason I'm doing what needs to be done. Please help Travis understand. I know justice is not the same as vengeance, and if that is how the courts rule it, so be it. I cannot live any longer with the thought of Matilda getting hurt, or Travis doing something reckless. This is the way it has to be.

Even if it's not Your way.

62

"Now, you're sure you know how to use a shotgun? Just in case you have any trouble with predators while I'm gone."

"Yes, Travis. I've used one before. Stop worrying."

It was as if he had a sense that something ominous was going to happen while he was gone, so Katie did what she could to assure him and not let her own nervousness show.

"We're leaving Tara here, just in case there's an emergency, and you need to ride to town." Tara was Caleb's horse. A beautiful bay mare that stood at least seventeen hands high. Katie had never ridden a horse so tall, but hopefully she wouldn't need to.

"I've brought in plenty of water. It should hold you until I get back. And if you run out of eggs, be careful of Henrietta. She likes to peck. And I know you like working in the garden, but I would prefer you stay inside most of the time and keep a look out while we're gone. You have plenty of kero—"

"Travis!" Katie didn't mean to snap; he was just making her so nervous.

"We've gone over everything at least a dozen times. Don't worry," she smiled and softened her tone. "I know what I need to do."

The three of them walked outside, the rising sun painting the sky with streaks of amber and gold. Caleb already sat on the buckboard, reins between his fingers, waiting while Travis said his goodbyes.

Katie held Matilda against her chest as Travis wrapped them both in a hug. His embrace said so much, it was all Katie could do not to cry when he pressed a kiss to the top of her head, then to Matilda's. He lingered a minute longer, before taking a step back. She could see the apprehension in his eyes.

"My goal is to be home Thursday by dusk, but don't wait supper. We'll have plenty of supplies with us to eat on the way. I have your list." He pulled a piece a paper from his chest pocket. "Are you sure there's nothing else you need?"

"Just for you to be safe . . . and to know how much I love you."

Travis walked toward the wagon but didn't get far before he spun back around, closed the distance between them, framed her face with his strong, calloused hands, and kissed her soundly.

Then, Katie watched as the wagon disappeared into the horizon, tears running down her face.

Please, God, don't let that be goodbye.

She allowed herself a few minutes, then cleared her throat of emotion, stood up straight, and took a deep breath.

It was time to put her plan into motion.

Knowing the element of surprise would work to her advantage, she intended to wait for Jethro and Wade in the barn. So, the first thing she had to do is get everything Matilda might need and store it in the hayloft.

With sweat trickling down her back, her heart beating a

thousand times a minute, and every limb of her body quivering, Katie stopped and took a breath.

She didn't know if she should attribute her light-headedness to exhaustion or the terror racing through her veins. All she knew was there was no turning back now.

The last trip up the ladder, Katie carefully traversed each rung—one by one—while clutching Matilda against her chest. Once at the top, she laid her in the blanket nest she'd created between hay bales, and watched as Matilda kicked and fisted the air, mesmerized by the wildflowers Katie had strung from the rafters. "I'm glad you like it. We might be here for a while."

Katie checked and double checked everything.

Then waited.

———— • ————

Clara watched as Jethro and Wade rode out of the yard. Jethro waited till this morning to tell her he and Wade would be gone for the day. Hunting he said, with a snide chuckle, his words chilling her to the bone.

"You weren't thinkin' of going anywhere, were ya?" Jethro had asked her over breakfast.

"Me? No." She swallowed deep.

Of course, if things didn't go as Katie planned, Jethro would know she lied. But Clara couldn't worry about that right now. She had things to do.

With Seth already on his way to school, she waited until Jethro and Wade were out of sight, then rushed to the backside of the barn.

Gasping, she just stood there, looking at the buckboard

and the broken wheel propped against its side.

Oh no. No! No! No!

How am I going to ride for the sheriff without a wagon?

It was part of Katie's plan. Though Clara didn't know all the details, it was her responsibility to let Jethro and Wade know Katie would be alone on Wednesday. If they took the bait, Clara was to ride to town, tell the sheriff what she knew, and get him to Travis' place as fast as possible.

Running inside the barn, Clara grabbed a bridle from the tack room and raced to Harley—one of their plow horses.

"Okay, boy. It's just you and me," she said as she looped the bridle over his head and threaded his ears through the leather straps. "I haven't done this in a long time, so I'm countin' on you to get me to town."

After tossing the reins over Harley's head, she quickly put the blanket in place, but the saddle was quite another thing. It was so big and bulky, it almost landed on top of her the first time she tried heaving it into place. But once she got her balance and took a deep breath, she gave it another try. When the saddle landed awkwardly on Harley's back, he neighed his disapproval.

"Sorry, boy. I'm a little rusty."

Clara thought for a second, realizing she hadn't been on a horse since before Katie was born. Once she had realized she was with child, she stopped riding.

And now I need to ride to save that child's life.

After tightening the cinch strap and adjusting the stirrups, she looked around for something to give her a boost. Using a milking pail, she turned it over, stepped on it, and vaulted herself onto Harley's back.

Harley bobbed his head and pulled on the reins while she

seated herself. Though she wished the stirrups were a bit shorter, she didn't have time to adjust them. Katie was counting on her, and she couldn't let her down.

With a silent prayer, and a click of her tongue, she steered Harley through the barn doors and headed for town.

The second they hit the open road, Clara felt the spirit and power that churned inside Harley. Though she was careful to keep a tight hold on the reins, his girth made it difficult for her to maintain her balance. She squeezed her knees as tight as she could but couldn't seem to get the hold she needed, and with her toes barely in the stirrups, Clara held onto the saddle horn for dear life.

"Come on, Harley, we can do this. I know we can."

Clara tried to stay positive, but it seemed like every time they found a good rhythm, Harley would stumble over a rut or a branch, throwing her off balance, causing her to accidently yank on the reins.

Not appreciating their little tug-of-wars, Harley would retaliate by dipping his head low or shaking it from side to side."

"I'm sorry, boy, I'm doing the best I can."

Please, God, don't let me fail Katie.

———— • ————

Katie heard something.

She was sure of it.

Closing her eyes, she strained to listen. It was the unmistakable sound of approaching horses. She looked at Matilda, sound asleep, then squeezed her eyes shut.

Okay, God. If You're really there, and You care for Your

children like You say, here's Your chance to prove it. I don't care what happens to me, but please take care of Matilda and Travis. If I don't make it through this, help him understand why I did what I did.

She held the shotgun to her shoulder and positioned herself in the far corner of the loft. Having a clear view of the large double doors, she planned to shoot the first person who stepped inside.

———— • ————

Clara reached the halfway point between home and town where the dirt road veered around Terrence Barton's property, taking them about a mile east out of the way.

She stopped, debating what she should do.

Even though Terrence told them they could cut across his land anytime they wanted to, she'd never gone that way, because the path wasn't big enough for a wagon.

What if I get lost or turned around?

She looked at the path clearly marked by the trampled down grass.

What if it passes too close to Terrence's house and he questions why I am in such a hurry?

She wasn't afraid of Terrence. He was a kind man. A widower. He came to the house on occasion to offer them vegetables from his garden. And when Seth was old enough, Terrence invited him over to fish in the creek that ran through his property. Clara let Seth accept his offers, but only on days when Jethro was busy or out of town.

Seth understood.

He learned at an early age what angered his pa. And

spending time with Terrence was one of them.

Clara looked back and forth between the two paths, time ticking away. Harley gave the reins a tug and took a few steps toward Terrence's property.

"Okay, boy, the shortcut it is."

As soon as they turned toward the narrow path, Harley's spiritedness came out in full force. Clara tried to hold him back, but he paid her no mind. He knew where he was going and wanted to be the one in control.

She trusted Harley, and since she needed to get to town as quick as possible, she decided to give him his head.

Hunkering down in the saddle, Clara white-knuckled the horn, her head nearly lying on Harley's withers, and let the horse lead the way.

All was going well until the moment Clara realized they were airborne. The only thing she had time to process was the gurgling sound of a creek, before she tumbled to the ground and her world faded to black.

63

"We'll leave the horses over there." Pa pointed to an outcropping of trees closer to Travis' cabin.

Wade rode up beside him and dismounted slowly, cradling his sore ribs. He'd done his best to hide his pain from Pa, but when he stumbled over an exposed tree root, he cursed out loud.

"Be quiet, you idiot," Pa groused under his breath. "I don't want her to hear us comin'."

"But I still don't understand," Wade whispered. "Katie must've told Travis about you . . . about me. How do you think you're gonna get away with this without him comin' after you?"

Pa shoved him against the tree, jabbing a finger in his chest. Wade wanted to puke but didn't dare show weakness.

"Because I'm smarter than Travis," Pa spit in his face. "I'll just say Katie's crazy, that we've had problems with her for years. Lying, making up wild stories, disappearing for days on end. I'll tell him I caught her more than once with men twice her age."

"But what if he don't believe you and decides to ask Ma?"

Pa swirled tobacco around in his mouth then spit a wad. "I'll tell him that I kept it from Clara because she's too weak and frail to handle such matters."

"And you think Travis will believe you over Katie?"

319

His pa just sneered. "It don't matter. Once she's dead, it will be my word against hers."

"Dead!" Wade gasped. "You're gonna kill Katie?"

"What did you think we were doin', havin' a tea party?"

"I just figured you'd threaten her. Get her to be—"

"No! Katie had her chance to keep her mouth shut, and she didn't. I warned her, and she didn't listen. It's time for her to go."

Wade had done some awful things, hurting Katie being the worst of them. But he wasn't a killer. And he certainly didn't want to hang for murder. "But you will be Travis' number one suspect."

"Not when he reads the note she leaves behind."

Wade looked at him, knowing if he didn't do what his pa said, he would be the next to die.

Better her than me.

As they slowly approached the house, Pa stopped and turned to him. "Okay, you go to the backdoor; I'll get the front. Make sure you don't hurt that brat of Travis'. He knows Katie would never hurt the baby, even if she was crazy enough to kill herself. For my plan to work, the kid has got to be okay."

Wade limped around the back of the cabin and waited. When he heard the front door slam open, he gave his a shove and hurried inside. Pa stood in the middle of the cabin.

But it was empty.

"So where do you think she is?" Wade asked.

"I don't know, but she's here somewhere. Go check the creek. I'll check the barn."

———— • ————

Katie heard the groan of the barn door's rusty hinges and scooted further back against the wall. She could still see the door from where she sat in the loft, and would know the minute someone walked in. Holding the shotgun with shaky hands, she waited.

And then she saw him.

With one eye closed and the stock of the gun against her cheek, she followed Jethro's every step, the barrel pointed at his head.

What are you waiting for?

Just do it.

Her inner hatred taunted her. She had Jethro in her sights, right where she wanted him. Just like she planned. This was the moment she'd been waiting for, plotted out. But now that it was here . . . she couldn't do it.

She couldn't kill another person.

No matter how vile or wretched that person was.

But what do I do now?

Jethro's here; he took the bait. Just like she knew he would. He'd come because he knew she'd be alone.

It's only a matter of time before he finds us.

Once again, Jethro held all the power.

64

Clara felt something over her left eye. When she tried to raise her hand to touch it, fire shot up her arm. She cried out as her mind raced for an explanation for the pain.

Then she remembered falling from Harley.

And the reason she was riding him in the first place.

"Oh no! Katie!" she gasped as she tried to get to her feet, but her body protested, causing her to crumble.

"Help me, Lord. I have to get help for Katie."

She took a minute to gather her strength. Then, with gritted teeth, she held her right arm to her chest and rolled to her knees. Her head swam, and her stomach tightened. She closed her eyes, taking deep breaths to push back the nausea.

How long have I been here?

Am I too late?

She looked at the cloud-filled sky, trying to judge the position of the sun.

Please, Lord, don't let me be too late.

She drew on strength she didn't have, but soon was on her feet. Harley was grazing under a nearby tree and perked up when he saw her move.

"Come here, boy," she said as calmly as she could, and was shocked when the normally ornery Harley leisurely ambled to her side. "That's a good boy."

Slowly, she gathered up the reins, then leaned against Harley for balance. Sizing up the monumental task in front of her, she groaned, "How will I ever get up into the saddle?"

With tears in her eyes, she lowered her head in defeat. Pressing her forehead against Harley's shoulder, she cried, "I need a miracle, Lord. Katie's life depends on it."

"Clara?"

She turned to see Terrence Barton on his Bay Mare trotting her way.

"Clara, what are you doing out here?"

Shocked and feeling woozy, she wasn't sure what to say.

Terrence dismounted and rushed toward her. "Clara, your head?"

She reached up to touch the knot over her eye and winced.

"And your arm."

She looked at her right shoulder. Her sleeve was torn, and blood stained the tattered material.

"I took a bit of a spill. I guess I'm not as agile as I use to be."

He shook his head and frowned. "Is that all?"

She looked at him, puzzled. "Yes. Harley jumped the creek, and I wasn't ready. It's just a bump and a scrape."

"Clara . . . you can tell me the truth. You don't have to be afraid."

"Terrence, I . . . I don't know what you mean."

"Was it Jethro?"

She didn't dare look at him.

"Clara, I've suspected Jethro of being heavy handed for some time now. Seth has said some things. I wasn't prying mind you; I was just concerned. If Jethro did this to you—"

"I fell, Terrence; that's all."

He ducked his head sheepishly. "I'm sorry . . . I didn't mean to—"

"No. It's okay. I'm fine." She looked away, unable to meet his eyes. "But I still need to get to town. If you could just give me a leg up, I'll be on my way."

"Why are you riding? Where is your wagon?"

"The wheel was split. I had no choice but to ride."

"Where's Jethro?"

She wasn't sure what to say, and the pain behind her eyes made it difficult to think. "He . . . he and Wade rode out early this morning."

"Well, you shouldn't be riding in your condition. You need to see the doctor. Let me hitch up my wagon and drive you into town. You can get checked out by the doc, and then I'll take you to the mercantile to get whatever it is you need."

She didn't know what to do. But every second she spent talking with Terrence meant another second Katie was on her own . . . with Jethro and Wade. The very thought of it made her vision blur, and her knees go weak.

"Clara!" Terrence caught her before she crumbled.

"I'm all right." Cradling her injured arm against her stomach, she took a step back from him.

"You're not all right. You're dizzy, and by the way you're coddling that arm, I would venture to say it's more than just a scratch. Come on, Clara, it will only take me a few minutes to get my wagon."

"Please, Terrence, I appreciate your concern, really I do." She forced confidence into her voice and smiled. "But you know as well as I do, if we show up in town together people will talk."

"So, we'll explain what happened."

"That won't silence the gossipers."

He looked truly perplexed. "Clara, I just want to help."

"Then give me a leg up and let me be on my way."

He looked at her with worry and shook his head in obvious disapproval. "I think this is a mistake, but I'll help you."

With Terrence's brawn, it took little effort for him to lift her up and over Harley's back. Clara bit her lip to keep from crying out against the pain in her arm while Terrence gathered up the reins. He handed them to her but didn't release his hold.

"What is so urgent that you would put yourself through such pain just to get to town?"

"It's very important." She looked him straight in the eye. "I promised Katie I would do this for her."

65

Katie didn't know what to do.

She quietly pressed herself against the wall of the loft and lowered the gun to her side.

"She ain't anywhere near the creek," Wade said, walking through the big barn door.

"Well, she's gotta be somewhere," Jethro snapped, then slammed shut the tack room door with a string of curses.

Out of the corner of Katie's eye, she saw Matilda's tiny body flinch, startled awake by the bang of the door. But before she could let out a cry, Katie leaned over and slipped her knuckle into Matilda's mouth. Thankfully, it worked.

Closing her eyes, she pleaded. *Please God, make them go away.*

"Maybe she decided to go with Travis after all," Wade said.

"No. Not if he was going to Quincy. The trip is hard enough with a wagon. There's no way Travis would take Katie and that yapping baby of his. No. She's here somewhere."

"Maybe she went to town?"

"Are you really that stupid, boy?" Jethro shouted then spit a wad of chew. "You think Katie would just up and walk to town carrying that baby for no good reason?"

"Maybe the kid got sick and needed to see the doctor."

Please God, make Jethro listen to Wade. If only this once.

"Then she would've taken that horse there. Katie might be stupid, but she's not senseless enough to walk when she could ride."

Katie's heart sunk; her prayer immediately dashed.

"She's around here somewhere. She might've gone for a walk further downstream, but she'll come home for dinner." Jethro turned and walked toward the barn doors.

"Let's go move the horses further south where they can't be seen. We'll just wait Katie out inside the cabin. We've got all day. She'll come home eventually. And when she does, we'll be ready for her."

———— • ————

Clara opened her eyes and saw the church steeple up ahead. *Thank you, Jesus.*

"Just a little bit further, Harley, we're almost there."

Drenched in perspiration, her dress sticking to her body, and her hair pressed against her forehead and neck, Clara winced with every step. The pain in her shoulder and head had caused her to blackout a few times, but with her goal in sight, she willed her eyes to stay open.

Slumped in the saddle, barely holding onto the reins, Clara wanted to lead Harley to the sheriff's office on the main street of town.

But it was no use.

With her strength gone, Harley headed to the place he knew best. The livery on the outskirts of town.

Clara could feel herself fading, the road ahead of her rolling like the wheat fields in spring.

Just a little further. I can do this. Please God, help me do this.

With all the energy she could muster, she held onto the saddle horn as Harley approached the livery. Her vision was blurry, but she made out several silhouettes, then heard garbled voices and rushing footsteps.

"Clara!"

Thank you, God; I made it.

Knowing Hank and Monty would help her, she tried to say something, but her words were a garbled mess.

When strong arms enveloped her and pulled her from the saddle, she tried again.

"Sheriff . . . I need the sheriff," she muttered, her eyes closed, consciousness slipping away.

"Clara . . . Clara can you hear me?"

She strained to open her eyes, shocked.

"Travis?"

She closed her eyes, thinking she was seeing things. But when she opened them again, Travis was still there. "You're supposed to be gone."

"Clara, what happened? I thought you were going to be with Kathryn today?"

"Katie . . . plan . . . help."

"Yes, you were going to help Kathryn today. What happened?"

"She . . . she needs help."

66

Travis felt his blood run cold.

"What's wrong with Kathryn? What kind of help?" he asked Clara as she lay limp in his arms, giving him no response. Jostling her slightly, he tried again. "Clara . . . Clara!"

When her eyes opened, she looked at him, panic in her stare. "Jethro and Wade . . . headed to your place," she said, then burst into tears, crying hysterically.

"Clara," he shook her harder, desperate to know what was going on.

She clutched her arm and cried out like a wounded animal. "Travis . . . you've got to go . . . you need to . . . help Katie. She plans to kill them."

It took Travis a second to grasp what Clara said, then started barking orders.

"Monty, stay with Clara. Hank, fetch the doctor. Once Clara's stable, have him get to my place. I have a feeling we're going to need him. Caleb, find the sheriff and get him there as fast as you can."

Travis pulled himself up onto Harley's back while Caleb ran to the wagon. When he returned, he tossed him the lever-action Winchester and warned, "Be careful, Travis. It's going to be two against one."

"But they don't know I'm coming. I'm hoping that works to my advantage." Travis spun Harley around. "Come on, boy, show me what you got."

With Harley traveling at top speed, Travis tried to come to grips with what Clara had said. He didn't want to believe it. He did *not* want to believe that Kathryn had set this whole thing up.

But everything pointed to just that.

The only reason he decided to go to Quincy was because she told him Jethro and Wade would be out of town. Kathryn convinced him that she would be okay on her own, and that her mother would come stay with her while he was gone.

Travis cursed under his breath, realizing it all had been an elaborate plan so she could lure Jethro and Wade to the ranch and kill them.

But why?

It didn't make any sense.

Kathryn was the one who wanted to put the abuse behind her, to move on, to let Jethro and Wade get away with all they had done.

He was the one who wanted justice.

He was the one who wanted to see Jethro and Wade pay and was willing to go to whatever lengths it took . . .

"God, no!" he gasped, realization finally sinking in.

This is my fault. Kathryn did this to protect me.

His heart seized. *What have I done?*

Travis heeled Harley hard, demanding every ounce of speed he had in him.

Let me be in time, God. Please don't let me be too late.

67

Katie waited in the barn for what felt like an eternity.

Where is the sheriff?

Mama was supposed to ride to town, tell the sheriff what had been going on for years, and let him know she was afraid Katie was in danger. He would then arrive at Travis' place and find Jethro and Wade dead. Katie would explain that she had no choice, that Jethro said he was going to kill her and Matilda, so she acted in self-defense.

But something was wrong.

The sheriff should have been here by now.

Feeling hope dwindling, Katie swiped at her tears, angry she had trusted Mama with something so important. This was her chance to make things right, to prove she was sorry for the wrong Katie had suffered over the years. but just like all those nights before, Mama ignored Katie's need for help.

Having wasted enough time on the sheriff—who obviously wasn't coming—Katie realized she had to come up with another plan. They needed to move before Jethro decided to take another look around.

After considering all her options, she decided her best chance of escape would be to take Matilda and head north on foot.

It was the only way.

If she tried riding away on Tara, she ran the risk of Jethro and Wade seeing her. And there was no way she would be able to outride them, not with Matilda in her arms. Walking was her only chance, but she couldn't use the normal route. All it would take is one glance from the cabin window, and they were sure to spot her.

No . . . her only hope for escape was to head north, away from the cabin, away from Jethro and Wade's view. Then, when she was sure to be out of sight, she would double back to town and hope Jethro and Wade didn't go looking for her.

She looked down at Matilda, momentarily overwhelmed with emotion. *I'll keep you safe, little miss. I promise.*

Then she looked up. *Please, God. Don't let me break my promise.*

Fashioning a sling from Matilda's blanket, Katie held the child snug against her chest. She stuffed the few things she would need for the trip into a burlap sack and tossed it down from the barn loft. Then, she painstakingly descended the ladder—one rung at a time—careful not to smother Matilda while holding the shotgun at the same time.

Standing just inside the barn door, she pressed her ear against it, to see if she could hear anything. She assumed Jethro and Wade were still in the cabin, but she couldn't take any chances.

Katie's body shook from head to toe as she slowly pushed the door open.

Protect us, Lord. I don't care what happens to me, just let me get Matilda to safety.

With a deep breath, she quickly walked toward the field, away from the cabin.

Travis took cover behind a rocky knoll, so he could assess the situation. He saw Jethro and Wade's horses tied to a tree, confirming his worse fears.

They were there.

Just like Clara said they would be.

From where he was hunkered down, Travis could see through the cabin window the silhouette of a man pacing back and forth. But if Jethro or Wade was inside the cabin, where was Kathryn and Matilda?

Travis didn't know what to think or do. Kathryn had to be somewhere. She was the one who orchestrated this whole thing. But if it was a trap for Jethro and Wade, where was she?

No sooner had he asked the question, did he see Kathryn emerge from the barn.

His heart stopped for a second before he breathed out a praise.

Thank you, God. She's alive.

He watched as she pressed her back against the door, and with a closer look, he saw the bundled tied to her chest. *Matilda.* Travis choked back a sob as Kathryn moved quickly across the yard, her head swiveling from side to side.

Is she trying to get away?

But it didn't make sense. If what Clara said was true, Kathryn would be going *after* Jethro and Wade, not hurrying in the other direction.

Travis didn't know what was going on, and he didn't care. All that mattered was Kathryn and Matilda getting as far from Jethro and Wade as possible, because when the sheriff showed up, there was sure to be gunfire.

Pulling his timepiece from his pocket, he wondered how long it would take for Caleb and Sheriff Chambers to catch up with him, if Caleb was able to locate him at all.

But as long as Kathryn and Matilda got away, he didn't care. He would wait until he had reinforcements before going after Jethro and Wade.

Keeping his eyes on Kathryn, Travis watched as she stumbled, then righted herself. She quickly looked around before taking another step.

You've got it, sweetheart. Just keep going.

No sooner had he thought she was in the clear, he heard the lever action of a shotgun. He turned and watched as Jethro step from the cabin and took aim at Kathryn.

"No!" Travis stood and shouted.

Both Kathryn and Jethro turned to him.

———— • ————

Katie couldn't believe her eyes. Travis left hours ago. Yet there he was, his gun pointed at Jethro.

She watched as the two men stood stock still, aiming at each other.

"Drop it, Jethro! Nothing good can come from this," Travis shouted.

"That's where you're wrong," Jethro yelled back, then pulled the trigger.

The single shot echoed in Katie's ears as Travis fell to the ground.

Screaming, she ran across the yard, not caring that Jethro now had his gun pointed at her. Collapsing next to Travis' body, Katie sobbed while Matilda screamed and squirmed against her chest. Travis stared up at her, shock turning his normally warm complexion gray, blood pouring from the bullet hole in his thigh.

"Get out of here, Kathryn!" He grimaced. "Run!"

"No." She shook her head, tears falling unchecked. She quickly pulled the tie from her hair and wrapped it around Travis' leg, trying to stop the blood. "I'm not leaving you."

"Hurry." He swallowed deep, his eyes fluttering. "You and Matilda need to get out of here."

"Don't worry, Travis, we'll take good care of her. Won't we, son?"

Katie turned to see both Jethro and Wade, guns drawn. Jethro's pointed at her; Wade's pointed at Travis.

Instinctively, she turned her shoulder, putting herself between Matilda and the barrel of Jethro's shotgun, even though she knew it would do little good.

"Don't . . . please," she begged. "I'll do whatever you say. Just don't hurt Travis or Matilda. I'll go home with you. I'll never tell a soul . . . about anything. Please . . . just don't let him die, please!" she sobbed.

Jethro sneered. "Well, isn't that sweet. Did you hear that, Travis?" Jethro stepped around Kathryn, pressing the muzzle of his shotgun against Travis' chest. "She'll do whatever I say. You see . . . your little wifey isn't as innocent as you think. Why, she's practically beggin' to go back to the way things used to be between us. She misses her pa. And I must say," he turned to her with a long lustful look, "I've missed her every night since she's been gone."

Travis swatted at the gun resting against his chest, then groaned from the pain. "You're a sick, lecherous animal!"

"Why?" Jethro laughed, clearly enjoying his taunting. "Because I want a young, supple body lying next to mine? Isn't that what you wanted? Isn't that what every man wants?" He swung his gun back to point at Travis' face and shook his head. "It's a real shame you didn't take advantage of having Kathryn in your bed sooner. Because now . . . now it's too late. She's mine. Always has been. Always will be."

Jethro's smug smile turned to a venomous scowl as he looked from Travis to Katie. "Take her to the cabin," he barked at Wade, "while I finish up here."

Wade jerked her up by the arm. She quickly covered Matilda with her other arm, protecting her. "No!" she screamed as he dragged her away. "No! I'll do anything! I'll say anything! Please!" she pleaded hysterically.

Trying to break free of Wade's hold, she yanked her arm and dug in her heels. But it was no use. Her will was no match against his strength.

She cried uncontrollably, "Please, Wade, don't do this! None of this is your fault. That's what I'll tell the sheriff, that Jethro forced you. I promise. Please . . . please stop Jethro before it's too late."

Pulling her inside the cabin, Wade pushed her to the floor. Katie twisted to her side, protecting a still screaming Matilda, her shoulder taking the brunt of the fall. She cried out as a splintered board dug into her shoulder, and when she looked at her torn sleeve, she saw blood began to spread across the tattered material. The pain made her dizzy, but she fought against it. She had to help Travis.

Somehow, someway, she had to get to him and stop Jethro.

When she looked up, she saw Wade slumped in the

rocking chair, looking like a scared little boy.

Maybe I still have a chance to convince him.

"Wade, please," she spoke softly. "You've got to stop Jethro. I promise, I will tell the sheriff that we were both victims. That none of this is your fault. I will never tell a soul that you laid a hand on—"

The blast of a gunshot cut her off.

Her body flinched.

Her heart stopped.

Her life was over.

68

Katie sat with her back against the wall, her eyes swollen from crying. She'd untied the blanket that held Matilda to her, and tried to soothe the hysterical child, but she felt numb, disoriented. She could hear herself whisper to Matilda, lulling her with words.

But how could that be?

How was it her body continued to function when her heart no longer beat within her chest?

She looked up to see Wade sitting in the chair across the room. His gun pointed at the ground in front of her, his face distorted from anguish or shock; she wasn't sure which.

"Wade," she whispered, "please don't let him hurt Matilda. I know Jethro is going to kill me. He has to. He can't have any witnesses. But Matilda is innocent. Please don't let him hurt her. Take her to Pastor Holt. He'll find her a home."

"Ma will take care of her," he replied, his tone lacking feeling of any kind.

"No!" She shook her head vehemently, knowing once Jethro found out Mama was in on her plan, he would kill her too. "Promise me, Wade."

He stared at the ground in front of her.

"Look at me!" she shouted.

He glanced up with empty eyes.

"Please. I beg you. Just give Matilda to Pastor Holt. Mama won't be fit to take care of her. Please."

Wade never answered; he just stared at the ground, clearly in shock.

Katie sat with her head back against the wall, eyes closed, wondering what was taking Jethro so long.

The veins in her head felt like they were going to burst from the blood rushing through them, and her body shook uncontrollably.

This must be what it feels like when a person is sentenced to death.

She thought about the hanging she saw when she was four years old. She watched as a man was dragged up the steps to the makeshift gallows. She remembered asking Mama why they broke the man's legs. She told her his legs weren't broken; he was just weak with fear.

Though Mama shielded her from the actual hanging, Katie always remembered the man looking like a rag doll, not understanding how fear could affect someone's body.

Now she knew.

Because the fear she felt for Matilda was stronger than anything she'd ever felt before.

When the door rattled, Katie jolted upright, and Wade jumped to his feet. She cowered, her body wrapped in a ball around Matilda, waiting for Jethro to burst into the room.

But nothing happened. There was only silence.

Katie looked at Wade, seeing the confusion on his face as he walked toward the door. Then, as soon as he turned the knob, the door flew open, knocking Wade to the ground, his gun skittering across the floor.

Katie couldn't believe it.

Terrence Barton walked in; his Winchester trained on Wade. She watched as Wade chanced a look at where his shotgun had landed.

"Don't do it, boy. No sense making this any worse on yourself."

Terrence glanced at Katie quick like, then back at Wade. "Are you hurt?" he asked her.

"It doesn't matter," she sobbed. "Travis is . . . he's . . ."

She couldn't say it. Because voicing the truth made it all too real.

"I know." Terrence said as he stepped forward and kicked Wade's gun out of reach. "I saw the whole thing. I'm just sorry I wasn't able to stop Jethro sooner." He backed up to Katie. "You know how to use this?" He asked as he held out his rifle.

She nodded.

"Good. I want you to hold it steady on Wade while I tie him up."

She looked at Wade, where he laid on the floor. His eyes empty. No fight left in him.

Terrence had Wade tethered to the table leg in a matter of seconds because Wade offered no resistance. Picking up Wade's gun, Terrence squatted down next to Katie and carefully took his gun from her shaking hands.

"How's this little lady doin'? Terrence asked as he looked down at a rosy-cheeked Matilda.

"Fine," Katie choked. "She was jostled quite a bit . . . but I think she's fine."

"And you?"

She looked up into Terrence's eyes, unable to answer because she didn't really know what to say. She was still breathing, but beyond that she felt like she had withered from the inside out.

"Come on," he said as he wrapped a sturdy arm around her shoulders, but when she cried out, he pulled away. "So, you *are* hurt." He looked at her, worried.

"It's nothing." She slowly got to her feet with his gentle assistance.

"Nothing or not, we'll have the doctor check that out. But right now, I need to get you to Travis, so he knows you're okay."

She turned to Terrence, stunned. "I . . . I don't understand. You said you saw the whole thing. Jethro shot Travis. Not once, but twice. I watched him. I heard it."

"No, Kathryn. What you heard was me . . . shooting Jethro. Travis has lost a lot of blood, and needs a doctor, but I think he'll—"

Katie didn't wait for Terrence to finish. She quickly cradled Matilda in her good arm and ran to where Travis was propped up against a large boulder. His leg was bloody and cinched with a belt. His eyes were shut, and his lips were colorless, but when she dropped to her knees next to him, he slowly opened one eye.

She grasped his hand and brought it up to her face, ignoring the pain in her shoulder. Pressing it to her cheek, her tears washed over his fingers. "I thought you were dead." She smiled and sobbed all at once.

"So did I." Travis turned to where Jethro lay, Katie following his stare. Jethro's shirt was stained red, and his eyes were vacant, but somehow, he still had the ability to make her tremble.

Travis stroked her cheek with his calloused thumb, getting her attention. "He can't hurt you anymore, Kathryn."

Matilda let out a squeal, bringing a smile to Travis' face. "Here," he held out his arms, "let me hold her."

"Are you sure?" Katie wiped her tears as she looked at his leg and the perspiration beading on his forehead. "I don't think you should. We need to get you to the doctor."

"He'll get here as soon as he can," Travis said as he reached for Matilda and cradled her on his lap. The emotion in his eyes when he looked at Matilda caused Katie's heart to catch.

"I don't understand, Travis." she said, still confused. "What made you come home?"

"Your mother."

"Mama?"

"She rode into town looking for the sheriff."

Katie saw the disappointment in Travis' eyes when he looked at her.

He knew.

He knew about her plan.

She turned away, feeling ashamed.

"Why'd you do it, Kathryn? Why would you put yourself in such danger? Matilda too?"

"Because I was afraid." She looked at him. "Afraid you wouldn't let it go, that you would go after Jethro and Wade. I couldn't let you do that. I couldn't chance something happening to you. I didn't want Matilda to grow up without her pa to love and protect her. I know what that's like." She stroked Matilda's cheek. "But in the end, I couldn't do it. I had Jethro in my sights, but I couldn't pull the trigger. I couldn't take another person's life. No matter what he had done."

Katie heard footsteps behind her and quickly spun around, wincing at the pain it caused her arm. She sighed with relief when she saw it was only Terrence.

"How's he doing?" He gestured to Travis.

"He's lost a lot of blood."

"What about Wade?" Travis asked.

"Don't go changing the subject, Travis. Wade's not going anywhere. It's you I'm worried about. We need to get you to town."

"Caleb will bring the doctor just as soon as he's done with Clara."

"Mama?" Katie whirled back around. "What's wrong with Mama?"

"I knew she was in bad shape when she left my place," Terrence said, "but I couldn't convince her to let me take her to town. She was too worried what people might think."

"What happened? I don't understand?" Katie was frantic as the men talked back and forth about Mama but didn't answer her questions. "What was she doing at your place?" she asked Terrence.

"She said she was getting something for you."

"But she was hurt?"

"Yeah. Harley threw her. She hit her head pretty hard; had a knot the size of a goose egg. I'm sure she blacked out for a spell as well. And she wouldn't let me look at her arm either, but I'm thinkin' it was broken. I told her she was in no shape to ride, but she said it was important she get to town . . . that she had to do something for you."

Terrence looked at her, discernment in his stare. "I'm guessin' she knew Jethro and Wade were over here bent on trouble. All I knew was somethin' wasn't right, so I figured I'd ride out and see for myself. When I got here, I saw Jethro with his gun pointed at Travis and Wade dragging you away. Jethro said some nasty things to Travis about you, confirming what I feared all along. I knew then there wasn't time left to reason with Jethro. So, I shot him before he could pull the trigger on Travis. I'm just sorry I didn't get here sooner."

Katie turned back to Travis. "Was Mama okay when you left her?"

He shook his head. "She was holding her own, but she didn't look too good."

Travis shut his eyes, the conversation obviously wearing him out.

"Here, let me take Matilda." Katie reached forward, grimacing to herself, not wanting Travis to hear her.

"I'll take the baby in just a minute," Terrence said. "You just be careful with that arm until the doctor gets here."

Travis opened his eyes, zeroing in on her bloodied sleeve. "Kathryn, you're hurt."

"It's nothing."

"It's a mighty bloody nothin'," Terrence said with a stern voice. Then, he bent down to examine Travis' leg further. He pulled back the wad of bloody cloth, causing Travis to moan. "If Doc ain't here in the next few minutes, I'm gonna have to get you inside and see what I can do about that bullet. I don't like the looks of your leg."

Terrence wiped his hands in the dirt, then brushed them off before gently lifting Matilda from Travis' lap. "I'm gonna go get some water. Clean it out some."

Just as Terrence stood, he turned toward the horizon.

"Praise, God. The cavalry is here," he said with a look of relief.

"What?" Katie asked.

"Three riders comin' this way. Doc, Sheriff Chambers, and your friend, Caleb."

69

Katie watched as Caleb and Terrence carefully carried Travis to the cabin. Sheriff Chambers held Matilda in his arms, while Doc Hammond cupped her elbow, obviously sensing she wasn't as strong as she claimed to be.

"How's Mama?" she asked with tears in her eyes.

"She's pretty banged up. I had to set her arm, and she has a concussion."

"A concussion? That's serious."

"I'm not going to lie to you, Kathryn. She's in pretty rough shape. Martha is sitting with her now. I normally wouldn't leave a patient in her condition, but Clara insisted. Somehow she knew I would be needed here."

Katie followed the men into the cabin, glancing quickly where Wade was tethered to the table leg, then immediately went to Travis' bedside.

Brushing her shaky hand across his forehead and down his flush cheek, she waited for him to look at her, but he didn't.

"Come on, Kathryn," Caleb said. "You need to sit down and let Doc do what he needs to do."

"I want to help," she said without budging.

"You're in no condition to help. Besides, Doc can't tend

to Travis if he's afraid you're going to pass out. It would be a mighty big distraction." Caleb smiled reassuringly, obviously trying to ease the tension in the room. "Come on . . . Travis is in good hands."

Doc Hammond looked across the bed at her. "Terrence can help me, Kathryn. I would feel better if you were off your feet until I can take a look at that shoulder."

"Besides," Sheriff Chambers chimed in, his voice controlled but direct. "Someone needs to explain to me what went on here."

70

It was nightfall by the time Terrence retrieved his wagon, loaded Jethro's body, and rode away with the sheriff, Wade in tow.

Doc Hammond had stitched up Travis and Katie, and left instructions with Caleb to send for him if either of them developed fever or heat around their wounds. The doc also assured Katie he would send word if her mother took a turn for the worse.

Katie was conflicted; her feelings for Mama were a jumbled mess. She shouldn't care about her condition, not after all the woman had allowed her to endure. But if it wasn't for Mama going for the sheriff . . . cutting through Terrence's property . . .

Katie didn't even want to think about it.

As soon as everyone left, Caleb was quick to start on supper. Though Katie insisted she could cook, in the end, she didn't have the energy to. So, they settled on eggs and buttered bread, the extent of Caleb's kitchen skills.

Exhausted and aching, Katie wanted nothing more than to collapse next to Travis but didn't think that was appropriate in front of Caleb.

With Travis' eyes closed, Katie reached for the plate

resting on his lap. He'd eaten propped up against the headboard, looking worlds better than he did just a few hours ago. Thankfully, the medicine Doc Hammond gave him took the edge off. Even so, he was still tired and hurting quite a bit.

When she lifted the plate, he reached out for her hand, stopping her from walking away. "You need to lie down, Kathryn."

She turned to where Caleb was playing on the floor with Matilda, then back to Travis, raising her brow.

It took him only a second to understand the gesture.

"Hey, Caleb, how about you call it a night? Kathryn won't lay down in bed until you're gone."

"Travis!" Katie was mortified he would say such a thing.

"I understand, Kathryn," Caleb said as he smiled and got up off the floor. "Do you want me to take Matilda for the night, so you two can have some alone time?"

"No," she said, knowing her face had to be red with embarrassment. "After today, and the thought of losing her and Travis, I think I want to keep them both close."

"Well, give me just a few more minutes. I'm sure I'll be able to rock her to sleep and get her settled in for the night."

She smiled. "I'd appreciate that."

True to his word, Caleb had Matilda asleep in a matter of minutes. He carefully laid her in the cradle and walked to the cabin door. Katie followed him, leaning on the door once he opened it.

"Caleb, thank you for everything. If you hadn't tracked down the doctor, I don't know how Travis would have fared."

"Well, you can thank God that Pandora threw a shoe. Otherwise, we wouldn't have had to stop at the livery."

"That's why you were in town?"

"Yep. And when we got there, Hank noticed a split in one of the wheels. If he hadn't, we might have ended up in the middle of nowhere with a busted wheel to boot."

"But I don't understand? Travis checked the wagon and the horses before you left."

"Like I said. We need to thank God. Because if it wasn't for Him, who knows what would've happened to you and Matilda today."

Katie closed the door, wrestling with Caleb's words. It was the only thing that made sense.

How else could she explain it?

Her plan had backfired.

After all Jethro and Wade had done to her, she was sure she would be able to pull the trigger, but in the end, she couldn't do it. She wasn't a murderer. Instead of getting justice or revenge she had put Matilda and herself in Jethro's crosshairs.

But God saved us.

The thought astounded her. After all she'd suffered, after all her unanswered prayers.

Why now?

"Kathryn, are you okay?" Travis asked, sounding half asleep.

"Yes . . . I'm fine."

Walking slowly toward the table, she glanced at Matilda one last time before lowering the lamplight, then moved to her side of the bed and sat on the edge with a heavy sigh. She listened to Travis' rhythmic breathing and smiled. It was music to her ears.

In the quiet, sitting with her eyes closed, she thought again about what Caleb had said; his confidence that God had orchestrated everything. A thrown shoe, a broken wheel, even Mama cutting across Terrence's property and falling. If any of those circumstances had been different, who knows what would've happened today.

She shuttered at the thought.

How could I have been so foolish?

Her plan had nearly gotten Travis and Matilda killed. And yet, even though she plotted evil, God showed her mercy. Not only did he save Travis and Matilda, but He saved her too.

It was more than she could comprehend.

Too tired to undress and not wanting to mess with her sore shoulder, she carefully pulled off her boots, then lay down and curled up on her side of the bed.

Travis sighed, then rolled closer to her. "What are you thinking?" he whispered.

"I thought you were asleep?"

"Just resting my eyes."

She waited, hoping he would drift off again, not knowing if she could have this conversation right now.

"Kathryn . . . you didn't answer me."

She struggled, trying to control her emotions, but in the end, she couldn't hold back her tears. "I'm so sorry, Travis. I know you're disappointed in me, and you have every right to be. I don't know what I was thinking, endangering Matilda the way I did. I never even considered that I wouldn't be able to . . . I mean, after all Jethro did. I thought I'd be able to pull . . ."

Emotion strangled her words.

Slowly and carefully, Travis moved closer to her, draped his arm across her waist and hugged her to his chest.

"It's over," he spoke softly, his breath warm against her neck. "It's time for us to start our life together. No more secrets, no more threats. Just the three of us."

"You mean the four of us."

"Four?"

Katie turned so she could see Travis' face. She looked into his warm, handsome, forgiving eyes. "I'm convinced now, if it weren't for God, I wouldn't be here. I don't know why He allowed what He did. Why I had to go through what I did. Or why you had to lose Mary. But He protected us today. All of us. I'm convinced this is where God wants me to be. This is where my life begins."

Epilogue
One year later

"Okay everybody, smile."

Everyone stood patiently in their Sunday best posing for a family photograph. However, as soon as the photographer took the picture, Matilda squirmed out of Travis' arms and went running across the yard.

"I'll watch her," Seth said, as he took off after Matilda.

Katie smiled, loving the relationship that had blossomed between the two of them. Seth was fiercely protective of Matilda, and it warmed Katie's heart to no end.

Clara turned to Katie. "I can't help but think we are leaving at the worst possible time."

"I'm fine, Mama," Katie looked up at Travis as she stroked her extended tummy. "The baby isn't due for another month, and I'm feeling healthy as a horse."

Terrence slipped his arm around his new bride's waist. "We don't have to go right now, Clara. We could go another time."

"That's ridiculous," Katie scolded. "It's your honeymoon. Besides, I have Travis to look after me. I'll be just fine."

Clara smiled at Terrence, tears on her cheeks. "Then I guess we should be going before it gets too late."

Terrence and Travis walked toward the wagon, discussing what needed to be done on Terrence's property while he was gone. Clara looped her arm through Katie's and held her close as they slowly walked toward the wagon as well. "I love you, Kathryn, you know that, right?"

"Yes, Mama."

Katie had spent the last year rebuilding her relationship with her mama. It had been difficult at first, but Katie finally came to the conclusion that Mama was a victim of Jethro's abuse too. Though her wounds were more emotional than physical, she was a victim just the same. Their relationship wasn't completely healed yet, but Katie was trying.

The year brought many other changes both good and bittersweet. Caleb had stayed with them for a few months, helping Travis finish the addition to the house before returning to North Carolina. He now oversaw The Clark Foundation and the numerous institutions Travis' grandfather had established. He promised he would visit after the baby was born and even hinted that he might bring someone special for them to meet.

Seth was growing into an amazing young man, and for that, Katie thanked God every day. Without the tyrannical rule of Jethro or the bullying from Wade, he was no longer the shy little boy who blended into the woodwork. He had shot up in height, carried himself with more confidence, and even had a few girls at church showing him a little extra attention.

Of course, Travis and Terrence were big influences on him, helping him deal with his feelings of anger and bitterness towards Jethro and Wade for what they had done to her. He had also started asking Travis questions about the fairer sex. Nothing too serious, just general curiosities. And Terrence . . . he was an amazing man of God. He treated Seth like a father should, with gentleness and encouragement.

Katie prayed nightly that Travis and Terrence would be able to reverse the emotional scars left behind by Jethro and Wade.

Unfortunately, Wade did not survive the effects of Jethro's ruthlessness or his own demons. Once in jail, he became despondent and depressed, even refused to eat. Then one night, he asked for a pen and paper, so he could write her a note. He apologized for the torment she had suffered at his hand but didn't ask for her forgiveness. He explained that his acts were unforgiveable, and death was the only just punishment. He then hung himself from the window bars of his jail cell.

It was difficult for Katie not to feel responsible. She couldn't help but wonder, if she had gone to the sheriff and told of Jethro's abuse, would Wade still be alive today? It was a struggle she had to turn over to the Lord daily, knowing she would never have an answer.

And then there was Matilda and Travis.

Her own little family.

Matilda was growing like a weed and was the most curious child Katie had ever known. She smelled every flower, picked up every stick, and loved to sit on the back porch and watch the leaves flitter in the breeze. She was adorable and precocious and had her daddy wrapped around her little finger. And when she squeezed Katie around the neck and pressed her cheek against hers, Katie's heart would melt every time.

And Travis . . . Travis was a true gift from God. He was an amazing husband and an incredible father. She was truly blessed beyond measure. And even though she still had nightmares from time to time, Travis was always right there to comfort her and remind her how much she was loved.

Stroking her tummy, Katie smiled as she watched Matilda and Seth run about the yard. Secretly, she was hoping for a son, someone to carry on the Clark name. But in truth, it really didn't matter. Having a child, *Travis's child*, was a true miracle. She was living a life that just a little over a year ago was unimaginable.

At times, she pondered why God had allowed her to endure so much pain, but instead of dwelling on it, she clung to the Psalms that reminded her, *weeping may endure for a night, but joy comes in the morning.*

She was experiencing joy.

True joy.

Something she thanked God for every night.

ABOUT THE AUTHOR

Tamara Tilley writes from her home at Hume Lake Christian Camps, located in the beautiful Sequoia National Forest. She and her husband, Walter, have been on full-time staff at Hume Lake for more than twenty-five years. Tamara is a retail manager. When she's not working or writing, she loves to read, spend time with her grandkids, and craft greeting cards. Visit her website at www.tamaratilley.com to read excerpts from her other books.

Made in the USA
Columbia, SC
01 June 2021